UNDERWORLD JUSTICE

Pete,

Thank you for all of the
books you have kindly
given me over the years.

Mark

Underworld Justice

Published by The Conrad Press in the United Kingdom 2021

Tel: +44(0)1227 472 874
www.theconradpress.com
info@theconradpress.com

ISBN 978-1-914913-04-4

Printed and bound in Great Britain by Clays Ltd, Elcograf S.p.A

Typesetting and Cover Design by The Book Typesetters,
www.thebooktypesetters.com

The Conrad Press logo was designed by Maria Priestley.

UNDERWORLD JUSTICE

MARK BLACK

I would like to thank the following people who have helped me on my literary journey: Mum, Dad, Caroline, Clare, Jean, Pete and Sarah.

My thanks also to The Conrad Press and The Book Typesetters.

Chapter 1

Early life

Born on the 23rd December 1946, Gary Jones was part of the baby boom after World War 2. Being born just before Christmas allowed his father to celebrate his birth into the new year, vigorously.

Fathers returned from service and immediately looked for solace with their family, before venturing down their local public house. Gary's father, George, used to frequent The White Swan in Romford Market Place, where he would spend all possible hours consuming pints of Mild for 1 shilling, before going home and demanding dinner. Gary never liked his father drinking. His fathers' breath would smell stale and he could become aggressive if his dinner was too hot, too cold or there was not enough of it. George did not realise, nor care, that he spent all the family' money down the public house, or with the unlicensed bookmakers based on the corner, outside pubs. He thought the country owed him, due to his efforts in the war. No one knew what George had done during the war. It was a subject no one dare ask, and one George did not volunteer, although many thought he had done little, if anything.

Gary understood why his father was like he was, and decided from an early age that he would never treat his family poorly. 'Family is family' was his motto.

George did not want to go to work. He informed all that listened that the war effort had exhausted him. Work was scarce, everywhere had been bombed, and if you had a job you looked after it. The only jobs available were in construction, although not all soldiers could be employed. Officers could become schoolteachers, although George did not enter this equation. This suited him. He would rise in the morning, have a mug of sweet tea, leave the house to buy a *Daily Mirror*, return, and select his horses for the days' meetings. This routine never changed.

Gary quickly became the money maker for the home at an early age, and his father hated him for it. Gary would always give half of the money he had *found* to his mother, and leave the rest on the window ledge knowing that his father would take it.

From an early age he realised his father was a wastrel. When his father had won on the horses everyone knew, he celebrated like a professional, although no money was forthcoming to his mother. The man was oblivious to household bills, and the fact money was required to purchase food and pay bills did not occur to him. The wins were quickly followed by losses, many of them, in which everyone was blamed; the jockey, trainer, course…even Rose was blamed.

Gary's mother, Rose, was a caring person who worshipped the ground he walked on. She had loved Gary from the moment he entered her world. Rose tried to ensure he never went without when schooling and defended him at all times. She had been called to the school on a number occasions for trouble involving Gary. The headmaster always said the same things to Rose, 'Gary is very intelligent, possibly the cleverest in his year, although he has an inner-strength that causes problems.'

Inner-strength, what the headmaster really wanted to say was Gary was just hard, fucking hard. Not one person could touch Gary. He had lightning reflexes, and fists the hardest prize fighters would be proud of. His stocky build gave the appearance of someone older, and his cold attitude aligned him with someone who knew they were destined for better things in life.

Gary never lied to his mother, he always told her what had happened, and whether he felt he was right once he had had time to consider his actions. Mother and son had a close relationship, both knew they only had the other for support, due to George's inconsistent behaviour and amateurish attitude to earning money, although he spent it like a professional. Gary looked at his pitiful father and thought he had champagne tastes but lemonade money. He vowed never to be like him; a waster, scrounger and loser.

Gary enjoyed going to school, although school was not keen on Gary. Many teachers were unqualified, and Gary found holes in their knowledge and zoned in on it. He was very bright, almost too bright, questioning teachers too often, which they did not always appreciate. They did not respect his fertile mind and its need to gather information. Gary's schooling carried on in the same manner.

The cane had become an inconvenient nuisance, one that neither hurt nor bothered him. During one severe beating he had the audacity to laugh at the headmaster, who had gone red during the thrashing. Gary turned, grabbed the cane and snapped it, before threatening the man with his life if he hit him one more time.

The headmaster was so shocked by the low-pitched ferocity that Gary made the statement in, he immediately stopped. In that instant the headmaster realised he had to take action as the pupil standing before him had an inner demon that would ensure danger for those who stood against him.

This had confirmed Gary's tenure at Marley School came to an abrupt end. The school had seriously considered their verdict as Gary was considered a pupil of high intellect. He was thought a boy who could reach university standard if he could control his inner monster. Sadly he had been unable to achieve this. Unfortunately, this reputation followed Gary. Residence at his next school, Triptons, also in Dagenham, lasted six weeks due to the severe beating he gave the head boy. Gary was fourteen, the head boy seventeen.

Gary decided school was not going to allow him to fulfil his lofty ambitions, although his force would. Many ideas were considered. Boxing was one seriously considered, yet Gary could not think of one fabulously wealthy fighter who had maintained his income without significant problems. He evaluated his options and thought protection could be his answer. He would offer a service for money retrieval. If someone had not paid a bill, he would go to the person's establishment and claim the money, charging them an additional 25 percent. If the debtor would not pay he would remove items until the bill was settled, including his fee.

Gary arrived home from work one evening and heard a terrible commotion indoors. As he ventured into the family home he saw his mother with a bloodied nose and a swollen eye. Across the room was his father. Immediately, his father shouted at him to fuck off. Gary stood his ground fixing his father with a cold stare that would have frozen the devil's soul. George turned towards Gary and beckoned him, 'You want some of this do yer?'

George ran at Gary like a crazed man, but before he could throw a punch Gary side stepped him and punched him just below the ribs. George fell to the floor, staring incredulously at the opponent who had given the blow, his hands clamoured wildly for non-existent handles, before re-gaining his composure with feelings of rage flying through his mind. He stood and stared at Gary, picked up the empty brown ale bottle and smashed it on the side. He then charged at Gary again. Rose screaming at the top of her voice. This time Gary's mental attitude turned on and he hit George with all the force in his body. Everything slowed, even sound, as George realised he was airborne, losing control, hurtling towards the solid concrete floor. Arms flailing desperately trying to soften the impact. George knew he had not survived this war. His neck acting as a spring, allowing his skull to crack against the floor and every wound was like sandpaper sanding his tired skin. He finally returned to where he had come from, without moving. Blood was running like little rivers from a head wound and little puddles were forming.

Rose was in total melt down. 'You've killed him, you've killed him!'

Gary looked at the man who had been a father in name only and replied coldly, 'You reap what you sow.'

The emergency services arrived. Ambulance men removed the body, and police officers interviewed both Gary and Rose.

Gary told the officers exactly what had happened. He knew he may get in trouble, but he did not care. George had finally fucked off, and he could get on with his life. Gary told the officers George was a fucking leach. They looked at each other as neither had heard someone so young, speak so coldly about death, particularly a father they had just killed. The officers asked Gary if there was anything else he would like to add to his statement, Gary replied nonchalantly, 'Do you mind if I have my dinner? I'm bloody starving.'

Gary was led away by the officers to the police station where he was charged with his father's murder.

Due to his age, he was sent to a juvenile correction unit called Leverton. Warley was a nice rural area. It was connected to Brentwood and surrounded with nature's bountiful supply of trees and open pastures. Gary decided immediately he would like to live in this area, which made him smile, as he would be for the next four years.

The security van entered an area called Dark Lane. This lead directly to Gary's new home. The dark wooden gates opened, and the security van entered. Immediately, Gary was led to the governor's welcoming area and informed of his rights, which were few.

The governor was an upright man, who looked like he had served in the army. His speech was very clipped and his attire modest, but perfectly pressed. He was then shoved out and lead to his sleeping quarters. On the way he heard someone call him a 'silly little cunt' very quietly. This was followed by 'understand, cunt? I'm in charge, prick face.' Gary understood this was code for '*do as you are told.*' Gary decided that this needed to be rectified quickly.

The following morning, he enquired who the person was who had spoken impolitely to him. Information led to someone who was seventeen, three years older than himself. This person was the *head boy*, a term given to the toughest boy in the unit. Everyone was terrified of him. Gary introduced himself to the lad known as *Mad Mike* when outside in the recreation area, which was situated close to the five-a-side football pitch.

Gary had already understood from discussions with other inmates where the meeting would take place, and had made suitable plans.

Mike told Gary to follow him to his inner sanctum, which was the sports hall. As both entered, the door was shut by a third party. Mike informed Gary what his commission was for safeguarding and security, whilst he spent the next few years inside. Mike began to shout at Gary, who continued to walk towards the end of the sports hall. Mike was now frothing at the mouth and charged at Gary for disrespecting him, yet before he could say another word a sharpened table tennis handle was shoved with such force at his face, it imbedded in one cheek and emerged from the other, tearing muscle to shreds as the handle was rotated. Mad Mike's cry was a brilliant sound, guttural chokes mixed with an agonized howl. Gary smirked, removed the implement from his now deathly white victim. Mike sank to his knees, continuing to scream, convulsing and trembling like a rabid animal, thick blood flowing freely from the gaping hole in his face. Gary calmly looked at him, 'who's a cunt? I'm in charge prick face.'

Mike's third-party assistant did not know what to do. Gary looked at him and forcefully growled, 'Put the word out. I'm head fucking boy, not him, or that silly old fucker in his office. Understand?' A swift sharp kick was administered to the injured participant's testicles, who rolled around like a crying baby.

The empire had started.

Security guards at the correctional unit found Gary very easy to deal with, a model inmate. Trouble was minimal, and it had been the easiest four years of their service. There had been no wars, stabbings and brutality. The worst scenario encountered was someone tied to a radiator that had been on for over an hour. The burns were severe, and the guards assumed it had been Gary who had inflicted them, although they did not mind as the person receiving the punishment had interfered with young children and was a juvenile nonce who preyed on spring chickens, a term used for pre-pubescent youngsters. No-one was supposed to know about the inmate, but Gary was whispered this information by guards. It was a mutual agreement that took place with Gary to iron out any problems the guards thought may escalate.

The four years came to an end. When Gary left, the guards wished him well. They understood their lives would be worse for having no Gary Jones inside with them. He had been known as the *quiet assassin* by the guards. He had become liked, respected and feared. The Warley holiday camp had come to an end, and it was back to work for them.

•

Gary set himself up as a small debt collector for local companies. His reputation had increased once he had collected his first debt from a very small company. Initially, finding work had been difficult. Everyone he had spoken to considered him too young and inexperienced. A one-manned company had given him his first opportunity. A debt, he was informed was huge to the gentleman he was working for, yet not excessive by most sizeable companies. Once he had collected the debt he understood why it needed collecting.

The debt of £300 was incredible. The largest amount of money he had ever seen. Collecting the debt had been surprisingly exciting. Having met the head of the company Gary laid down his terms and why the visit had been required. The gentleman speaking to him laughed immediately telling him to 'fuck right off and get a paper-round'.

Gary fixed the man a steely stare and calmly replied, 'Calm down, it'll be for your benefit.'

'My benefit? Fuck off. Who do you think you are, Mr Paperboy?'

The debtor was looking flushed red, and his palms were placed directly on the green ink blotting paper. Immediately, Gary reached for the letter opener lightning quick, and with incredible ferocity bayoneted it through the man's right hand, embedding it into the wooden desk through the blotting paper. A trail of red ink began to run onto the paper.

The debtor let out a loud, deep howl, which no-one heard as everyone had gone to lunch.

'Now, getting back to the money. You owed £300, that has just increased to £375. Two cheques will suffice. One for £300 and another for £75. You are left-handed, so you will be able to sign the cheques before I leave.'

Gary returned to his customer and without delay handed

over the £300 cheque, 'Job done. I believe you now owe me a cheque for £75.'

The cheque was signed and passed over swiftly. Gary was thanked for his service and informed he would be used again. The debt career had started very successfully.

The smoke twisted in its artistic way, forming curls in the gloom, illuminated only by the dust-speckled bar lights. Along the wall was every alcoholic known liquid in their inverted bottles; every vice that the locals craved. Each drink offering temptation, like the devil.

He stood with his arms in his pockets contemplating which drink to have. He decided it would be a pint of Double Diamond or Ben Truman, both had a hearty taste he enjoyed. He noted the foul-tasting lager in their bottles, Harp. What chance did that have against British Bitter? He raised a weathered finger to call the barmaid, she instantly saw him and came over. The barmaid looked no older than twenty, she had an innocent look, although looks were usually deceiving. She had been cleaning the bar top, this impressed Gary. This indicated she took pride in her job and wanted the place clean and organized. Having evaluated the pretty barmaid, he chose his drink, Ben Truman, it cost 1/5d. He took a first refreshing slurp from the tankard. The brown liquid barely touched the sides of his mouth before its journey into the depths of his stomach. Instantly he felt energized.

The pub was full of men regaling stories of their day and how they had fared. Some were there for a period of time, whilst others for one swift pint before they went home to their families. All appeared decent hard-working people. The place was full of builders and clerical staff. This would be perfect to visit for a quiet drink where no-one knew him. He would ask to meet no one and bring no one. It would be his sanctuary. He read the sign on the wall that indicated the pub was built in 1762. Gary was intrigued by local history. He considered two other local pubs, The Bull and The White Hart, and decided he would trace their origins. His eye went back to the bar maid. He heard someone call her Gill. It was the opening Gary required. Over the ensuing three hours Gary peppered the bar maid with sweet talk and innuendo's. When her shift finished, she agreed to go back to Gary's home in Dagenham East. Once through the door both parties ravaged the other. Gary was shocked that an innocent looking girl could be so experienced. She suddenly got on her knees and told him to stick his cock in her arse. Gary was momentarily confused. Had he heard her correctly? He looked at Gill and she was on her knees baying him over. He got behind her and slipped his cock into her tight arse. She let out a passionate scream. He then fucked her hard. After two minutes she asked him to stop but he would not. She wanted it – so now he was finishing it. Five minutes later Gill was sobbing. He told Gill to have a bath and clean herself up.

Crumpled flannelette sheets on his bed looked like they had been to war. The olive green colour was fading, making them appear lifeless. Gary lay there with his Capstan cigarette hanging from his mouth, its smoke gently floating toward the ceiling like dancing angels. The ceiling was stained, dirty and brown, just like the River Thames. He considered his day. He had collected some debts, had a beer, found a nice pub and fucked a young barmaid. Overall, a successful day. He considered his way to the top. Having removed some obstacles, he only had the Smith's standing before him and the whole of London could be his. Having considered this, he decided they would need to be removed. No one could be trusted so he would do it himself. He was known as a lone wolf who could get anything done. He was friends with no one, and people heard of him through reputation. This was the reason why the Smith family had not ventured into Essex.

At twenty-four, Gary still had the verve and vigor of a young man, although he had the strength of ten. Being mentally strong made him a dangerous proposition. Gary considered all angles when forming a plan. He would contemplate all scenarios, those that would go right and those that could go wrong. He felt this gave him an edge as those in his line of business only believed things would go right, which was their weakness and undoing. A man in his position must consider and evaluate all areas of strength and possible weakness. This would prepare him for any pitfalls he may encounter.

He suddenly heard the rumbling from his belly. He had not eaten since breakfast. Gary considered his options and placed the burnt end of his cigarette into the overflowing ash tray. He would have Fish and Chips from Tony's Fish Bar. One thing you could guarantee from Tony's was fresh battered fish. Gary always paid, although Tony offered it to him free every time. Every man has to make a living so pay people promptly, although he smiled when he considered he had made his business collecting debts, or as he liked to call it…aiding people in need.

He rose from his bed like Goliath and admired himself in the mirror. He was a good-looking fit man that both sexes were attracted to. His mystical manner intrigued ladies, and empowered gentlemen. He strode to the bathroom to bath and shave. Having cleaned, he chose a nice white shirt and navy-blue suit. Gary applied some Old Spice aftershave and left his flat. Tonight, was the night he would make discrete enquiries about the competition. This would be risky in case he bumped into someone he knew, but it was a chance he would have to take.

He arrived in Roman Road at nine o'clock and decided to enter the John Bull pub. It was a miserable looking place with a traditional horseshoe bar that was dark brown, almost black. Striding to the bar he asked for a light and bitter. The barman quickly pulled him the half pint of bitter and passed the bottle of courage light ale. He had noticed Kelly's pie and mash shop when walking to the pub and asked the barman what time it opened. Gary was informed it opened at 11am and was the best pie and mash shop in town. Gary thanked the man and made a mental note to visit the establishment. He absolutely loved pie and mash, although he knew it would never better his mother's steak and kidney pudding or her pies. He began to think of his mother and her tragic battle with cancer and how she had finally succumbed to it having fought so bravely. It was the only day he had shown emotion. Every day he thought of his late mother and wished she could see him now. He missed her always. She was a great woman, an honest woman, the only person he had ever loved.

Suddenly the bar doors opened, and two brothers walked in. Many people called over hello to them, whilst one or two finished their drinks and left. It was the two men he hoped to meet and here they were standing next to him. The barman offered a greeting to the brothers who both asked for their usual. They were given their beers, free of charge. Gary noticed this straightaway. These brothers never paid their way. A weakness to exploit. Greed and power was their undoing. Both were immaculate in their dress sense. Similar to Gary, although they wore black suits, white shirts and black ties. Gary thought it gave them the look of pallbearers. How apt they dress this way, as it could be where they both end with his friend, the Gravedigger.

The brothers began a conversation that could be heard by many people within earshot. Gary understood this to be a warning to those listening. Suddenly Gary's drink fell from the safety of the bar and hit the floor with the brown liquid flying over his trousers and the brothers. Immediately, one of the brothers turned around and apologized. He said it in a sarcastic manner, mentioning it had been his fault and no hard feelings. There was no mention of replacing the drink. The barman scurried from behind the bar and began to wipe the mess from the floor. Gary noted a sense of terror in the man's operation. He had noticeably changed colour. He did not appear to be a person who enjoyed the sun, yet now he looked a man who had never seen the sun. He had become ghostly pale. The barman offered to replace the drink. Gary thanked the man but said he would buy his own. He knew this would be noted by the two men standing nearby. They would look at each other and consider what had been said. They would immediately decide whether he was taking the piss or being kind to the barman. They chose the latter. Today had probably been a good day, and a day where no trouble was required, unless it was required.

The barman poured the drink and passed it to Gary who offered the correct money. Gary saw the barman had given him three quarters of a pint of bitter instead of the regulation half along with his bottle of Courage Light Ale. This was a silent thank you from one man to another. Words were not needed.

Gary had seen enough. He finished his drink and began to walk to the door, as he opened the door someone called, 'Aven't you forgotten something?'

Gary looked back and one of the twins was holding his change. He strode over to the gentleman, thanked him and took the money. He eyed the brothers and asked if there was a charity box. They mentioned a Barnados box based behind the bar. Gary called the barman and told him to, 'Sling the change in the charity box'. He turned to the twins who were looking at him with curiosity and said in a gentle manner, 'I didn't even notice I'd left it behind, so let some poor kid benefit.' He then removed himself from the pub and made his way back to the Kings Head.

On the way home Gary had a distinct feeling he was being followed. He departed the tube at Dagenham and watched a number of people disembark. One in particular caught his eye. It was the less masculine of the two brothers. Gary had caught the man looking at him in the reflection of the mirror placed behind the bar. Gary had also thought the man had given him a knowing smile. This had been something he had not considered. One of the brothers was queer. Gary decided he wanted no part to play in this man's deviant world, yet knew the possibilities of bringing him down had increased substantially.

He knew the back streets of Dagenham, and assumed the man from the tube would be seeking him, going from pub to pub. He would start at the Railway, onto The Bull before settling in Dagenham's best public house, The Cross Keys in Dagenham Village. Gary briskly walked through the back streets of Rogers Road and Reed Road, that offered refuge to the local hardworking population, before arriving at the Matapan public house, where he supped a few pints of Charrington's Brown Ale before making his way home. Never one for small talk, he was happy standing alone listening to everyone's idle gossip, each believing their news was significantly more important than those they were with. Using this technique had paid handsomely for Gary when he overhead pieces of local gossip about certain individuals and the area. Gary believed in keeping your mouth shut and your ears and eyes open. During his one hour stay in the pub he had heard the name of the hardest man in Dagenham and Barking-...which had made him smile, a place where nice 3-piece suites could be bought at Andrews Corner, and the worst pub in the area...evidently The Fiddlers. All information was key to a man's success or failure.

He decided to leave before closing time, and strode home thinking about the Smith brothers and how detestable they were to all who unfortunately came into contact with them. They were pariahs of life. They never enhanced persons wellbeing, in fact, the opposite. They bled them dry, feeding on a person's fear. The world did not need these fucking arse holes. They were a complete waste of skin. Every breath of air they sucked depleted someone else from using it. The rage began to rise, although it quickly tempered down.

Reaching his mid-terraced home, he entered, heading for the kitchen, popping the kettle on before flicking the switch for the wireless and tuning into Luxembourg. 123 by Len Barry began to play. A song for all generations. Gary stood listening and thought how it had a warmth and innocence that would earn the songwriter money forever.

He had a penchant for music, and his knowledge was incredible, yet no-one knew it. It was a side of his life he kept quiet. He was a fan of *The Beatles* and *The Rolling Stones*, although the *Beach Boys*, and in particular the *Bee Gees* had caught his ear. Both were a little more melodic.

Gary was proficient at playing the piano. It was something he had been able to do from a young age. He could hear a song and play it immediately. His mother always got him to play at parties. He had hated it, yet performed to please his mother. One of his mother's cousins had said he was a genius and should play professionally. Straight away his mother had defended his honour by declaring, 'He plays for his mum only.' Thinking back, it had made him appear a little soft, yet the secret had remained with him. Anything related to music he kept secret from all. It was his private playground that no-one knew, witnessed or considered.

Chapter 2

Bob Burns, The Gravedigger

B ob Burns was six feet seven, clever, strong and meticulous. No one knew much about him. He rarely ventured into public houses, despised gambling and attended church every Sunday morning. He was considered perfect husband material by those who knew him, although few did. Only a couple of people really knew anything about Bob, and one of those was Gary Jones.

He had been born Robert Burns in 1948. He was unsure of his exact date of birth as he had been left on a pew in Our Lady of Dolours Servite Church, wrapped in a dirty white shawl, discovered by the priest who took pity on him straight away. The priest ensured he was found a bed in a local home. Bob attended church every week, becoming friends with the priest. When the priest passed on he had requested Bob read the eulogy, which he had considered the greatest honour he could imagine. The priest had been a good man, educating Bob on the rights and wrongs of life, and how respecting everyone and forgiving all was key, although he never mentioned drinking. He loved a tipple, something Bob did not replicate.

Bob had come across Gary when both were nineteen. Bob had witnessed Gary service a debt for someone and had been intrigued by the initial kindness shown, followed by the ferocity and speed of Gary's temper once the debtor had tried to make a fool of him. It had excited him, so he had introduced himself to Gary. From that moment they had become friends and work colleagues. Gary always referred to Bob as 'Big Boy'. No one else did.

Bob, although an educated man, enjoyed working alone. He felt people complicated everything and life became unbearable. He could not understand why people would moan and groan about everything, it was either; too hot, too cold, not enough, too much. He felt like screaming, choosing instead to watch them with distain, like they were rats scuttling amongst the dead. He considered life to be a blessing and one that should be cherished and loved. Attending church allowed him to consider words of wisdom and hymns of praise and joy. After each service he would sit in his pew and study the magnificent architecture. The power he gained from such austere and inspiring surroundings made him want to weep with joy. He believed the Lord had aided the creator to erect such places of beauty and worship.

The local people considered him below intelligence due to his employment. He had applied for the role as Grave Digger as he knew work would be constant and a high percentage of his work outdoors. Weather made no difference. If it was cold he would wrap up, if it was warm he would unbutton his shirt, although not remove it, that would be disrespectful to the dead.

During a passing conversation with Gary he had mentioned wishing to own a Mini, yet they were £600 and how he thought the sum was huge for 1970. Gary immediately offered the money, this was rebuffed by Bob as he believed a man had to earn a wage. Gary offered Bob a chance to earn the money, this he had done nine times since. Each time his choice of vehicle improved, as had his savings.

Grave digging was a specific enterprise and one Bob took seriously.

A standard grave had to be six feet deep, eight feet long and just over two feet wide. These dimensions took into account the coffin size and headstone.

The dead deserved a final resting place that showed respect. Bob could estimate the graves measurements within two inches, and have the grave dug in ninety minutes. It would be perfectly rectangular and sharp looking.

The vicar would often watch to acknowledge the strength and nature of the man digging the grave. Bob thought the vicar was a poof who liked a bit of rough. Having finished the grave, Bob would busy himself ensuring the graveyard looked pristine and tidy for the upcoming service of remembrance. Why films depicted graveyards as bleak places, overgrown with long spiteful plants amazed Bob. The ones he had visited were always well tended and crafted with beauty. Respect was a commodity not often given, yet everyone sort. If the grave-yard was untidy the public would mention it straight away. It was a sanctuary away from their morbid lives and one they expected to be different, clean and perfect.

Having heard Gary's idea for the purchase of the mini he sat aghast. He sat as if frozen. Gary, his friend, had just pro-posed he bury people under coffins. The idea appeared simple enough, the manner in which Gary had described it astoun-ded Bob, 'I'll supply a stiff, sling it in the 'ole, fling a load of mud on it, pat it down, job done.'

Bob was amazed. He was in shock, had he heard this correct? Gary would supply a body to be disposed of under a coffin. Had he not considered how disrespectful it would be to the persons final resting place?

'Bob, you all right, you look like you've seen a ghost?'

Bob woke from his dream like state, 'Yes. I am fine. A Mini you said? All right I will do it. I will need to organise it as the vicar can be a bit troublesome.'

Gary jumped on the reply quickly, 'Don't worry about that shirt lifter. He likes a few young 'uns. If he gets busy I'll have a word in his ear.'

A word in his ear. Bob understood this to mean Gary will sort the problem out thoroughly. The thoroughly part concerned Bob.

The statement kept spinning round in Bob's mind. The lack of respect shown to the dead amazed him. Gary had just trivialized death. He understood the person being buried under the coffin was not an up-standing individual of the community and probably deserved his comeuppance, yet everyone deserved some dignity, even villains.

The plan had been easy enough. Instead of digging a six-foot hole, he dug nine. This would ensure three feet of soil and earth would cover the corpse. The body would be placed in the grave early morning before the remembrance. Bob would dig the grave the previous day. Covering the body with soil would finish the job. He would guard the grave until the service.

Gary arrived with the body at 4am. As he removed it from the boot of his car he considered why graveyards were always cold. Even when the temperature was high during the day they were always chilly. What was it with these places that did not allow heat to gain entry? The body was wrapped in a thin black cotton sheet and weighed heavily. The occupant was not a big man, but weighed like he was a horse.

Bob had told him a dead weight basically meant the centre of gravity is wherever you are supporting the weighted load with no support, whether this was correct Gary was unsure, although it sounded plausible.

The spade sliced the dirt majestically. Fragments of earth spluttered onto Bob's ankles, hard and dense, like miniature pebbles. Muscles strong and practiced, stuck in their own perpetual motion, drove at the earth. The tough soil made soft by his spade, and by the strength of his arms. It was hard work, made easy by the man excavating the hole.

Finally, the two men carried the body over to the grave, where it was unceremoniously thrown into the grave.

Bob eyed Gary as he tossed the body. He had treated it as if it was garden waste.

The person now in the grave had been born to a world where his mother who would have loved him, fed him, bathed him and protected him, yet events had taken him to a path that had led to his life being cut short. Who the person was he did not wish to know, obviously someone who had annoyed Gary?

Bob then got busy ensuring the body was facing up and the mouth open. This allowed soil to enter the mouth so it would decompose quicker. Lye had been placed under the body to aid the decomposition. The earth was compacted across the body. This was done meticulously so if assessed by the vicar it would look as sharp and professional as any other grave. As dawn began to break the job had been completed. Bob stood up and recited a pray quietly and made the sign of the cross. Gary looked on and realised he was watching a man pay his respects to someone he had never met, yet felt deserved a final send off to their next journey.

Gary did not wish to tell Bob the person they had buried was a paedophile who had abused two brothers from Bow. He had overheard the boys' father telling someone in the cafe that he was going to serve justice for the man who had removed both his sons' dignity.

Gary had made some discrete enquiries and been informed the man was a known nonce who had made a career in avoiding the law, although they knew his fetish. He appeared to frighten his young victims to the extent they were paralysed with fear and would not testify against him. The father need worry no more. Gary had drugged the paedophile and removed his penis before ramming a nine-inch knife into the man's rectum. He had located the residence of the boy's father and left a note compiled from letters surgically removed from the daily newspapers. He also placed the man's penis into the envelope before posting it through the door. The note simply said, 'Justice has been served, G'.

The boys' father was immediately pulled in for questioning, but his alibi was totally watertight, and he showed the police officers the note he had received along with the dried penis. Having considered the facts and evidence, the officers allowed the father to leave and thought a vigilante may be scouring the streets. The paedophile's death would be placed at the bottom of their investigation list. They had decided it was a job to analyse when things were quiet, until such times it would remain on the 'to do list'. No body, meant no thorough investigation, yet a posted penis had to be looked into-…sometime.

The job been surprisingly easy, yet he surprisingly felt no remorse. If Gary felt the need to dispose of someone in this way, then he obviously believed they were people not fit to walk the earth. The priest had told him to respect and love all, but had a quietly said, 'There are exceptions to this rule, which I am sure the Lord would forgive.' Whoever he meant, was anyone's guess. So hopefully he would forgive himself and Gary now.

Bob selected his car and agreed to carry on the enterprise. He was rather pleased with his new white mini. It looked rather dashing. Death and taxes were certainly an avenue that paid well.

Chapter 3

Putting it together

The time had come to remove the twin brothers from London – forever.

People who lived close by said they were angels who stopped all local trouble, although those with businesses were terrified of them. Money with menaces was their profession. Simple shop keepers or pub landlords were expected to pay for a non-existent service. There was no trouble in the area, so they did not require protection. The protection money was to ensure the brothers left you alone.

Gary thought this was disgrace. He understood people had to earn a living, but a living for providing no service was unjustified. It was the sort of thing his waster of a father would have been involved in… if he had had any arse-hole.

The brothers had begun to hear whispers of someone called 'G' who aided those with justice. They had no idea who this superman was, although rumours were sweeping it was a rival villain. Anyone known locally who had been in trouble was given a face to face meeting with the brothers to ensure their loyalty was to them. No one dared argue, and all said they would aid the brothers plight to find this *superman*.

Gary had been in the Bakers Arms public house in Leyton reading the *Sporting Life*, which he had purchased from the paper stall outside. He heard a group of men talking about the brothers and their search for the *G Man*. He had listened to their conversation intently and understood a bounty of £200 had been placed on his head for those who could name him and his whereabouts. He now had to take action to remove these two men, for good.

Having met the brothers once he had a considerable advantage, he knew them, whereas they had no idea who he was. They were creatures of habit. They both wore black mohair suits – which were identical, crisp white shirts with cuff-links and ties to match their suits' colour. The routines they followed never changed. They would go to the same cafe, visit some local establishments for easy money and call into the snooker hall. Having spent three or four hours there, they would leave and have a beer, for which they never paid.

Every time Gary saw them he grew angrier inside. He was like a mountain of lava ready to explode. The time had come to remove these pariahs of London. They were no good fucking ponces who preyed on the weak or defenceless. He was going to do them both, one after the other, and he would like one brother to watch the other executed. This would be a magnanimous gesture to all in London. The people of East London would celebrate.

The Smith Brothers will shortly be known as The Dead Brothers. The thought excited Gary. He would then begin to gain control of London. He would ensure local villains answered to him, and any wrong doing by them would be met with such severity they would never cross him again.

The Gravedigger would need to be informed, and he would

want a sizeable fee due to the quality, and quantity of the burial.

Gary began to think of ways to end the twin's reign. Drugs would be required to put both into an induced state, although he would have to lure them into a false arena. This would be difficult as both brothers relayed their movements to all who could hear, although both had different tastes in sexuality.

Gary had heard that one of the brothers, Dave, frequented men only parties. The sort of parties where anything goes. Discreet enquiries had told him Dolphin Square was the venue. An opulent set of flats where wealthy patrons included politicians, civil servants, peers and security personnel. The flats stood very proud and housed the wealthy.

Robin Shaftsbury, a hedonistic bisexual, was the man hosting the party. It had been rumored that Shaftsbury had been involved in a long-running affair with the wife of a well-known politician, many thought it was the wife of the former Prime Minister.

Through contacts, Gary had found out that Shaftsbury had struck up a friendship with Dave Smith over their shared taste for very young men. It appeared they had met at a previous sex soirée and had enjoyed the ample pleasures on offer. He had also established both men were hunters of men, and both had vivacious appetites of lustful greed.

Eliminating one of the twins could be done during the evening of the party. He assumed everyone participating would drink heavily and consume drugs, therefore, increasing his chances of success. He had also been informed all men present wore masks to hide their identity, which heightened the thrill of expectation and anticipation. Gary did not understand the thrill of being fucked in the arse by another man, nor would he ever understand it, yet it would allow him the chance to remove one half of the East London brotherhood.

There would be repercussions for those involved at the party, specifically from Steve Smith, but if he slipped in and slipped out, no-one would know he had even visited the sordid banquet of flesh. Yet, if he could remove both brothers within seventy-two hours, neither would know.

Drugs would be the easiest way to end a life, specifically nitrate or methamphetamine, although he had been informed a new drug called Gray Death would kill someone instantly. If he could source Gray Death that would be his weapon of choice. He could inform Dave it was nitrate, the muscle relaxant, and watch his lifespan ebb away when he gorged on it. Gary would enjoy listening to Dave's shallow breathing and loss of consciousness until heart failure finished him. It would be interesting watching someone die, knowing you can save them, but not wishing to.

The idea appeared practical enough, although a little basic, yet simple plans were often the best plans.

He knew the gravedigger would remove the body from life itself if required. This left two obstacles to overcome, sourcing the drugs and gaining entry into the party of deprivation.

Sourcing the drugs would be tricky, but something he could over come, but gaining entry to the party could prove troublesome. He only knew one name, and that was the person he intended to eliminate. Robin Shaftsbury would have to be his entrance. He was the weak link. He would be suspicious, but his morals may be his undoing. Young men and drugs would be required.

An idea was beginning to form. He would host a male only party full of escorts. They would be paid to have sex with whoever was available, this included Shaftsbury. Drugs and drink would be plentiful. Hiring a flat in a prestigious part of London would be expensive, but worth it. He would drop a letter to Shaftsbury, stating a private party had been arranged and his presence would be welcome. The man had the morals of an alley cat, so he would attend. Drink, drugs and lubricated arse's would ensure he stayed.

Gary was in a private gentleman's club in Piccadilly taking a sauna, having had a nice relaxing stress-free day. The door was suddenly opened, and two men walked in. Gary noticed they sat close together. He suddenly became very interested when he noted one of the gentlemen was Robin Shaftsbury and the other was Malcolm Mason the Arsenal player. He immediately thought it an unusual coupling. Shaftsbury was whispering to Mason who suddenly screamed out loud, 'A party, just like the last one, far out?'

Gary pretended to act surprised by the sudden outburst. Shaftsbury swiftly chastised Mason and told him to calm down. This was all the information Gary required. He finally knew how to remove Dave Smith without being known. It was like the stars had aligned to aid his progression. Shaftsbury was hosting his own party, and he had also learnt Malcolm Mason and Shaftsbury were 'friends'. A nice day had become an amazing one.

The three men sat in silence for a further ten minutes before Gary left, leaving the love birds together.

Having showered and changed, Gary decided to dine at the club. Seating in a scrolled wingback chesterfield he picked a newspaper and ordered a whisky and dry ginger from the steward, who was immaculately dressed, as usual, in his starched white jacket and jet-black trousers, his shoes shone like two mirrors. Gary considered how a boy from Dagenham could lavish such luxury on a club like this. Whenever he entered the establishment, he felt he did not belong there, which amused him, as he knew one or two of the members felt he did not belong there either.

Whilst waiting for his table, Shaftsbury and Mason immerged, looking rather red in the face. They sat in two chairs close to Gary. Shaftsbury turned to Gary and spoke in an uninterested fashion, 'Hope the yelp did not disturb you in the sauna?'

Gary looked at both parties replying, 'I was in my own private world. Sorry.'

'I'm Robin Shaftsbury. Forgive me for asking, but I don't know your name?'

'Gary Jones.'

'I'm Malcolm Mason, the Arsenal player.'

'I support West Ham.' Gary replied in a matter of fact manner.

All three men laughed.

'Are you dining alone?' Shaftsbury asked inquisitively.

Gary did not wish to dine with the two gentlemen. He wished to keep them both at arm's length, having just met them. Turning he answered, 'I am, it's something I enjoy when I come to White's. The sense of peace gives me thinking time.'

Shaftsbury was trying to calculate the man standing before them. He appeared decent, although he felt there was an edge to him, possibly military. He was also considering whether he was party material. He noted there was no wedding ring, that was suspicious, a good-looking man…unmarried!

Gary was saved by the steward who came to inform him his table had been prepared. Gary stood, shook both gentlemen's hands, and left, thinking of the Devilled Kidneys on Italian bread he was planning on devouring.

Shaftsbury swiftly turned to Mason whispering, 'What do you think of the Jones gentleman?' He did not expect a plethora of magnificent vocabulary to escape from Mason's unintelligent mouth.

'He's well fit, I'd knob him.'

Shaftsbury raised his eyebrows.

Mason did not understand whether he had said a good or bad thing to Shaftsbury, what he had said was honest. His mum had always told him to be honest, which he sort of was, apart from the fact he was supposed to be seeing Carly Jens. As if he would like her. For one she was blonde, the second being he liked blokes and the third, she was in a relationship with her manager – another woman. The press lapped it up when they went out. It suited Mason as no-one knew he was gay, although he knew Jens was a lesbian, as he had been paid a substantial sum to be her beard, in an attempt to dispel rumours of her sexuality. Only Shaftsbury knew totally about his sexuality, having caught him in a compromising position in the toilets of The White Bear in Kennington one Sunday evening.

Mason had been attracted to Shaftsbury instantly. He liked

his persona; the way he dressed, the way he spoke and how he instantly commanded respect. Mason wanted to learn from this man, and learn he had. He had met ministers, sports stars, television personalities, minor royalty, the list was endless, they all had one thing in common. They had a secret that needed guarding, a secret so explosive it would finish them all. A secret of double lives and outrageous, perverted parties. Shaftsbury was the man. He knew everything about everyone. He could get anything or anyone, quickly. What a man.

Shaftsbury eyed Mason, 'Do you only think with your groin? Lovely though it is. You need to broaden your horizons.'

'Broaden my horizons, yeah, that sounds all right. How shall I do it?

Internally Shaftsbury wanted to shake this barbarian of a man into a new world, but he knew he loved him equally. Slow and lacking in vocabulary as he was, there was something beautiful about him, and he was incredibly kind and honest. Plus, he understood Mason felt the same towards him.

Both understood love for the other, although the thought of having something on the side was enjoyed by both. As long as it did not interfere with their life together, that was accepted.

Jones was thoroughly enjoying the Devilled Kidneys. They were succulent, and the homemade bread heightened the taste. He had decided to follow it with Baked Alaska. The sweet taste would link nicely with the livery taste of the kidney. The meal was beautiful, light and refreshing. He finished with a black coffee, paid the bill and left. He made sure Shaftsbury did not see him again. He sensed Mason was a predator and would like to get to know him better, although that had zero chance of happening.

Leaning against the polished bar in the Golden Lion public house in Romford, Gary noticed a plaque on the wall that informed drinkers Dick Turpin and Wilfred Owen had frequented the establishment. Gary knew Owen had been stationed in Gidea Park at the beginning of World War 1 in Hare Hall, but the Dick Turpin information made him smile. This public house must attract a certain kind of bad boy with the occasional good one thrown in for good measure. Another picture offered information on the history of Romford Market. The pictures were incredibly grainy, yet showed there had been a market since 1247.

He eyed the clientele. It was the first market day of the week – Wednesday, therefore, a few traders were enjoying a mid-morning pie and pint, and retired husbands were savouring a quiet beer away from their wives, who were probably busying themselves in the market having given their husbands an errand to do, which they had failed to achieve.

Gary was waiting for the Gravedigger to arrive. He had already purchased his drink, a pint of Bitter Lemon. When he had ordered it, the barman had asked if he had heard correctly. When the drink had been served it had looked refreshingly nice. He considered trying it, but thought it would be poor taste to try another man's beverage.

The door of the bar opened, and a large man stooped to enter. He immediately strode up-to Gary, lifted his drink and slurped half of it in one magnificent gulp, wiped his mouth with the back of his hand and said, 'Wotcha Gal'.

A man of few words. The Gravedigger had arrived.

Gary pointed to a table for them to sit and discuss business. The table was situated in the far corner away from prying eyes and drinkers with a penchant for listening to other conversations.

Both parties made themselves comfortable. Neither believed, nor wished to engage in small talk.

The Gravedigger eyed Gary and asked in a matter of fact manner, 'The usual?'

The reply he received shocked him. His overactive and precise brain quickly calculated the dimensions. The information he had just been given still reverberated uneasily. The Smiths, both of them.

He eyed Gary and spoke directly, quietly and precisely, 'In my experience there aren't many evil people around. Just ill informed, ignorant and misguided ones, but these brothers are cunts!'

Gary was shocked at the terminology used to described the Smith brothers. He had never heard the man sitting in front of him use any form of profanity. He considered his reply and curtly replied, 'A friend in need is not needed, and these two have no friends, therefore, they are not required.'

Gary took a sip of his refreshing beer and pondered how to extend this barren conversation. Before he could form a sentence his acquaintance began to speak.

'These men are notorious; we will be doing life a justice ending their reign. They believe they are tough, ruthless and powerful, yet they are not. People are afraid of the reputation, not the man. Gary, people will be frightened of you, but equally respect you at the same time. This is why you will rule London. You will be like Robin Hood.'

Gary stared at his friend and considered what he had just been told and sarcastically rebuked, 'Robin Hood, a bloke who wears tights. Bollocks to that Bob.'

A roar of laughter escaped their mouths. Tears streamed down Gary's cheeks, and his body shook. His friend began to laugh raucously with a mouth full of throat numbing bitter lemon.

No-one paid any attention to the men laughing. Once both had composed themselves and finished their beverages they bid the other farewell and went their separate ways.

Gary strode down the street taking purposeful steps. As he strode passed Our Price record shop in South Street the music playing was distasteful. The men were wearing makeup and calling themselves Punks. The song being blared out was 'London's Calling'. All the radio stations were playing it. It was dreadful. He made his way to the paper stall on the corner and purchased a copy of the *Daily Mirror*, handing over 10p to the old man who worked the afternoon shift for the business.

Fifty yards further on he entered the snooker hall and bound up the steps. Opening the door, he was immediately hit with the stale smell of smoke. The smoke appeared to float in the air with an invisible force, its grey look giving a menacing feel to the already busy, yet quiet den of gambling and *unofficial* business taking place amongst those in the legal enterprise.

Gary immediately went to table 8 that had one competitor. This person was known locally as Mr Bigtime. He had received the moniker by his often-exaggerated mannerisms and his big booming voice shouting 'bigtime' when he thought something, or someone was too minuscule for his attention. He noted Gary walking over; confident, purposeful, successful...and dangerous, fucking dangerous.

He arrived at the table and lifted a cue. Those on the surrounding tables looked on, unsure whether trouble was brewing. Previously, someone had done something similar and had been snooker-balled leaving the hall minus their front teeth and a fractured cheek bone, although this may have been caused by them losing their footing down the stairs.

'Johnny, I'm feeling lucky today, tenner sez I win.'

Johnny 'Bigtime' smiled, 'You silly fucker, I'll demolish you.'

Both men laughed and began their frame. Thirty-seven minutes later it was completed. Johnny had won on the black ball by 5 points. It had been close, very few people had the bottle to challenge Bigtime and run him close. He had enjoyed the contest, now it was down to business.

Both men were brought over a cup of steaming hot tea in white china mugs. Johnny signalled for Gary to join him in the dark corner, an area known to his colleagues as 'the business corner'. Everyone understood to not disturb Johnny when he was in the corner until he stood up. One of the younger employees had gone to pass a message and had been met with a glass ash tray across the face that had required twelve deep stitches previously.

Gary had met Johnny at Boyles Court. He had served a one-year term for robbery and violence; he had been thirteen.

Johnny was one of the people trusted by Gary, and this was reciprocated. Johnny knew the ferocity of violence served by Gary if you crossed his negative pathway. They very rarely saw one another, but when they did, the past was never spoken of, as the future was all they cared for.

When both men were comfortable, and happy no one was listening, the conversation began, 'What you after Gal?'

'I need entrance to a select, but strange party taking place in London, Dolphin Square.'

Johnny nodded, unblinking, 'I assume this party is so special no one must know who you are?'

'You read my mind.'

Gary had always been a man of few words, and when used, they were selected carefully, giving nothing away.

Johnny appeared deep in thought, 'How special?'

'This party is about as special as it gets without the royal family being present.' Gary whispered, emphasizing the word special.

'There'll be a cost, plus the entrance fee to the party.'

'What sort of cost am I looking at Johnny?'

'I don't want nothing financially, although I want information about anyone present at the gathering, although you will have to pay the cost of entrance, whatever it is. I won't stiff you, you know that.'

If there was one man who would not have Gary over for anything it was Johnny. It was known he was harsh if you fucked him about, but straight and to the point if you wanted anything and had the cash.

Gary looked at Johnny and passed an envelope, 'There's 10k there, you may need to sweeten a few people.'

In the pit of his stomach Johnny had a feeling Gary was going big time, and this party idea was something that had to happen. It also meant it was something that could be fucking explosive, in good and bad ways. He just hoped the positive side would expunge the negative. 'Fuck. Now I need to be Johnny Bigtime' he thought privately.

Gary stared at the man in front of him and asked if he was all right.

Johnny quietly asked if there was a contact for the party.

'Robin Shaftsbury.'

Johnny blanched, 'Did you say Robin Shaftsbury? The poofy bloke, who's in with all the top brass?'

This was met with an immediate, 'Yes.'

Gary was not going big time. He was going to the top. There must be something going on at this party with so much importance money was no object. Yet Gary was no fairy, so why was he going to a fairy party?

'Gal, whatever you're getting involved in, be careful. Shaftsbury's a slippery cunt, in fact a total cunt. He'd sell his own mother to earn a few quid. Me and you have been friends many years. Just be careful.'

No-one spoke to him in that way. He realised Johnny was showing a softer side, a protective side, almost brotherly. It also showed for the first time in existence – Johnny was worried.

'Give me 48 hours, and I'll have some information for you'.

•

'Robin Shaftsbury?'

He stood perfectly still, and turned serenely, almost cream like. Showing complete confidence in himself. His piercing eyes bore into the man requesting him, 'I am he.'

'We need to talk about a party you're holding.'

'A party? I have no idea what you are talking about.' His curiosity peeked.

'Does five grand spike your memory and curiosity?'

Immediately Johnny noticed a flicker in Shaftsbury's eye and knew he'd been hooked, therefore, greed was his undoing.

'£5,000, it must be a good party you wish to gain entry?'

'My client considers it one he very much looks forward to attending, oh, I nearly forgot, there's another £5,000 for a list of the people attending. All cash.'

'List? Why would he require a list?'

'He's hoping there's someone on the list he'd like to get to know a lot better, anally.' Johnny looked at Shaftsbury and winked and raised his eyebrows, 'I think you know what I mean.'

Shaftsbury began to feel a stirring in his loins. He considered the proposition, 'Is this person of serious wealth?'

'Fucking serious.'

Shaftsbury detected the heavy London accent in this man's manner. This ruled out security services. He guessed he was representing a high-level banker and this man was his security advisor, his heavy.

'What is the name of your client?'

Johnny had already anticipated this question and decided shortening Gary's name and using his mother's name as the surname.

'Gary Rose.'

Shaftsbury considered the name and quickly calculated it was a new one to him, therefore someone who could be another high-ranking contact.

'I want the money in cash, and can give you the list tomorrow.'

The man standing opposite placed his hand inside his brown overcoat, in which time Shaftsbury had a vision he was about to be shot. An envelope was suddenly offered to him

'There's your readies.'

Shaftsbury was shocked, although showed none of it. For a man to be carrying £10,000 in cash showed confidence, wealth and above all – ruthlessness. This man was worthy of being a contact alone, so who the fuck was Gary Rose?

Shaftsbury did some checking for Gary Rose and had come up with nothing. This man was a ghost, therefore he thought he was someone famous who would be recognised instantly. He became excited and considered the possibilities. He had been told Rock Hudson was gay, although the film industry kept it quiet and paid people off. Imagine it was someone like that. He had that stirring feeling again. For someone to be able to pay £5,000 cash showed considerable wealth. He finally settled it was someone high ranking within the entertainment industry. His feelings were usually correct.

Johnny met Shaftsbury at 10am. It was cold and damp with pedestrians carefully dodging the droplets falling from the dark sky. One such pedestrian was Robin Shaftsbury, who was in a hurry to get to Piccadilly Circus. He hated being late for a meeting, and this had ten-thousand reasons to not be late.

Johnny was standing by the statue of Eros. He had laughed at the agreed meeting place, as the statue was also known as Shaftesbury Memorial Fountain. Robin Shaftsbury obviously enjoyed aligning himself with the great and good, and this included statues sharing the same name. Fucking oddball.

'Hello man with no name. How are you?'

Johnny stared unblinkingly at Shaftsbury, which in turn made his nemesis uneasy. 'I'm good, got the list?'

'You need to improve your interpersonal skills. It will allow you to get on in life and introduce you to a better standard of person.'

'If you're trying to fuck me off, or mug me off, tiptoe very fucking carefully you no good little cunt.'

Shaftsbury was shocked to the bone. No one dare speak to him in that dreadful manner in such an overt and aggressive way. He now knew the man standing opposite him was dangerous, incredibly dangerous. This changed everything. He now understood the person he was representing was powerful, therefore ruling out someone from the entertainment industry. This confused and excited him. It added danger to scenario.

'I'm waiting.'

Shaftsbury passed Johnny a small plain brown envelope, similar to those used by thousands of people each day. 'There you are; patience is a vir…'

He did not have time to finish the sentence before the man had left him and marched off into the gloomy distance.

The Kings Head smelt of cigarette smoke, it was like a perfume that clung to clothing, skin and furniture alike. There also lingered the smell of stale beer and body odour.

Many conversations told in loud voices, all of them competing, believing theirs was the funniest or most important.

Johnny saw Gary sitting in the corner reading a copy of the *Daily Mirror*. He fixed him in a look that would make any character other than his friend shrivel. He met his gaze with the smile of one who knows the upper hand should be his, although unsure if it was. He lit a cigarette to add to the hazy cloud, lingering, spiraling in stagnant air and sat on the dark wooden chair opposite Gary.

Immediately Gary sprang up, 'Pint?'

Johnny was shocked at the immediacy of the question and reaction, 'Yeah, nice.'

Gary placed the light and bitter in front of Johnny, who took a huge slurp from the glass, downing half of it, before topping it up with the remnants of the Courage Light Ale. He then placed his hand inside his jacket pocket and produced the envelope Gary obviously craved. Johnny studied Gary's reaction. It was everything; desire, passion, danger, greed. He had never seen him like this. It was a little un-nerving. Something had changed in Gary's persona, and it could be bad for the receiver.

'Everything go all right? How was Shaftsbury?'

'Five grand got you in, your list was five-grand. I didn't like him, wouldn't trust him. As soon as I mentioned the money, a slight smile grew on his face. He's the sort of bloke who'll sell you out. Be careful Gaz, this bloke is a cunt of the highest echelons. He has no morals. He'll grass to save his skin. Whatever you're up-to, just be careful of this snake.'

Gary was amazed by the passion Johnny had shown for protecting him. He knew he was solid, but it was brotherly.

He genuinely meant it, 'Don't worry about me. I know what Shaftsbury is like. He is a money man, loves the stuff. He can be bought, and he'll sell anyone, you're right there. Slippery and untrusting is how I'd describe him.'

Both men began to laugh.

'So, he won't be welcome in this watering hole?'

Chapter 4

DCI Jack Philips

Who was this man? He was a vigilante the public loved, almost craved. He killed the killers, which was no bad thing, yet lawlessness was not what the Metropolitan Police required. A modern-day Robin Hood. Why could it not have happened in seven years when he would have retired? Bloody typical.

He sat at his old wooden tired desk with his unpolished, black brogue shoes resting on it. Leaning back in his chair like he was on a long overdue sunny holiday. He was pondering the effects of the recent spate of killings. He had been trying to work out how this person had learnt about the hidden dark practices of those murdered, even the police did not know about three of these. Who was he? Where had he come from? Why did he wish to kill these people? Who was HE? Another problem worried him. Over the years many people had gone missing. The people missing were non-desirables. Yet they had just – gone missing, but where had they gone. He had a nasty feeling, that experienced police officers have, the person responsible for it was the same man they were looking for. His thought process was broken by the new shapely WPC walking in. She looked at him and nervously said, 'Mornin' sir.' He looked at her in a salacious manner that most of the men in the station gave her, yet she appeared to like him, he had no idea why.

'Would you like a tea sir?'

Jack looked at her appraising the question and responded with a simple nod of the head. She laughed.

Sylvie had been based at the station for six months. During that time, she had been asked out on a date seventeen times, yet the one man to not ask her on a date was the man she was making tea for. He was a handsome man in his early forties, who had a rugged look about him. His shoes were never polished, but quality, his suit lived in – yet not untidy. His general demeanour unwholesome, yet manly. He had something about him that made every lady at the station want him, old and young. He was unmarried and did not live with anyone. Rumours had circulated that he may be queer, but these did not last long. He had supposedly heard the rumours and his response was, 'They think I'm queer, so what.' He was a real man. Sylvie passed him the tea. Jack picked it up and studied it before quietly muttering 'Builder's tea, just what the doctor ordered.' He took a sip from the dark grey mug and carried on pondering.

Sylvie was bursting to say something to him, yet did not know what to say. Jack turned in his chair and removed his feet from the desk, and looked directly at her, 'Cat got your tongue?'

'No sir. Sorry.' Sylvie replied in an innocent yet childish manner.

'Sorry for what you daft mare? You have haven't done anything wrong.... have you?'

'No sir, never' she stammered. Knowing she was making

herself look foolish. She composed herself quickly and responded 'What are you thinking about sir, if you don't mind me asking? You were miles away when I walked in. Totally different planet. Every man in this nick notices me, but you didn't, makes a nice change.'

Jack smiled inwardly. This cheeky young WPC had a bit about her. He liked that. She had balls. Most, no all, WPC's were too lightweight and timid, yet this one had arsehole. She was questioning him.

He faced her and replied in a matter of fact way, 'These murders are getting on my nerves, they need to be solved, but there is nothing to go on. The last person we brought in for the sketch artist described Dennis the Menace, and another Roy Race. This person has become a cult hero and it needs to stop sharpish. There, rant over.'

She looked at him and felt she was going to melt. He was so manly.

'You all right love?'

Sylvia came out of her hypnotic love trance, 'If you need a WPC on your task force sir, consider me.' She turned and left Jack to his own devices without waiting for a reply.

He returned to the missing person reports. They all had one thing in common. The radius was ten miles from Dagenham East police station, which lead Jack to understand it was a local person who knew the surrounding areas incredibly well. They would know alleyways, car parks, transport links, parks, pubs, short cuts…everything. It was definitely a local person, he knew it, he was sure of it. A person who would blend in with everyone, had respect and the likeability factor. This was going to be tricky. Someone must have an idea who it is. No one covers their tracks that well, unless they are a loner. A loner! He had not considered it. They had interviewed every low-life and underworld connected person, but not one person had been alone. They had come in pairs or gangs. It's a LONER.

He bounced out of his chair and made his way to the Chief Superintendent Taylor.

Twenty minutes later Jack left the office.

The chief super had considered his points, mulled them over and agreed quickly that this angle was certainly one worth pursuing. The man did not need much persuasion. Jack was one of his senior and trusted officers, and if he thought this was the correct course of action – then it was. Jack was a pit-bull, and if he felt he had a small opening, then that opening usually snowballed quickly.

Taylor had known Jack many years and considered him a career officer. He had dedicated his life to the force. This dedication increased when his childhood sweetheart had drowned when they were in their early twenties and Jack had been unable to save her. From that moment no one stood in his way. Many had recommended Jack for promotion, yet he always turned it down citing one reason or another; it was never the right time, wrong department, too busy, the list was endless. Yet he was considered the best, and if any officer was going to crack this case, it would be Jack. He had a calculating mind that appeared to be working constantly. All angles were considered, and nothing was left unchecked. MI5 had monitored his progress due to his lack of family and diligent behaviour, yet Jack had informed them he was a copper, not a spy.

Jack was tasked with assembling a team to crack this mysterious case about a mysterious man aiding the affected, and killing the infected. This puzzled Jack. Why would a lone man help those who suffered at the hands of the mentally unstable, yet took a no payment for his trouble?

This man must be connected or known somewhere. All men enjoy a pint, and most a bet. These could be avenues worth pursuing, although they would be time consuming. Local low lives would be pulled in for questioning, hopefully a shakedown would worry a few into spilling the beans on whispers they had heard in their community, yet the information supplied was often unreliable.

The station was a cauldron of activity and the heat inside C.I.D was immense. The telephone was red hot with officers trying to contact informers, or locate them. The silence was broken by a deep manly shout that offered information.

'We've heard there's one of those odd ball parties taking place at Dolphin Square sir.'

Jack looked at the officer and considered what he meant by it. 'Is there?'

'Yep. It'll be full of fruits from parliament and theatre.'

Jack now understood the connection between oddball and fruits, 'What are you suggesting? You wish to attend?'

Everyone in the room laughed out loud at the sarcasm supplied from their DCI.

The officer stood his ground with purpose and replied in a controlled, yet officious manner, 'Oh, and Dave Smith will be attending sir.'

Suddenly the room went silent. The atmosphere changed immediately. Heads spun round; it was like time had stopped. Jack considered this information and stared coldly at his officer, 'Are you sure?' There had been rumours, strong rumours that Dave Smith enjoyed pleasuring the male species, but nothing had surfaced, and no-one would confirm it. Now a golden opportunity may have been sent from the gods.

'Bloke I know said it was a party similar to a previous one. It's an invite only bash. Costs a few quid as well to gain entry. Men only. Drugs, drink and sex are the themes.'

The information supplied by his officer was pondered, calculated and evaluated immediately by Jack's methodical brain. A photographer would be noticed, and entrance to the party would be near impossible. The only feasible avenue would be hiring a room at the complex...if possible. The budget would need to be taken into consideration and Jack was sure the security services, specifically MI5, would be having a nose. This would be tricky, but mouthwateringly tempting.

'What do you think sir? Do you think it has legs?'

Jack eyed the officer and replied in a non-committal manner, 'It may do son; it may well do.'

These opportunities showed themselves infrequently, and when they did you had to pounce. Jack looked squarely at the officer from his old wooden chair and gently spoke in a commanding manner, 'How sure are you this party is taking place? And when is this den of disgrace supposed to be taking place? Also, try to find out how someone gets invited to such an event.'

The officer nodded and walked away, knowing this could be the break he needed to push his career forward.

Jack eyed the officer walking away. He assumed he would be bouncing with joy inside, not understanding the problems he could face with such a party, and those attending. Participants at the party would have friends in high places – the highest, and probably attended the same masonic lodges, allowing them to hear one word and understand two. They would believe that life is a bridge, cross over it, but build no house on it. These people would be untouchable, yet this may be their downfall. Over confidence and lustful greed could bring the house down. It may also produce a few unexpected treasures along the way.

Ambition is a magnificent thing for all concerned, but sometimes caution was the best form of defense. Jack understood all constables wanted a big break, as did those employed within C.I.D, yet sometimes it was worth standing back and considering all the possible implications of a case, particularly a case like this, which could make or break a person's career.

The strength of the opponents worried Jack inwardly. Knowing who was on his side, and knowing who was not, could prove difficult and tiresome. Favours, money, sex, politics, gambling…it would all be used to aid and develop the fight against Jack and his team of honest officers. Honesty and hard work would be the elements to win the battle, and it would be a battle. Jack turned and faced his team, looking at them he knew what a professional and loyal outfit they were. He was proud to serve alongside them.

Chapter 5

Dolphin Square

Shaftsbury was organizing his show stopping party for the great and the good who enjoyed a special night – with a few edible treats thrown in.

The Golden Boys had been booked. They were well-known for their muscular physiques and magnificent arse's, that were great receivers of cock. They were also clean and discreet. At the prices they charged, they needed to be.

Substances to heighten all imaginable internal male powers had been ordered, along with the regulation bowls of cocaine that were expected by all who attended.

The drugs thing always made Shaftsbury smile. Those who gauged on the powder were those who were forever proclaiming it should be banned.

500 bottles of non-vintage champagne had been delivered. He knew his clients enjoyed the non-vintage variety as they enjoyed the fresh and acidic taste along with its fizzy content. During a previous party he had witnessed one bottle being poured into another man's arse, which in turn created an incredible explosion of darkened liquid spraying everywhere. A fantastically disgusting, yet amusing viewing, enjoyed by all those who witnessed it, specifically by the MP who had the beverage poured into his backside.

The seven bedrooms were spotlessly clean, and pure white, almost virginal. How ironic he thought.

Every sexual device known was added to each room, along with the regulation lubricants, although it was barely used.

Music had been arranged. His clients enjoyed a slow start to the evening, but when the booze and drugs began to kick in they enjoyed the ferocious up-tempo type and the lights dimmed down. It gave the party a demonic dark feeling, with corruption and sleaze thrown in.

Shaftsbury pondered how during the day many of these people made rules for good, but as soon as the sun set, they became deviants, and selfish for flesh.

Shaftsbury needed EVERYTHING to be correct and high class, with low class morals. He was charging £1000 to gain entrance. The coded invites had been sent out, and all invited had accepted and paid. Bibles had been sent as an invite, and a code was written inside. This party's code was;

Exodus 20:14:060669:2200:10000:

These were quickly read by those receiving the gift. They all understood the double meaning behind the message. Shaftsbury loved his humorous double meanings on the invites. Exodus 20:14 stood for 'you shall not commit adultery'. Many of the men attending visited church regularly, alongside their families, who had no idea about the double lives their husbands were leading. The code in the bible meant: date, time, price of entry. The one hundred extremely wealthy and powerful men consisted of; politicians, lawyers, sportsmen, pop stars, actors, security personnel, gangsters, newsreaders...the list was endless. All had one thing in common, they were depraved behind closed doors and had false smiles outdoors.

Shaftsbury was salivating at the thought. The power it would give him over those who attended, the secrets he would learn and use against them when required. Some had called his parties *chemsex*, as many men stayed within the environment for days on end, able to continue having sex for long durations of time. One politician had missed a meeting with the Prime Minister as he was so off his head with drugs, and did not care as he had been breaking in an eighteen-year-old pop star from the latest boy band.

•

Jack Philips sat in deep thought considering Dolphin Square and the rudiments and problems it could offer. This operation could go everywhere and anywhere. It was a once in a lifetime campaign that could start and end careers. Neither bothered Jack, although he had to consider those who had families and individuals who did not want involvement in a high level or high-risk case. Having considered the endless possibilities, he knew he required young ambitious officers and those nearing pensionable age. Those stranded in the middle were in the safe zone and plodded along with their young families. Having never been lucky enough to have been granted the fortune of being a father, he always ensured those who had remained safe and happy. There was a lot to be said for being safe and happy. Jack smiled to himself. He was a wily old fox, and he knew it. He reached out and grabbed hold of the coffee mug, and took a swig of the contents that had now gone cold, its bitter taste lubricating his sand-like mouth.

Some of the experienced officers were looking at Jack from the corners of their eyes. They knew he was plotting and planning. Whoever was the recipient of the plan being formed had best be careful. When Jack was feeling alive, no man was safe from conviction, whoever they were.

He sat quietly thinking about the party and Dave Smith. To think, one of the country's hardest criminals had a penchant for gay sex. It went totally against the grain. Having considered the possibilities, he wondered whether they could enter one of the neighboring flats and drill a small hole and listen in. They would not gain facial recognition, although they may learn some useful information. The idea was not fool proof, but had semblance of an idea.

Sitting there he realized he needed first-hand experience of Dolphin Square. Understanding the layout of the local streets, bars and restaurants could prove essential, knowledge was a powerful tool, and this required every piece of knowledge he could muster. He needed fresh eyes, a different perspective; he pondered his question and knew the answer was staring him in the face, WPC Sylvie. She was young, ambitious, sharp and female. She may see something a male colleague could miss, plus she was fresh, she had not been tainted with years of police work. Jack was satisfied she had the qualities for which he was looking. They were also the ones he admired in a policing: intelligence, courage, discretion and common sense, anything else was a bonus.

Having had a brief meeting with Chief Inspector Taylor, he

found WPC Sylvie and spoke to her Sergeant, who understood what was required. He had not informed Jack that Taylor had already informed him what was happening, and it had been an order.

Jack briefed Sylvie quickly at the station, before informing her they needed to leave. On the way to Victoria Station he quietly fed her further information on the what he wanted her to do. He could tell by the way she was gazing at him she felt it was her big opportunity. Maybe it was. This could be explosive for all involved, and career defining.

Jack had researched background information on Dolphin Square, and found it had a colourful history. During World War 2, 'black shirt' leader Oswald Mosley was arrested in his Dolphin Square flat and driven to prison. MI5's Maxwell Knight recruited Ian Fleming to the Secret Service from a flat a few doors down. Charles de Gaulle based his Free France government in the square during the war. It had an unusual history and appeared to attract a specific person.

Arriving at the square, both Jack and Sylvie were struck with a feeling of wealth. 1200 flats set around a garden courtyard, each having views of trees and a dolphin-shaped fountain. Sylvie tried to imagine how it must feel to live in such splendour in the middle of the world's greatest capital. Jack noted that each block was named after someone connected to the United Kingdom's distinguished maritime history. Accommodation was provided in 13 blocks, each named after the famous navigator or admiral; Grenville, Drake, Raleigh and Collingwood were some of the names used. Both noted how each building had a form of uniformity, they stood like guarding soldiers.

'Sylvie, this could prove tricky, everything is identical. One building resembles another; this could leave it open for anyone to enter the wrong block. What do you think?'

'Sir, I'd get lost in here. It is so beautiful in a mysterious way. It's like it's an oasis that hold secrets forever. Secrets that never surface. Do you know what I mean?'

'It's too perfect, just too nice. Something's not right here. I feel it.'

Walking past the entrance to Duncan House; both admired the timber double doors. It offered a feeling of opulence, grandeur and luxury. The garden's lawn was perfectly manicured, and the overhanging tress looked like arms trying to caress the perfectly cut grass.

'Sir, this place is pretty tight for security. How is everyone going to get in without being noticed? I know people can enter and sit in the garden, but a party, that's a different ball game all together.'

'Go on.'

'Well. My friends are trainee nurses and have parties in their flats, so invite the neighbours. Yet this party appears to remove all elements of neighbourly contact. It's un-neighbourly.'

'That's a fair point WPC. So, we could be looking for a number of flats left empty during the week.'

'The higher the better sir. If it were me I'd want the penthouse. No distractions, quiet, people could be offered gifts to go away…if you get my meaning sir.'

Jack looked at her. She'd gone from calling him *guv* to *sir* in under five minutes. The informal friendliness had left her; she had grown into a woman in three hundred seconds. This girl could go far, very far.

The two officers walked out onto Grosvenor Road in a comfortable silence and turned left. Approximately one hundred yards further on Jack detoured into The Grosvenor public house without saying a word to his assistant, who manoeuvred herself next to him swiftly. 'Pint of best and a coke with ice and lemon please?'

'A coke?' Sylvie raised an eyebrow.

'You're on duty. Anyway, something's not right. I have no idea what it is, yet I know it. I feel there is a big hand yet to be played.'

'What do you mean guv?'

The informality had come back. 'I don't know. I'll sort it. I'll sort it, and bring every fucker down.'

Sylvie looked at Jack and felt a sense of fear run through her body. He was the real deal. He was going to crack this case and bring everything and everyone down. She had to stay on this case, whatever it took.

•

'Hello.'

'Robin, it's me. Don't say a word and listen. Jack Philips is all over you. He knows about Dolphin Square. No idea about a date. Got to go.'

The telephone call was swift and to the point. Sylvie was proving to be a nice contact. Having a niece working within the force was beginning to prove dividends. The information she provided had allowed him to keep abreast of the investigation. He now needed Sylvie to be part of the investigative team. She had to up the ante, and if it meant sucking some cock along the way, then cocks she would have to suck. Jack Philips would be one she'd have to dirty her knees for.

Jack Philips was becoming an irritant, yet one he dared not remove. The cardinal rule was police officers were off limits, even if they got to close. If an officer was *removed*, serving officers in the force would be ordered to find and arrest the perpetrator, and this would create chaos amongst those not abiding the law. Shaftsbury knew he would have to play the game, all be it dangerous, and possibly reckless. The adrenaline was still firing through his body due to the excitement of the impending party, yet nerves were still prominent because of investigation. Whatever was happening, was making Shaftsbury feel increasingly randy and eager for sex.

Chapter 6

Steve Smith

S teve knew where his brother had gone, although he thought it disgusting and immoral, he never said. He understood it would cause problems that need not have been caused. Anyway, he had a meeting with a new contact who could be useful to the business. He had been told a man called Gary had five F1 submachine guns for sale. Where he had got them was what interested Steve. He had been trying to obtain a machine gun for some time, yet here was a man, who he did not know, selling five. He wanted £100 for each gun. £100, as if he was going to pay that, he smiled, as if he was going to pay anyway. He felt the smooth leather security casing of the knife in his jacket pocket.

One of his colleagues, Patsy the Paddy, had told him about Gary. Patsy had met Gary at Walthamstow greyhound stadium one evening, and they had become gambling friends over a period of time. Patsy felt Gary had military experience, he had an air of importance with a laddish, yet professional manner about him. Conversations were always low key, apart from the evening Gary had mentioned armoury. Patsy immediately became alert. Gary continued to have small wagers on his selections, yet Patsy's mind had been tempted into other arenas. Over the course of that evening Gary had told everything he wanted Patsy to know, he knew he would want to earn the ear of Steve Smith. The following week Patsy informed him Steve Smith wanted to meet about the weaponry he had.

The journey took thirty minutes to reach the Spencer's Arms public house from his home in Bow. The pub was incredibly big, red bricked and had a large area at the front facing the road with a school on the opposite side. The area looked middle class affluent. It was the sort of place he could imagine settling down in. He had agreed to meet the contact at 7pm. He walked into the sparsely populated bar and noted a man holding a copy of the *Sporting Life*, with a pint placed on the dark wooden circular table in front of him. He had been told his contact Jones would be reading this specific broadsheet newspaper. He strode up to the bar and ordered a pint of Bass Worthington. He took an incredibly dip swig from the beer and sat opposite his contact.

Both men eyed one another in a suspicious, yet inquisitive manner, Gary spoke first 'Steve?'. Gary knew it was him.

Steve had a feeling they had met somewhere before. 'One and only, you're Gary right?'

Gary nodded and whispered quietly, 'Drink up, and we'll sort our business, I don't want the merchandise left where it is.'

Steve considered the news and a deep curiosity got the better of him, 'Where's that?'

'Graveyard.'

Steve studied him and realised this man was shrewd, no pushover. In fact, he had an uneasy feeling that this man could be dangerous, very dangerous. He was unnervingly calm, something members who worked for the twins had said Steve was, yet here was a man facing him who could be his nemesis. It was exciting, he could feel his nerves dancing in anticipation. He felt alive. It felt better as Dave was away on his three-day bender, with the benders. He still had the feeling that they had met, he was certain of it, like a sixth sense. It was beginning to consume his mind. Yes, they had certainly met, but where? 'No problem, I'll neck my beer and we'll go.'

Gary was analysing the man in front of him. He was calm, but looked a little uncomfortable. Not having his brother alongside was unusual, he probably felt a little lost. Gary knew he had the beating of the man in front of him, physically and mentally. In fact, he felt the man sitting in front of him was a little out his depth. Gary suddenly stood, 'Time to make a move.'

Both men entered the grounds of the graveyard. The vicar was away, and as a strange twist of fate had attended the same party Dave Smith was frequenting at Dolphin Square. Funny how life turns out Gary considered.

Steve sat in the car still thinking of a past meeting without success. His concentration was broken by a low whistle and a beckoning hand. He removed himself from the car and carefully bowled over making he sure he missed all the soft, dark, muddy puddles, Gary stood waiting for him. Gary went behind the car and opened the boot. Steve came over and lifted the oil skin cloth to inspect the weapons. Instantly he felt liquid running down his neck. He turned, and his now bulbous eyes were staring for the final moments at his executioner. 'The pub, he was in the fucking pub'. He knew his throat had been cut. He was screaming silently. Pain sheeted through him with a terrible intensity. The trunk of the tree he landed against felt rough against his back and the cold rain was beginning to land on his blood sodden body. The grass, heavy with rain looked like glistening pearls, and the trees were dancing in the night-time breeze. The sky had a dark serenity that offered peace. The moon was fighting to touch everything with its outstretched fingertips. This English graveyard was a picturesque place. This was the end, but it was a beautiful place to die. His eyes were becoming heavy, and he thought about his brother. My lovely brother. He then fell to his side like a dead weight. Gary stood alongside Bob the Gravedigger, looking at one of East London's most feared men. He looked like a tramp about to be consumed by the tree.

'I didn't even hear you! You're like flannel feet, a fucking phantom. For a big man you move quietly.'

The Gravedigger eyed Gary and smiled, 'You must respect all, even no good cunts like him. Anyway, less about my movements, we need to move him over there, no-one will see us. We'll start at 8am, can't do anything until then.' The body was dragged to a quiet wooded area and covered with heavy camouflage netting. Both men then retired to their cars to rest until their morning work began.

Fuck! The body was heavy. Gary unceremoniously dumped it at the base of the woodchopper. The Gravedigger picked it up and began to feed it into the hungry machine.

Nothing made Gary sick, but this had. He thought the body was going in a grave, yet this was something he had never considered, never imagined, could never imagine. It was depraved, yet ingenious.

The head of Steve Smith was being fed into the hopper, followed by his body. Immediately the chipping blades appeared to slow like a lion stalking its prey, before speeding again as the bone crunching sound of Steve's head, followed swiftly by the body was greedily severed, crunched and pulped, before being spat from the chute. It was truly disgusting. The process of feeding lasted twelve hypnotic and mind-numbing seconds. Steve Smith had gone from being a six-foot thirteen stone man, to a thick globule of red paste in under one minute. Even Gary considered it a gruesome way to end.

Opposite the chute was red juice and tiny particles of bone. This landed within a radius of eight feet. The Gravedigger had brought along a tank of water and grass seed. He then soaked the area before using a fork, found in most household sheds, and began digging the area. In under five minutes the ground had been broken up, turned over and replaced beautifully. It looked majestically manicured as if a professional gardener had tendered it.

Gary looked at his friend and realised; one – he needed paying, and two – he was dangerously insane.

Gary thought to himself, 'One Smith down, one to go.'

From out of the early morning gloom the vicar loomed. Gary's face blanched. He thought the vicar would not be home. He had acquired a copy of the list of those attending the bash at Dolphin Square and the vicars name was number 53 on the inventory.

The vicar spoke in an eloquent and playful manner; he had obviously had a good time with all the poofs at Dolphin Square. He asked what was going on and what the red juice was on the ground. Having listened to the explanation he accepted the ground was lifeless, and for roses to bloom over time the ground needed to be cared for and loved. This included ground fertiliser from fish be added to the ground. The Gravedigger had explained fish fertilizer was made from whole fish and carcass products, including bones, scales and skin. Rather than let unusable fish products go to waste, they were converted into nutrients for the garden. The vicar had grimaced at this, but understood the benefits. He began to spout that roses were as beautiful as life itself and offered a life-force for insects to thrive in their environment. He suddenly turned and strolled away dreaming of wild roses and how the Lord would smile upon their beauty.

Gary then began to laugh heartily. Imagining the roses would bloom with Steve Smith's head as the flower. The vicar would absolutely shit himself and consider them triffids.

A large deep yawning bellow awoke him from his daydream. He was told to feed some small trees into the hopper which would clean the blades. The chippings would be spread around the circumference of the church grounds, therefore removing all evidence.

The trees were munched and spat out at an incredible speed. Gary had to feed twelve trees into the device. All that was left was a pile of wooden chips which showed the occasional stain of red.

Steve Smith was an earthy type of a character, now he literally was.

Gary was immensely pleased with the evening's work, and the new day's start. He had removed one significant problem, yet may have acquired another. The vicar had seen his face;

therefore, pressure may need to be applied if he became a little too curious. Fortunately, the vicar's attendance at Dolphin Square was the leverage required, although he hoped it would not be needed. He did not really care to be honest. This was a problem that could be easily fixed. In the scheme of things, this was small fry.

Chapter 7

Dave Smith

Dave Smith lay there, paralysed, like a frozen fat whelk. The drug had kicked in now. Whatever the poofs at the party had given him had certainly worked. His entire body was relaxed, specifically his arse hole, that was waiting for a big veiny cock or ten.

He could move his eyes, hear, smell and probably taste. Yet something was wrong, badly wrong. Drugs never affected him like this. This time he was helpless, and in the wrong hands it could be dangerous. His mind was working like a well-oiled machine, trying to fathom out who would do this. Finally, he came to the conclusion that as it was his turn to be the pillow biter or the sword swallower for LOTS of men. They had made sure he would be accommodating. He smiled. They would be shitting themselves as they fucked him or ejaculated over his face, not realising he fucking loved it.

The door opened and a handsome man walked in, who gracefully turned and locked the bedroom door. This one wanted privacy. He was tall, bespoke, muscular...just how he liked them, yet there was something about the man's demeanour. The mask was removed and he felt he knew him.

'Good evening Dave. I would say it was a pleasure to meet you. Funnily enough, I suppose it is. Oh, and by the way. I've come to remove your penis and watch you choke on it.'

Dave eyed him and felt the anger reaching an explosive level. He was like a mountain lava ready to explode, although he couldn't. He was totally helpless, like a fish left on the sand.

Gary slowly strolled over to the king size bed where Dave was placed. He began to laugh. Being trussed up made Dave look like a Christmas turkey.

Dave kept his eyes on the man and wondered why he was walking over to the heavy dark oak table placed along the magnolia wall. The man got on his knees and appeared to be gliding his extended hand under the top of the table.

Gary turned, and in his hand he had a pair of spring-loaded scissors. He opened them and watched as they snapped shut like an alligator's jaws. Dave understood the implications. He privately prayed that someone would walk in and save him from the incredible indignity that was going to be bestowed upon him. Dave 'no cock' Smith they would say, and they would be fucking laugh…cunts.

Gary turned Dave round and asked if he wanted some cock. Dave was confused until he understood it to be his own cock. This madman was really going to feed him his own cock.

Gary calmly and slowly walked to Dave, 'Anything you want to say to your cock before I lop it off?'

Dave was terrified. His face was blood red.

Gary went over to Dave and lifted the now flaccid penis. He opened the scissors, so they resembled a large mouth and let go of the spring. In under one second Dave Smith had gone from a man with a 4' flaccid penis to a eunuch. Blood was pumping out like an oil well. The blood oozed down the inside of Smith's leg. Thick droplets spattered on the cream fluffy luxury carpet. The blood that had flowed so freely from the severed member now lay in drying pools around the soon to be corpse that resembled a Halloween dummy. But this one was real.

Dave was screaming, but his vocals chords were paralyzed. His body would make no sounds, yet his mouth was open wide. Wide enough for the fatty flaccid deposit being fed into his mouth. Dave for the first time in his life wanted his brother to walk in and save him from this undignified humiliation. The metallic liquid taste slowing oozing down his throat made him gag, yet there was no escape. This time he was receiving a punishment he had given to many others. The fucking irony of it. His final thoughts were of his twin brother, and his final moments were with his executioner and a mouth full of his own beautiful penis.

Gary looked at the corpse thinking how peaceful it looked. He knew no-one at the party would realize, they were too off their heads on strong drugs and booze. In fact, one final indignity would be watching a few perverts fuck the corpse. Necrophilia.

He unlocked the door, having positioned the body on the bed how he wanted it found, tying the wrists to the bedposts, arching the body so it was on its haunches. No-one at the party could refuse such an opening of a free fuck with England's most violent gangster.

He retraced his steps and placed the expensive looking Persian rug over the blood-stained carpet.

He replaced his mask and opened the door. The sound of

hearty moans, the sordid smell of corruption, sweat and shit hit his nose holes. Fuck, it was horrendous. He laughed, at least he knew he did not have a cold. He walked towards the room where guests had placed their clothes on entrance to the den of iniquity. He noted a huge bowl of cocaine on the McIntosh coffee table, that had an MP's face immersed in it, a footballer being sucked off – whilst the man sucking was being fucked by someone connected to the Royal family. A party full of influential perverts.

He entered the changing area, dressed and left in a very casual manner.

The following lunchtime Shaftsbury awoke. His head was pounding, and his cock was red raw. He went to the dining area and took two Nebs with a pint of water. Fuck, he ached all over.

There were naked bodies everywhere. It had been an incredibly successful party. Sportsmen, politicians, members of the Royal household, high ranking civil servants and the very wealthy. The blissful exchange of love energy that flowed between two men, or more at the party, in a healthy intimacy gave a specific stale odour. It was not unpleasant, just a smell of old semen.

Shaftsbury walked into each bedroom to ensure everything was in an acceptable behavior. Walking into the final room he was greeted by the site of Dave Smith tide up and still on his haunches. The stench of stale sweat walked in with him. There was blood and faeces covering the bed, a usual offering. He appeared to still be sleeping. Shaftsbury decided to untie the restraints. They were bound tightly, and it was a struggle to undo them. Eventually they loosened and the 'sleeping' body rolled over. Shaftsbury immediately felt a sickening feeling grow in his abdomen. He turned and the green offerings from it flew from his mouth. Dave Smith was dead. A penis was hanging from his mouth making him look like a Swiss cuckoo clock about to chime. The body was as white as falling snow.

Sweat trickled down Shaftsbury's back, free flowing like condensation on a window-pane, it beaded on his forehead and began to form on his chin. A muscle twitched involuntarily at the corner of his right eye and his mouth formed a rigid grimace. He tapped his foot furiously and all the while stared at the dead man who lay on his back, not three feet from him, covered in dry blood and shit. It gave the room a sickly smell of an abattoir.

His mind was racing. He would have to use his database of contacts to clear this up. More frightening would be the repercussions from the twin brother Steve, although he was more diligent, he was still a complete nutter, although nor frenzied like the one in front of him. How could a mother give birth to two complete mad men? Fortunately, those connected with the party were the people he needed NOW. How did Dave Smith end up like this? Everyone who attended the party was security vetted. He understood that a couple of whispers may have got out, but this was on another scale. He could not check the security camera feed as he had paid to have them disconnected so there was no footage of those arriving and leaving.

Many people had left, although when – he had no idea. the Golden Boys had been paid until 6am, so they would have cleaned up, changed and left to go on vacation to rest their

arse's until the next showbiz party they attended.

This magnificent night had been ruined by someone who was a deviant. He would find out who and ruin their lives.

There was only one person he could call. It would be an expensive call, but a call that needed to be made. 'Giles, I have a problem, quite a major fucking problem.' The receiver of the call was someone employed by the security services clean-up team, and had been on Shaftsbury's retainer for many years. He knew about the parties but never uttered a word. He was discreet, known by many to clear away a problem as if it had not appeared. Shaftsbury always booked him for celebrity gatherings and paid handsomely, although he knew by the tone in his voice this was a significant problem.

'How may I help sir?'

'I have a body in my bedroom and it's Dave fucking Smith,' he shouted in a hushed tone.

Did he say Dave Smith was dead...in his bedroom? What have they been up-to? His mind was calculating costs. 'You will need a removal, disposal and clean up team. Cost is £10,000, and it needs to be in the usual denominations.'

Shaftsbury considered the price, and knew he would have paid one million pounds to remove this eye sore in front of him. Dead bodies make a lot of noise. 'It'll be paid. When will you come?'

Giles was expecting this question and heard the panic in Shaftsbury's voice. This could bring everyone down unless it was handled quickly, cleanly and decisively. 'One hour, lock the bedroom. No-one goes in.' The call was disconnected.

Exactly sixty minutes later the clean-up team of three men

arrived. Each dressed in navy blue overalls and blue shirts like they were caretakers, they also bore clothe caps. The entire uniform would be incinerated within thirty minutes of leaving the location. They walked past the still sleeping naked bodies, not commenting on the sight or smells beholden to them. The bedroom door was opened and to work they went. Ninety minutes later the team emerged from the sanctum each pushing a traditional laundry trolley used in hotels. They blended in with their apparatus like they were ghosts. They vacated the flat, never to be seen again. No names, no descriptions…absolutely nothing.

Shaftsbury entered the room when they had left. The room looked pristine, absolutely immaculate. He only had one problem left. How to explain the missing whereabouts of a certain Dave Smith?

As hours progressed the guests woke and left, no-one mentioned Dave Smith. Shaftsbury assumed no one could remember after their busy night of excess. Many great contacts had been made, and secret filmed footage showed it.

Across the road in yellow General Post Office van was Jack and his team of officers. They had been given a pass to work until the following morning. Many names had been jotted down, one of two causing discussions on whether the person was attending the party. Super Malcolm Mason, the Arsenal player, was decided not to be attending, as he was going out with Carly Jens – the pop star who was currently number one, in both England and America. Jack told the officers to pop Malcolm Mason down in case he was needed as a witness. A number of civil servants and politicians were seen entering; their names went on the *those attending list* straight away. A couple of pop stars from a band were seen entering, they also went on the list. A single man was seen walking into the building, alone. He looked a resident, although warning signals went off in Jack's head. He told the officers to make a description of him.

Gary Jones was in The Bull Pub located in Romford, enjoying a nice comforting pint and a meat pie. He was thinking about Dolphin Square, interestingly, nothing had been in the papers, and not a soul had mentioned Dave Smith. It was like he had disappeared up his own arse. He assumed prominent people at the party had made the body vanish from sight. He was going to the West Ham v Arsenal football match that evening and wondered how the Arsenal defender would play, having consumed many men, drugs and booze the previous night. How ironic. The player was dating a prominent female pop star, adored by many, yet was queer. He never thought there would be a fairy footballer.

His daydream was broken by two gentlemen sitting nearby. They looked like plain clothed police officers. Gary's ears suddenly perked up when he heard the name *Steve*. One officer was chatting to the other in a very hushed tone, 'No-one has seen him, he's sort of vanished.'

His colleague listened intently, occasionally nodding his head in a robotic manner. Suddenly he announced, 'East End will be better without him, all he caused was death and chaos.'

Having taken a huge slurp from his tankard he replied quietly, almost whispering, 'Funny though guv, but the other brother hasn't been seen either.'

'Both of them missing. Are you sure? They're never further

than six feet apart usually. Now that is bloody odd. Quite a coincidence.' His toned walked the line between surprise and incredulity, and it was clear it was anything but.

Gary considered the news he had heard. These officers would either go about their day and forget their meanderings to each other, or share ideas with colleagues.

Chapter 8

Freddie Stone

Freddie Stone was a hard-working popular person, who was liked by all who met him. He lived alone, although had been dating Penny for two years. He understood time was looming for him to settle down and start a family. He had pondered this scenario for some time and had finally decided to ask her. It was the right thing to do, and something he wanted to do.

Occasionally, he would pop into the Thatcher's Arms on the way home for a quick pint. It was convenient as it was just a short distance from Boyles Court, and only locals used it, as it was a little out of the way. He would sometimes bump into other officers, who like him, were refreshing themselves for the arduous journey home after a long, and sometimes difficult day. Having left the pub, he would mount his bike for the ride home. During the dry months this would be a beautiful and scenic route, yet during the cold winter months the bike was put away and he chose to get the 347 bus that would drop him near his home.

Freddie was a man who believed if you were on time you were late, yet if you were early you were on time. Everything was precise and had meaning. His black shoes were polished every day, ensuring they looked new and professional.

Appearances were paramount to Freddie. His late grandfather had always told him 'clean, smart clothes gain you entrance to a party, yet a fast and disgusting mouth gets you removed from it.' He always adhered to these rules, and they had proven to be correct.

Freddie had been 21 years of age when he had entered the Youth Offender Institute as a novice. He had wanted to be a Police Officer, but had struggled with the exams, finding them a little complex. He believed to gain someone's trust you needed to find out their interests and build from there. Now 35, and having looked after many inmates at Warley, he felt an officer needed to be positive, and find ways to aid those staying to break away from their current negative behaviour. He also believed this environment required honesty, although he had heard some of his colleagues would supply *goods* needed by those housed in the institution, for a price he assumed.

One person had intrigued him, Gary Jones. Gary had become the *Head Boy* almost instantly, something unheard of. It was known he had battered Mad Mike with a sharpened table tennis paddle, leaving the recipient of the attack with life changing injuries. Gary had been placed in solitary confinement by the governor for his punishment.

Segregation is the hardest form of imprisonment. It was accepted for most prisoners as it had a negative impact on their emotional and mental wellbeing. Inmates were allowed a daily half an hour out of their cell for association ... and 20 minutes' shower time. Yet this had been welcomed by Gary, he positively thrived in segregation.

When Gary had been released after 4 weeks' segregation, he looked refreshed, dangerously refreshed. Gary positively thrived at Boyles Court. He treated it like a four-year sabbatical. Everything was controlled. No-one disturbed the peace, no one dared disturb the peace, otherwise it was met with swift recompense.

During his tenure at the institution Stone taught Gary to play chess, something he grasped quickly, and something he became proficient at.

Gary and Stone had a mutual respect for each other, although Gary felt Stone was different to the rest of the guards. He felt he was careful, and would not break the law. He was straight, totally straight. Someone who could not be bought, someone who could be a dangerous adversary, someone to avoid, although someone to play chess with.

When Gary left the unit, Stone gave him a chess set and quietly adviced, 'Every move you make is a decision, and for every decision there is a consequence, choose wisely Jones, be like your chess decisions, a winner.' He then turned and entered his place of employment, leaving Gary waiting for the bus. He had hoped these wise words would stay with Gary Jones. He also hoped to play chess with him again.

Stone had given up on the idea of joining the police force, although he had become friendly with many officers who said he should still join. When speaking to some officers they had spoken to him about many strange crimes happening to people who were scum bags. The officers had joked the person committing the crimes was clearing the streets of all the criminals and they would lose their jobs. It had created a laugh amongst the group, although it had left Stone with an uneasy feeling.

He asked what was strange about the crimes in a dour,

almost uninterested manner, and had been told sex cases, nonce's and hard-core criminals had been removed from the streets, many of which the police had no idea about. To make it even more peculiar, this person or persons was beginning to enter folk law as a kind of Robin Hood.

Stone considered the information and remembered when Jones had tied a young 17-year old paedophile to a radiator and attempted to boil him. It had left horrific melted scars on the man's back. Jones was an enforcer who righted wrongs, particularly when those in the wrong were deviants.

Freddie casually remarked he would listen out for any murmurings amongst the inmates, and who should he report it to if anything came along?

He was met with a shout from the departing officer, 'Jack Philips, Dagenham.'

Jack Philips. He would go and meet him. It may lead to nothing, yet there was something about it that smacked of Gary Jones, a modern-day Robin Hood. This moniker would appeal to Jones.

Stone had not heard of Jones, so had hoped he had gone straight, although when juvenile offenders were released the recidivism rate was very high, similar to adults. This in turn concerned Stone, no-one had heard – or seen Jones, which in itself was unusual, therefore something was amiss in Stone's mind.

Stone left Dagenham East station and marched left up Rainham Road. The station had recently moved from the old site situated at Rainham Road South to the new offices based by the railway bridge. As he walked along he noted the factory site owned by May and Baker, who were known for developing the drug quinine to combat malaria.

Finally, he reached Dagenham East Police Station, it looked unspectacular in its appearance, yet it was still the local *nick*.

He bounced up the four steps and entered the station. He was immediately aware that it appeared to be calm and clean, which told him it was a well-cared for station.

The constable behind the counter became alert and enquired if Stone needed any help. Stone eyed the man and noted his nervous look, he appeared to be new to the realms to policing. Stone asked if Jack Philips was available. The officer replied he would enquire if he was about, and who should he say was asking after him. Stone replied in a nonchalant manner 'Freddie Stone. He won't know who I am.'

A message was relayed up-to Jack Philips who called he was too busy to see anyone.

The constable informed Freddie, who thought this behaviour incredibly poor. He may, or may not, have key information. Yet to be dismissed in this manner was like going back to school and being told to leave the classroom by the teacher at the end of day.

The constable asked if he would like to leave a message and handed Freddie a pad with lined paper.

He considered the pad and wrote a simple message 'I may have an idea who is removing your problematic individuals.' He then handed it to the constable and asked him to give it to Jack Philips as soon as possible. He then left the station and headed to the station.

The constable eyed the message and immediately bolted up-to Jack Philips and passed him the message. Jack read it and made straight for the door. When he reached the station front office he asked the constable where he had gone. The constable appeared nervous and cautiously replied, 'He left as soon as he gave me the message, telling me to give it to you as soon as possible, he appeared displeased as no-one had given him any time.'

Jack looked at the young police constable replying, 'Fuck it' in an aggressive and annoyed manner. He then barked, 'I'll go left, you go right. If you see him, bring him back here.' Both men departed the station as if looking for prey.

The constable caught a glimpse of Freddie entering the tube station, hoping a train would not arrive for a few minutes. Having just arrived from Hendon he was in peak fitness. Immediately he pushed harder on the ground ensuring his speed increased. As he approached the top of the stairs he saw a train beginning to pull in and his prey getting ready to vanish into the ghost like carriage. There was only one option, 'Sir, don't get on. Your presence is needed at the office,' he bellowed out, hoping he would be heard.

Many people on the platform turned towards the commotion, as did Freddie Stone. His eyes immediately fell upon the constable who was waving his hands like scarecrow in the mid-day wind. This amused Freddie, as he had gone from someone with no information, to being chased down the street almost Laurel and Hardy style.

'Thank you for coming to our humble crime fighting offices.'

Stone considered the welcoming, and decided immediately he liked the man standing before him, who had a smart, but severely lived in, shabby look. He had a masculine look to him that would appeal to many females.

'Thank you for considering my information and sending your officer after me.'

Jack was mulling over the man sitting across the table to him. He had a feeling he could be a fellow officer, although there was something not quite right, although security was certainly involved, 'Don't think I'm being rude, but you are?'

'I am Freddie Stone.'

'How and where did you hear of me?' Jack was now looking at the man suspiciously.

Freddie noted the change in the man's manner. He had seen it with inmates at Leverton. They were friendly, difficult, then friendly again. Some called it the shit sandwich approach. He knew Jack Philips was weighing him up, but had also underestimated him.

'Through continued conversations with office's at my place of employment in Leverton.'

'Leverton, Leverton, yes Leverton, Warley. Secure unit for young offenders. Is that right?

'Yes Mr Philips. You have a fine memory for secure units.'

Both men smiled at the humour offered by Freddie Stone. Jack Philips instantly liked this man. He would welcome him on his team if he were an officer. He had a hard working, methodical ethic that appealed to him. He also considered facts, and obviously had a mind for linking pieces of a puzzle. He would make a good detective.

'You mentioned to my officer, problematic individuals. What exactly did you mean by that?

'Shall I start from the beginning?'

'Yes please.'

Twenty-five minutes passed in which Jack did not move.

Freddie Stone was very engaging, and regaled the information incredibly well. He was succinct with a confident manner that was not laborious. Having considered everything, he was sure Jones needed to go on the list. A list so short, it only had Jones on it.

Having finished, Stone looked at Jack expectantly. 'What do you think, could he be the person you are seeking?'

'To be honest, yes. The way you told it was amazing. Do you think it could be him Mr Stone?'

'I do not know the facts, but from what I have read and heard from officers. Modern day Robin Hood would appeal to Jones massively. Being a righter of wrongs is something that would stroke his ego.'

'If it were Jones, what would be his downfall?'

'Nothing. He is too careful, wise beyond his years.'

'I do not believe nor accept that. Everyone has one weak link.'

'Seriously, if it is him. I taught him chess, and he will lay out his life like a game of chess, always two steps ahead of everyone. Thinking ahead, very wily, like a cunning fox. He'll consider every scenario – good and bad. You will have to out fox a fox. One thing I have forgotten; Jones is a near genius pianist.'

Jack considered the conversation and realised this really could be their man, although there was nothing linking him to any crime. In fact, any crime whatsoever., could any man fly under the radar that low to ground. if so, it would be a miracle. A master criminal of the highest calibre. A criminal with an incredible IQ who was a genius musician and chess player to a professional standard. This would be one to ponder and check...thoroughly.

Chapter 9

Michael Dawson

Michael Dawson's life had been difficult from the start. He had been conceived after his mother, Mary, had been raped by Graham Round. Throughout her pregnancy she was going to give the baby up for adoption, but as soon as she saw his wispy blond hair and piercing blue eyes she was in love. His first steps were greeted with a major cheer and clap of the hands, and each smile bought joy to her life. Little did she know the demons held within the bundle she cradled and cared for.

His grandparents, Celia and Jack never had any involvement with him. They could not cope with his sudden outbursts. Grandpa Jack's answer to everything was a swift slap round the legs and a deep bellowing, 'shut yer malf.'

School had been difficult as he was constantly in trouble for fighting, bullying and theft. Eventually, in his last year at school he had lost control and beat up one teacher...severely. The man had needed to be rushed to hospital with multiple fractures to the face and a punctured lung.

This resulted in him being sent to Boyles Court where he gained the title Mad Mike. He loved the name as it gave him a feeling of notoriety. He quickly became *Head Boy* in the community. This allowed him to make money and command inmates, although this changed forever when one specific inmate linked into the arena.

Gary Jones had arrived with a fearsome, cold reputation, although this had not bothered Michael. He had seen many tough boys come to his castle and stay. Yet none had caused him any problems. The meeting with Jones changed his perspective forever.

It had been agreed, more of an order, they would meet in the sports hall for a chat about the rules Mike had created, similar to the ten commandments. He was unsure if the guards liked him, although he did not give a fuck. Jones had turned up in a too confident manner, and ruffled Michael's inner demon, 'I expect you're wondering why I ordered you here today, Jones,' he intoned slowly, fixing his nemesis with his steely blue eyes. Yet he had seriously underestimated Gary Jones. He charged at Jones, who produced a sharpened piece of wood and plunged it into his cheek, which sliced through and protruded from the opposing side. The pain was immense. It had sheeted through him like hot coals.

The scars left, made his cheeks resemble the Japanese flag, and were a constant reminder to never underestimate anyone. Jones had taken charge of his castle, yet vengeance would be had, it had to happen.

Upon leaving Boyles Court Michael made his mind up to locate Graham Round. He wanted to pay him back for raping his mother, who he still loved dearly. Having made a few discreet enquiries, he located his scum bag father to pubs in South London. He had been easy to find as no-one liked him. He was a pick pocket who preyed on those unfortunate, yet would not go to the West End, as he considered it hard work and a long way. He would frequent The Ivanhoe and The

Morning Star pubs daily, drinking himself into oblivion. Michael decided he would pay his father back for all the wrongs he had committed.

Graham Round eyed the man who had offered him a drink and accepted. He looked like someone who had a few quid, and someone he could dip later. When studying the man's profile, he looked familiar, yet unfamiliar. Yet, there was something about him. Sod it, he would drink the man's money, more fool him. He turned around to eye the new barmaid who had her tits on show like a hanging basket when he felt a pain of electricity fly through him. He also heard the barmaid scream. He looked at his right hand and it had been nailed to the bar surface with such force the nails head was pinching his skin. As he began to shout the left hand was grabbed and smashed with a hammer. Those drinking in the pub quickly left their beer and vacated the premises. Graham Round eyed the man who had done it and shouted, 'Why?'

Michael looked at his rapist of a father and calmly replied, 'You daddy, are a fucking rapist.' He then plunged a six-inch nail into the top of his skull that pierced his useless brain.

Strangeways had been a learning experience. Michael was given 10 years for the murder of his father. The sentence should have been significantly longer, yet he had protested he had done the public a service, and he had found one of the judge's cousins had been attacked by his father. Therefore, leniency was given by the judge, who appeared to offer a nod of thanks to Dawson when he left the courtroom. He did not care about going to prison, although it was rather barbaric and primitive.

The prison cells did not have plush amenities. There were no toilets, so everyone had to use a bucket. If you had an upset stomach, tough. All prisoners had to slop out their cells each morning to remove their human waste. This in turn could cause problems. So much shit and piss was being poured down the sink it would sometimes overflow causing fights amongst the inmates who had been unfortunate victims of dripping excretion and splash back.

If an inmate was considered someone who could grass, they were sugared. This was an incredibly painful experience. One litre of scolding water mixed with the equivalent of sugar. It was then thrown on the prisoner's legs as a warning. It caused a red scar that would remain for two years.

Many high-profile prisoners were put on the ghost train. This was done to ensure they could not start an enterprise to make money and run the prison. During the night they were removed from their cells and sent to another prison in an agitated manner.

Violent and difficult prisoners were given liquid cosh, which reduced movement, and induced sleepiness. It was injected in a forceful manner, which usually involved three prison guards holding the recipient down to restrain them. The chemical kicked immediately.

Any inmate based in C Wing was in segregation, they were hated by all prisoners. This area housed sex offenders, specifically rapists and child abusers. Every person at Strangeway's tried to harm someone on C Wing. It was a badge of honour if you could slice, stab or harm them in any way. Prison Officers occasionally mentioned to someone discreetly, when someone may be in the exercise yard from C Wing. Michael had witnessed many serious beatings.

Some jailbirds, who had been custodians of the correctional system for some time, changed their sexual persuasion over their term of incarceration. They saw it as a temporary change during their term inside. They would seek one of the prisoners who was queer, and pay them tobacco or drugs for sucking them off. Michael thought it disgusting. The man performing the sex act would have a mailbag placed over them, with a mouthpiece hole cut out. He would then perform fellatio on up to six men, earning the magnificent amount of six cigarettes.

During his tenure within the reform system Michal had asked about Gary Jones, yet no-one had heard of him. It was like the man was a phantom, maybe he had gone straight, yet a man like Gary Jones could not, would not go straight. Michael knew he had to learn from Jones, and he had. Patience had made Jones top dog at Boyles Court, plus people liked him. Both he had learnt during his adult years. Recklessness had been replaced with cunning. This had allowed him to become a main player at Strangeway's. The guards saw him offer no violence, yet knew he was a menace, whereas the prison population heard of his menace and violence. They had also heard what he had done to his father, therefore his reputation came before him.

When the steel doors of Strangeways closed offering freedom for the first time in eight years. Michael knew he had to get back to London. A burning desire to fulfil the wrongs against him. He gently caressed the red round scar on his cheek, a constant reminder of revenge. A punishment he would enjoy exacting on Gary fucking Jones. A punishment so magnificent it would go down in record books as a thing of incredulity, astonishment and disbelief. He, Michael

Dawson, would be in the record books as the most dangerous person in history. A dangerous smile formed. The dull dark light in his eyes spread through every part of him. He was out. He was back and he was very, very fucking dangerous.

He departed the train at Euston after a three-hour journey. The trip had given him time to consider his first moves. He had decided the first thing required was money. He would visit Midland Bank, and make a substantial withdrawal from his account. He smiled when he had considered his last visit to his bank. He had tried to explain to the manager that no money would be entering the account for a number of years. Eventually, he thought the manager was taking the piss and had to explain that he was doing some bird. As soon as he mentioned 'doing some bird' the manager had blanched and asked him to refrain from using such abhorrent language. Michael realized the man facing him did not understand that 'doing bird' meant going to prison, therefore he had to explain. He then gave the manager a steely stare and menacingly growled, 'If anyone touches my money, I'll be touching you.' He then stood up, shook the man's hand and left. It was bloody superb. He so hoped Mr. Swales was still there.

He decided to base himself in a hotel, New World Inn, Brentwood. His choice was apt as it was near Boyles Court. The establishment maintained many of its original beams and had a feeling of grandeur. It was a little pricier than expected, but after eight years in Strangeways, Michael felt he deserved some home comforts.

Michael strolled to the Thatcher's Arms and ordered a Light and Bitter. Sitting at the stool he admired the pub's interior. It was old, yet clean, plus the beer tasted damn nice.

He felt strangely at peace here. He remembered being driven past the pub when he had been admitted to, and released from the institution. Seeing the pub for the first time as a youngster, he had promised himself he would return one day and have a drink at the establishment. He was now pleased he had. It was like returning home. For some unknown reason he felt closer to Gary Jones. The feeling un-nerved him slightly, he had no idea why, but something made the hairs on his neck rise. Gary had been here. He knew it.

Michael began a conversation with the owner. He had told him he had been based at Boyles Court many years back, and had promised himself to visit the pub, and he had not been disappointed. This news had pleased the owner, who had informed Michael quite a lot of previous visitors to Boyles passed through for a beer. He assumed it was a memory trip. Some even came in for a quick pint when they were released. The owner informed Michael he knew they were a little too young, but felt one beer would not harm.

Michael liked the barman. He had shown respect and did not take sides. The part about a memory trip had interested him. Why would anyone want a memory trip of prison? He pondered it, and decided they would be like himself. Warley was a lovely area, and the first thing they witnessed was the pub, therefore, a watering hole they would feel obliged to visit upon reaching the correct age, although it appeared the landlord was very laid-back concerning age.

Michael finished his beverage and bid farewell to the land-lord, before making his way back to his accommodation to formulate his next move on Operation Jones.

Chapter 10

Betrayal

Mason returned to his home in Upminster, having been given an extra training session. He had showered after his exercise, yet his muscles were still aching. It had only been twenty-hours since the 5-0 defeat to bitter rivals Tottenham Hotspur, in which his manager had squarely laid the blame at his doorstep for three of the goals. The manager had shouted in his face with spittle flying everywhere, that he had been seen coming out of a *special bar* at 2am. When he had made this accusation, many of his team mates had eyed him suspiciously. *Special bar*, that would intrigue them. They would not leave him alone. Fuck, this could be a fucking nightmare. How would he explain he had been visiting a gay bar with Shaftsbury, his partner? He had left the training ground speedily.

The night had been eventful. He and Shaftsbury had serviced a young male model in the toilets during the evening. Drink and drugs had encouraged the man to allow them to fuck him one after another.

Whilst running the bath he heard the doorbell ring. He ran down the stairs and opened it, to be met with a punch on the nose, that knocked him to the floor, and had obviously broken it. Blood was pouring down his face. He then received a swift sharp kick in the bollocks. He heard the door slammed shut, and was dragged into the large orange and white laminate kitchen, where he received a harsh kick in the ribs. He then passed out.

Mason woke fifteen minutes later to find himself in his bathroom. He adored this room. He had recently had it renovated, the colour avocado he had loved instantly. He often lay in the bath thinking he could die in this room. He became aware he could not move his feet, and his hands were tied together, 'Un-tie me now!'

'Shut up. You fucking big mouthed, loose lipped, queer cunt.'

His eyes, although blurry, were beginning to focus. He noted the man who had struck him. It was the man from the sauna, Gary Jones. Why had he hit him?

'You are a fucking low life. If you are a fairy, be a fairy. Just don't fuck with people like me.'

Mason mumbled in a barely coherent manner, 'What have I done?'

'The model you fucked last night had to be taken to hospital because of the drugs you provided and the internal you gave him with your disgusting poof cock.'

Mason knew this could end badly. He needed to save himself, 'Shaftsbury gave him the drugs, it wasn't me. I wouldn't know where to get them.'

Gary studied the man and believed him. Mason was a sexual predator and a footballer. Yet he was still a grass. He had just proved that.

'Do you know what your problem is?'

Mason was hoping this was a rhetorical question, it was not.

'Well do you?'

'No Gary. I don't.'

'You should have stuck with hanging about with footie players. Politicians are not your thing. They are not to be trusted. Specifically Shaftsbury, he's an absolute wanker.'

Mason gave Jones a steely look and shouted with all his energy, 'He is a great man, and he loves me, as I do him.'

'You need to listen, because I'm going to tell you why I'm going to kill you.'

Mason began to cry and scream hysterically, 'No please don't, I beg you. I'm a footballer.'

'You told the model my name. Don't tell me you didn't, as I was pulled in by the police this morning for a shake down.'

'I promise you I didn't, it wasn't me.'

'You're a fucking liar as well. The filth told me a prominent footballer had been bragging about a party in Dolphin Square to the model, and Gary Jones a man he'd met at the sauna was there.'

Mason suddenly went quiet, and gulped. He hoped Jones did not hear it. He did say those things to impress the model, although why he had mentioned Gary's name astounded him.

'So, you are aware. The model's dad is really high up at Scotland Yard, you fucking idiot. As soon as he heard his son was in hospital, every favour was pulled in. Just like I was, and every Gary Jones in London probably.'

'How was I to know?'

'Well you should've found out. What is your favourite room in the house?'

'This is, why? Why can't I move my legs? I can't move anything. What have you done to me?'

'I heard you like giving people Ketamine, so I've given you a nice big dose, as big as it gets. I am caring, so I've cooled the bath down.'

'Cooled the bath down?'

'Yes. I'm going to pop you in your new avocado bath and watch you drown,'

Mason began to speak but the words would not form. The Ketamine was kicking in, he was frightened, terrified. Tears began to stream down his face. He was truly sorry, he was not a bad man, just a gay man with a big mouth who played football. He felt himself being picked up and laid in the bath. The water began to jump and down over his face and float into his lungs. His final thoughts were of Shaftsbury and how much he loved him. He understood what love was, these were his final thoughts.

Shaftsbury arrived at Mason's house just after 7pm. The walk from the station was lovely, and Fairways was a beautiful road to live down. Malcolm had invested his money wisely in this property.

He enjoyed their quiet nights together. Both of their lives were organised and busy, so quiet time was enjoyed by both. They would prepare a meal together and have a mug of tea. Shaftsbury smiled, a mug of tea, how common, but with Mason it was normal and perfect. Watching television quietly on the sofa was considered loving. At 9pm, one of them would make a mug of hot chocolate for the both of them. Shaftsbury knew he loved Mason, although he was child-like in some ways, in others he was kind, loving and beautiful. He knew they would be together for life.

As he approached the house he noticed the door key was still in the lock. For some reason this concerned him, and his pace picked up. Turning the key, he entered, calling Mason's name. There was no response, although there was a dreadful feeling of calm in the house, that was un-nerving. It did not feel right, something was not right. Shaftsbury was worried.

Having searched downstairs, he bounded upstairs. He opened each of the bedrooms without success, the final room was the bathroom. He tentatively turned the cold brass handle, the hinges still required oiling. As he entered the room he noted the steam on the mirror. The panic began to flow, his heart started pounding at an increasingly rapid pace. One pace further on he let out a cry.

'My beautiful Mason, what have they done?' Tears were streaming down his face. The body was ghostly white, and the skin pinched like a prune. He could not remove his eyes from his one true love. 'Why? Why? Why?' He yelled in a river of tears.

He knew this was not a job for the clean-up team. Beautiful Mason was too high profile, plus Shaftsbury felt justice needed to be served. For the first time in his life he knew everything had to be handled correctly. The love of his life deserved nothing less. Still the tears cascaded down his face at an incredible rate. He knew he would never love again. He was nothing on his own.

From across the road Gary, sat in his car watching Shaftsbury enter the house. He could only imagine the feelings running through Shaftsbury. He did feel some sympathy for both Mason and Shaftsbury. It was obvious how they felt about each other, but business was business. He assumed

Shaftsbury would contact someone who could hide and lose the body like he had done with Dave Smith, although this time he was wrong.

In the distance, he heard the sound of sirens, many sirens. Shocked, he began to drive off just as the emergency services entered the road. He had read Shaftsbury badly wrong. He never considered he would make the correct move and contact the establishment.

The officer stood at the door watching the blubbering man. He felt like telling him to shut up. It was beginning to grate. Men crying appeared to be weak, it was not manly to cry, and this man had not stopped, 'Sir, would you like a drink?'

'The whisky is in the decanter downstairs.'

'I meant, tea sir.'

'Fuck tea. Whisky, and lots of it, and then I am going to find out who did this and this and fucking kill them.'

The officer looked at the man. Suddenly, he had become an aggressive man with a vengeance. A dangerous brew.

The door opened and a senior officer stood there. 'Mr Shaftsbury?'

'Yes.'

'I am DCI Jack Philips, and I am leading this investigation, and dreadful situation.'

'DCI Philips?'

'Yes sir.'

Shaftsbury knew the man. He was perfect, although it would be dangerous. He was dogged, someone who uncovered secrets, bringing everyone down. He was a man who would solve this case, but someone who could bring the house down. He considered his thoughts and made his decision, fuck the house. His Mason had been killed, and that was too much, too fucking much.

'DCI Philips, please find the killer of my partner.' An immense feeling of relief fell from Shaftsbury, it was magical, like tidal wave of joy. He did not care if anyone knew about the two of them. He noticed the young officer look at him. It would be headline news. A well-known gay footballer. It would also make the murderer nervous. He would also put a bounty of his head, and make it known.

'Your partner sir?'

'Lover, boyfriend, whatever you wish to call it. I do not care.'

Jack eyed the man, and knew he was telling the truth. There was passion in his voice, and his manner was of bereavement. The man looked broken, yet he sensed some resilience. This man was educated, wealthy, sought justice and had the contacts. A heady brew for revenge.

Having spoken to Shaftsbury, and looked round the property, he was more than sure that Malcolm Mason had known his murderer. One thing kept nagging him. Why murder a well-known footballer? It was obvious he and Shaftsbury had been partners for some time. The house was nice. Even Shaftsbury appeared reasonable enough, although one to keep at arms-length. This was one investigation that could lead anywhere, absolutely anywhere. He would first of all need to understand Mason's pattern of life; where he went, who he saw, favourite haunts, friends, recent parties, colleagues. The colleagues thing he thought pointless, although he knew it would have to be checked. The Arsenal players would assume he had been seeing Carly Jens, and would say he was a 'top bloke'. This offered another question, why was he seeing Carly Jens when he obviously was not? This could be a strange investigation. It was like a story written for a soap opera. Presently, every investigation was a soap opera, and Shaftsbury appeared to be the central character.

There was something strange about the murder. Why do it to someone who appeared to harm no-one? Jack sat in the station canteen pondering. Taking a bite from his third sausage sandwich, which was his dinner, he considered all the facts, but kept coming back to the same question, why? Malcolm Mason was not a bad man, he was a footballer who had a secret…was that it, the secret? Jack's mind began processing the facts. Shaftsbury, it had to be Shaftsbury. Something they had seen or done. That was it. In two swooping gulps he swallowed the sandwich and bound to his office. Instantly he gathered his team round. 'Shaftsbury, it's Shaftsbury.'

'Guv. What is Shaftsbury?'

'Sorry everyone. This Mason murder has been spinning round my head. Shaftsbury took it really bad.'

'Which was expected sir.'

Jack began to speak excitedly, 'Yes I know that, but remember the look he had. It was grief linked with an overwhelming sense of revenge. Shaftsbury and Mason shared a secret, something so large, one was murdered and the other will be unless we work it out quickly. We need to find out EVERY-WHERE they have been together in the last month, plus who they have seen. Start with clubs. I am positive Shaftsbury is a member of some upper-class place in the West End, which, I have no idea.'

The team scurried in all directions. This would be a night for overtime and not much sleep. They all knew their jobs, and set about their tasks immediately. Clubs were called and favours pulled in.

Two hours later a cry was heard.

'Guv, quick.'

Jack marched over to the desk quickly, 'What have you got?'

'Shaftsbury was a member of a club called Whites in Piccadilly, used to frequent the place with Malcolm Mason often. They would use the facilities there.'

'That's our in. Tomorrow we start banging on some important doors to gain entry to this *well to do club.*' Jack could feel the adrenaline bubbling like exploding lava. He had a feeling this was the opening they needed. He had no idea where it would lead, and he did not care. His motto was; *if they don't commit a crime, they won't serve time, and if they commit a crime, I'll make sure they serve time.* He had it written on a large sheet of white paper in his sparse looking office.

The following morning Jack visited Whites with one of his Sergeants.

Sergeant Drake had been chosen as he was diligent, and a man. He was a person who noticed small things and mulled them over. He was considered dour and had few friends, but was respected by all at the station. He was a career person, just like their DCI.

Today was a day when ladies would not be admitted to the club. It was a club for wealthy gentlemen. Royalty had visited the establishment, and enjoyed its treats. It housed gaming rooms, a majestic bar, and a menu replete with British game, along with a traditional pool and sauna. The club were not expecting them. Jack hoped the element of surprise would confuse those in the employment, although he assumed they would be sharp and accommodating to a point, without being too forthcoming. He also guessed it would ruffle many feathers, of note.

Arriving at St James Street, they both admired the magnificence of the building they hoped would allow them insight into how the *other half lived*. Jack strode over to the black glossy imposing door and rapped hard. The door was immediately opened, taking Jack by surprise.

'How may I help you?'

Jack eyed the extremely well-spoken man. He was dressed perfectly, and looked like a doorman, 'I need to speak to someone who can help with some official police business.'

'May I ask how official sir? And may I view your credentials?'

Jack handed the identification.

'And yours please sir.'

Drake handed his begrudgingly.

'How official. How does murder start to begin with, and we can work from there?'

The doorman of the club studied both police officers. They were a little rough, dressed in a primitive form with the manners of barbarians, particularly the one who did not wish to impart with his identification. He stood there thinking about the members. He guessed the dead footballer, shifty man – who knew everything and the quiet man who looked tough would be who they required. He then pondered how they had become members, specifically the tough man, although he was respectful, polite and honest. There was a distinct edge, he never spoke with any members, and never tried. He enjoyed his meals, lavishing praise on them. Which showed his upbringing was not from the class expected of Whites. He had only seen him speaking to two people briefly since being admitted to the club; Malcolm Mason and Robin Shaftsbury. It had been implied in the newspapers they were lovers. It did not surprise him; over the years he had heard many snippets of information from married individuals about the extra-curricular activities they enjoyed. Some made you blanch, although he could not say anything as he would lose his job and struggle to gain employment elsewhere, plus he was financially rewarded for keeping his mouth shut if members felt he had heard too much.

'Officers, I think murder suffices in this case. Please come this way.'

Jack and Drake could not believe the opulence of the hallway. It was magical, with high ceilings and a spiral staircase leading to floors above. They were shown to a Coffee Room, where tables were spread with white linen and glass chandeliers dangled from an extraordinary, barrel-shaped roof.

'Bit different to the station canteen guv.'

Suddenly the door swung open, 'Gentlemen, sorry to keep you. I am Nigel Morgan, and I believe you have some questions about a murder.'

Jack looked at the man. Stood six feet, was immaculately dressed in a black suit, waistcoat, white shirt and black tie, and had an air of wealth about him. He reminded Jack of an adult Bambi jumping about all exuberant and happy. 'Thank you for allowing us to speak with you. I realise your time is precious.'

'As is yours officer. If I can aid you solve this heinous crime, I jolly well shall. What do you wish to know?'

'Robin Shaftsbury and Malcolm Mason.'

'A rum fellow Shaftsbury, Interesting coupling don't you feel? Sorry, I did not catch your name?'

'Philips, DCI Jack Philips.'

'How shall I address you?'

'Jack will be just fine.'

'Well Jack, as I was saying. Shaftsbury is a rum sort of chap. No-one really knows what he does. I have heard he is a Mr Fixit. What he fixes I have no idea. Certainly not our plumbing.'

'A Mr Fixit?'

'Yes. He is friendly with a few chaps here. All honest decent gentlemen. Civil servants and MP's.'

'Anyone specifically?'

'If you name an MP or civil servant he is probably friendly with them. I believe he loves hosting parties somewhere, where, I have no idea.'

'Parties?'

'I believe some of our members go, not many, half a dozen at the most.'

'Any names?'

Morgan looked at Jack and whispered quietly, 'This is off the record?'

Jack considered the question and knew he needed further information 'Yes'

'Some male members of the cabinet attended and some

seriously wealthy people. Apart from that I know no more.'

'When Shaftsbury came here, was it always with Mason, or anyone else?

'Just Mason. I would assume it was there secret rendez-vous.'

'You said he never spoke to anyone. Not ever?'

'No. He never spoke…hold on. He spoke to Mr Jones for ten or so minutes recently.'

'Jones? Who's that?

'Unusual gentleman. I am not quite sure how he obtained membership, although he did with flying colours.'

Jack's eyed widened, 'Why unusual.'

'Unless I am mistaken, he comes from Dagenham. A working-class area with downmarket taste. Do you know it?'

Jack grimaced and considered what the man had just said *working class area and downmarket.* He loved Dagenham. He had been bought up in the environment all his life and knew no different, yet Morgan was implying it was a shit hole, 'Yes, I know of Dagenham?'

Morgan's mouth was on fast dial now 'It is rather peculiar that a man from Dagenham has the financial clout and grav-itas to become a member of White's. I have never known any-thing like it. Very strange. He must have some powerful friends.'

Jack and Drake looked at each other. Both believing the man they sought was this Jones character.

Drake, who had been silent throughout, suddenly asked about Jones, 'Was he a well turned out man. Did he have the look of wealth?'

Morgan considered the question and thought about Jones,

'He looked a man who had status. Smart suits, immaculately turned out and softly spoken.'

'Have you an address for Mr Gary Jones?'

'Now this is where it gets jolly strange. No, we do not currently hold one. When he became a member, the secret board, no-one knows who is on the board – so you are aware, gave him an official pardon, meaning no details required. This is only done for royalty of the highest calibre.'

'You have nothing?'

'That is correct gentlemen. The only thing I do know, is the name Gary Jones, new members have to show official documentation when joining the club. We cannot have any old scallywag joining our esteemed establishment.'

Both officers looked stunned. This esteemed club had allowed someone with no credentials to join their establishment. Only royalty was allowed to join with no credentials, yet mister elusive Gary Jones had been granted favour.

The officers thanked their host and departed the building. Jack was first to break the silence, 'Can you believe what you just heard? A secret board, no-one knows who is on, and Gary Jones, the phantom Gary fucking Jones, is allowed a free pass to join this elitist club. This case is getting weirder and stranger by the hour. In all my years I have never been involved in such an odd case, involving so many oddballs and secrets covered with secrets. Fancy a quick pint?'

Drake spoke in a thoughtful and considered manner, carefully selecting his word, 'Sir. I think Nigel Morgan was truthful throughout. He appeared to tell us everything he knew like a naughty schoolboy. I also felt he didn't like the secrecy part of the club. May be wrong, but I don't think I am. I also think he knows a little more than he's told us.'

'I agree Drakey. But how did Jones become a member, and more importantly. Who is he? The only thing we have is; he possibly comes from our neck of the woods.'

Nigel Morgan sat perfectly still, having not moved since the officers had departed. How did Jones find out about his past? He had got caught out at a party some years back. How was he to know the girls were fourteen, they looked eighteen at least. The party having been arranged by a friend of one of his chums at university. It was going to haunt him forever. He never found out who organised the shindig. It had been a damn good night. The stirring began. Fourteen…they were broad minded girls, and incredibly pliable. Jones had been a perfect member since enrolling at the club. He paid his bills on time, was quiet, courteous, respectful and popular, although he did not mix. One or two of the members had grumbled about ruffians trying to gain entry to the club, they had no idea the roughest one of all was amongst them. He knew this was going to go one of two ways; it would blow over, or the shit would hit the fan in a magnitude never experienced by man before. He had an epiphany of what would happen.

Whenever Jack visited Chief Superintendent Taylor he always felt he was going to receive a telling off, although he had no idea why. They had been friends for many years. He probably respected the rank, although it was only a man in a uniform.

'How did it go Jack. Any advancement on this case?

'To be honest sir, this is becoming the strangest case I've ever worked. There are secrets covered with secrets, people of no known address, high ranking ministers, money, power, unusual parties, the list is becoming longer by the day. It's almost like a James Bond film, but better.'

Taylor looked at Jack and his brain considered the inform-ation. If the best officer he had known found it bamboozling, then a minefield it must be. Jack had to stay on the case as he was as good as it got. He would solve it and keep him updated, of that he was sure, and when he did there would be repercussions for all involved.

'You'll have to be Dagenham's 007 then Jack' he said light heartedly. 'Now go and catch some criminals, and by the way, there is ketchup on your trousers, from one of your sausage sandwiches I would assume?'

Jack left Taylor's office having learnt two things. One, his governor was giving him cart blanche to solve the case, and two, he hadn't noticed the tomato sauce.

'Robin, it's Nigel. We need to talk, now.'

Shaftsbury did not like the tone he had used. Nigel Morgan was ordering him to a meeting. How dare he. Fucking jumped up little arse hole. 'What benefit would a meeting mean for me?'

Morgan was gripping hold of the phone tightly. Sweat was forming on his palms, 'For starters, how does the police sniffing around grab your fucking attention! Thirty minutes, Red Lion, Parliament Street.'

The police asking questions had gained Robin Shaftsbury's attention. 'Ok.' He put the phone down and considered the information, deciding it had to do with the death of his beloved Malcolm. He had been offered £1,000 by the *Daily Mirror* to write a piece about his relationship with Malcolm Mason, although for the first time in his life he thought it bad taste.

The Red Lion was a small pub with tradition. It looked just as you would expect an old public house to look; creaking floorboards, rich oaks all over and wooden pub style seating. It oozed old school charm.

Nigel Morgan entered the bar and immediately ordered his drink. Shaftsbury had already arrived prior to Morgan, and had been eyeing Morgan knock back three Jameson's in under ten minutes, whatever the police had asked him, concerned him mightily, and that worried Shaftsbury.

'Nigel, good to see you. Another?'

'Yes, and make it a double.'

Sitting in one of the alcoves was Jack Philips. He had seen a beer mat in Whites that Morgan kept fiddling with. He had taken the plunge and decided this was his favourite haunt for drinking. What now interested Jack was the appearance of Robin Shaftsbury, and Morgan knowing Shaftsbury, this case was getting more intriguing, all be it strange, by the hour. Looking at the two, he deduced Nigel Morgan's feathers had been ruffled by the earlier visit. He was currently on his fifth drink, whereas Robin Shaftsbury was on his first Gin and Tonic. Their meeting, although quiet, appeared a little heated. Shaftsbury looked in control, yet concerned. Morgan kept jabbing his finger on the table, obviously to emphasize a point. Suddenly, Shaftsbury grabbed the finger and bent it backwards. A cracking noise could be heard that resembled a small dry twig being snapped. Morgan's face contorted in pain. Jack now understood Shaftsbury was a big player in the game. He finished his pint and quickly departed leaving no trace of his existence.

'You've broken my finger you fucking prick.'

'It'll be a lot more than that if you open your fucking nonce mouth.' Shaftsbury mouthed quietly and aggressively.

Morgan suddenly realised the organiser of the party had been Shaftsbury. All this time he had wondered who had set him up, and it was this fucking low-life sitting in front of him. The time had come to finish Robin Shaftsbury. Inside, Morgan was ready to explode, but outside he was ice. Now he knew, he had a slight edge, and he would maximise it to its fullest extent.

Outside Shaftsbury was annoyed with himself. He hoped Morgan had not understood, nor realised his mistake. It had given him a continued edge over him. His only hope was Morgan's rage controlled his mind set meaning he was not alert, although he thought not. Morgan was a wily fox. No-one held the position he had by being a fool.

Shaftsbury felt something was out of place. He had no reason to feel it, yet he felt like he was being watched. He had a sense for it. He pondered the situation and thought the security services may be keeping tabs on him, no-one else had any reason…unless Morgan had broken the unwritten allegiance.

Jack had finally found the leverage required; it was Morgan. He obviously had a problem with Shaftsbury, and could be an important player in the game they were about to play. This was turning into a play no man could have dreamed of.

Morgan's temper was simmering when visiting the hospital. Shaftsbury, fucking Shaftsbury, was all he kept rolling in his mind. He had been played by that fucking low-life, who proclaimed to be friends with everyone, well that snake had finally reared its head, and he was going to remove it. He had decided to speak to the police officer, Jack. Morgan felt he was an honest man who could not be bought off, something many officers had been through links to Shaftsbury, with the occasional Masonic handshake thrown in.

Shaftsbury reached his London home, having calmed down. He had lost his partner, and now his empire was beginning to show a few cracks. The time had come to pull in many favours given over the years. These would ensure his longevity would continue. The fly in the ointment was the policeman, Jack Philips. He was dogged, careful and worst of all – honest. There was something about Philips that concerned him. The security services had tried to employ him, and he had been offered promotions in the police force, yet had turned them all down. Contacts had told him he was a 'good old-fashioned officer who never gave up and believed in right'. Shaftsbury had thought it ridiculous when he had heard it, but having met Philips, he now understood, although he was pleased he was the officer investigating Mason's murder, yet being investigated by him could prove troublesome.

Chapter 11

To catch a rat

'**A**m I speaking to Jack Philips?'

'You are, who's speaking?'

'Nigel Morgan. We need to meet. If you want Shaftsbury, meet me tomorrow in the Cheshire Cheese, Fleet Street, 12.30pm.'

The phone disconnected. Jack Philips sat there considering the unexpected piece of good news. How it would help them was anyone's guess, but it was the sort of lead they needed. This investigation was becoming more complex and stranger by the day, yet one of the leading players in the game, Nigel Morgan, wished to jump ship. To catch a rat, you need a rat, and Shaftsbury was the biggest rat of all, and hopefully, Nigel Morgan was going to be the one who ratted on them all.

Unbeknown to Morgan, Shaftsbury had heard the telephone conversation he had just made with Philips. Morgan had not known he was in White's. Shaftsbury's instincts had proved correct. He had guessed Morgan would pounce over his mistake in the pub. He would have done the same. This required action, although getting it arranged by the following lunchtime would prove impossible. Time to start calling favours in.

The evening had lost is golden feel, and a kind of dark that helps the orange and gold blossom across the sky had loomed upon the capital. Morgan left White's and placed one foot on the pavement, before he could make another step he was lifted from his feet and forcefully thrown into the back of a van. A damp cloth was vigorously placed across his face, he felt himself drifting away.

Nigel Morgan woke to find himself naked, with his hands bound and placed in the small of his back tied to his ankles. He was on his side and the position was incredibly uncomfortable. A disturbing shiver entered his body like a bolt of electricity. Immediately he became aware of a voice he knew very well. He turned around, only to see said man at his door, tilting his head back and cackling with brutal, malicious laughter – the laughter of a madman, 'What the fuck are you doing Shaftsbury?'

'The rat has woken. You've been out cold for four hours. We thought you may have expired and gone to meet your maker.'

'How's Mason? Oh, he's dead isn't he, you pair of fucking poofs.'

Morgan was the receiver of a swift kick in the stomach. A watery yellow trail began to form about his waist.

'He's pissing himself.' A nervous laughter was made by others in the area.

Morgan quickly regained his breath, and composure, 'Seriously Shaftsbury, did you love Malcolm Mason the faggot footballer?'

'Speak like that again and I'll…'

'You'll what? Kill me? You're such a fucking arse-hole that you'll get someone else to do it, and when you get caught,

116

you'll name them.' Morgan knew those in the room would consider the information.

'Shut your fucking mouth.'

Morgan knew he had hit a nerve and decided to press on, 'Those of you in the room, he will grass you all up, he will save his…' Before he could complete the sentence, he received another kick, but before this was administered, he had seen two men look at each other in the reflection of a window. Suddenly, and ferociously, duct tape was placed across his mouth. He was lifted and thrown onto a carpet, where he was unceremoniously rolled up and carried away.

Morgan could hear water splashing close by. He was lifted abruptly and carried down a set of stairs carefully. Through a hole in the carpet he noted a sign *Town of Ramsgate*, he was in Wapping. The men dumped him on the damp sand tersely.

'Do you know where you are? Probably not. This area was known as Execution Dock, some believe it was elsewhere, but who cares? Quite apt do you not think?' Shaftsbury stood watching Morgan. He was proving mentally stronger than he had imagined.

The tape administered around his mouth and head appeared to be seriously stuck. He was then hooked up to the side. He slowly moved his head up and noted the Thames was coming in. It was just below his ankles. He heard Shaftsbury call out.

'Been nice knowing you Nigel. Enjoy the swim. Toodle pip.'

The water was now up-to his knees, and it was cold. His teeth chattered together relentlessly and uncontrollably; he couldn't stop himself from shaking. He had never learnt to swim, it made him laugh. How he wished he had gills. The ties were cutting into his ankles and wrists. Fortunately, the cold water was removing much of the pain., although there were clouds of crimson liquid Jones could see through the murky tidal waters.

The tide was rapid. He had never realized how quick the tide turned in The Thames. He could no longer hold his breath, the cold water was engulfing him, all illusions of survival diminishing. Life had been good. These were his last thoughts as the water plunged its hand down his throat and strangled at his lungs. Mason let loose a final gurgle, entering an eternal sleep.

C.I.D was filling up with staff, and officers were milling about with mugs of tea talking quietly about the day's work that lay ahead.

'Guv, a body's been found.'

'Where abouts ? Anyone we may know?'

'Nigel Morgan.'

'Fuckin' 'ell. Fuck it. How?'

'Drowned in the Thames. He was bound.'

Jack had to compute the information. 'Bound, did you say bound, as in tied up?'

'That's right guv.'

'I was talking to him yesterday. He was going to set Shaftsbury up to help us nick him.'

The officer studied Jack, and for the first time since he had known his DCI, noted a change about him. He obviously believed Morgan was the tiddler who was going to catch the big fish, plus it appeared he felt obvious sorrow for the man's death.

Jack made his way to the place where Nigel Morgan had been found. Due to the tide, all evidence had been washed away and the area cleansed. Still, forensics were trying to collate evidence from the steps leading down to Morgan's final resting place. One of the team asked to speak to Jack, 'Are you the lead man on this investigation?'

Jack eyed the man. His white overalls had discolored from the search and he appeared to require a night's rest, 'That'll be me'.

'Whoever did this knew the area well, and understood the place would be sterile.'

Yet they did not know something Jack had kept to himself. A well-known snout lived opposite, and had told Jack he had some incredible news for a price. The price given was £50. He had decided to not inform Taylor, who usually sanctioned these payments. Something was nagging Jack about his superior, and he did not understand what.

Jack also felt there was a mole in the department, He had had his suspicions for a while. Shaftsbury always appeared to be one step in front of his team's investigation, and it concerned him. He also had a feeling who the grass in his department was, and he hated them. Being two faced was not a good trait to have, yet to snare this person he had to play their game.

Jack left the team and wandered off to where his snout lived in Wapping High Street. He rapped hard on the black wooden door, which had a coating of dust living on it. A loathsome, unkempt looking man who required a shave and smelt of whisky opened the door.

'Don't stand there, get in. I don't want anyone to know I know yer.'

Jack considered the welcome. It was rather brief, abrupt and rude, yet it was to the point, which is what he wanted from this man. Neither had time for pleasantries. This was strictly business.

'You got the dosh Jack?'

'£50 as requested. Now, what do you know?'

'Let me see it first.'

Jack carefully placed his left hand in his pocket, and slowly removed the quantity of £1 notes, bound with two elastic bands. He then threw the bundle on the table, 'There's your money. Talk.'

'Last night about 10, four blokes and a bird went towards the river carrying a plastic bundle that was wriggling like a worm.'

Jack evaluated the information, 'What did they look like?'

'One was the arse wipe Robin Shaftsbury, or whatever his silly fucking name is, the two blokes looked like heavies, the bird was interesting.'

'Who's that?'

'She was standing next to you about thirty minutes back. I assume she's a bent copper, also I think the next piece of information will blow your fucking mind and prove the £50 was worth it.'

'Tell me then?'

'The bent copper bird is related to… are you ready…Mr. Arsewhipe himself, Robin Cuntface Shaftsbury.'

Jack nearly fell from the dirty chair he was perched on, 'Are you fucking sure?'

The anger showed on the snouts face; he looked like he was about to explode.

'Fuckin' sure, fuckin' sure, that fuckin' slag who works for you tucked me up four years back and I did eighteen months in Sheppey cos of 'er. That cunt of an uncle put 'er up to it. So, am I sure? Too right am I fuckin' sure.'

Jack left and made his way back to the station, still in a state of shock. Even though he had suspected Sylvie, to have it confirmed made it even worse. She appeared to be a person who had a future within the force. She had intelligence, looks and charisma, yet she was a traitor. When she did time, and she would do it, Jack thought he may even put the word out who she was, that would totally ruin her life.

He went straight to Taylor's office and walked in without knocking, such was his mind so preoccupied that he did not note the meeting taking place. As he rose his head, he was speechless, Robin Shaftsbury sat opposite his superior.

'Speak of the devil. This is the chap you need to speak to.'

Jack looked squarely at Shaftsbury, which made his nemesis feel uncomfortable, 'What are you doing here?'

'This is the sort of aggression I have come to expect from officers like this man. Is it normal Mr. Taylor?'

Taylor faced Shaftsbury 'I will look into your concerns and you'll hear from me forthwith.'

'I do not feel you are taking my complaint serious enough.'

'Please close the door on your way out, and my receptionist will show you to the exit. Goodbye Mr. Shaftsbury.'

'What was that weasel doing here sir?'

'He wanted to put in a complaint about harassment, namely you.'

Jack stood still like a block of ice-cold stone. He could not believe what he had just been told, 'Did you say complaint?'

'Yes Jack.'

'Ok. Let him do it. Once you have heard my news, things will never be the same again for one or two people.'

Having paid close attention to Jack's findings – Taylor leant back in his chair and puffed out his cheeks. 'Fucking hell Jack. This is going to be massive and explosive. Especially WPC Sylvie and her relationship to Shaftsbury. We need to be watertight sure about that, although it will be easy to find out. I will look into that myself so no-one else has an inkling regarding the operation. I ask one thing Jack, be careful. I believe Shaftsbury is a bad penny who will do anything, and I mean anything to win this battle.'

'Sir, I believe Shaftsbury has two problems; over confidence and greed. One or both will be his downfall.'

Jack headed down towards C.I.D and entered the department. Discussions were taking place; phone calls being made, and typewriters were tapping away like tap dancers on the stage. He noted WPC Sylvie in the corner talking to one of his officers, 'Everyone gather round.' Immediately twenty people descended towards Jack like a pack of lions, 'First thing, any news on the murder last night?'

One of the officer's hands shot up, 'Nigel Morgan, employed by White's gentlemen's club, respected by those at the club and considered hard working, looked like he had been beaten before drowning, appeared to be a one-man band – kept himself to himself.'

'Well done. Good information. Everyone try to look for people he'd come into contact with; family, friends, drinking partners, lovers…anyone. I'm going to delegate some roles to people. If I give you that role, stick to it, don't deviate.' He went through some roles finally playing his trump card, 'WPC Sylvie, you look into friends he may have known or colleagues he had. Righteo, off to work everyone, busy bees.'

He eyed his WPC, she immediately left the room and headed to the telephone in the empty office. 'I've been told to look at Nigel's friends and colleagues, Robin.' The receiver was put down, but the call had been recorded.

Shaftsbury replaced the receiver and considered the information. The investigation appeared to be growing in stature. Jack Philips now had a sizeable budget to work with, which had been signed off by those in loftier climes. They obviously felt they had a case against someone, or had suspicions. He understood the need to tread carefully, particularly after the party that had gone so gloriously bad in the end. Nothing had been said about Dave Smith, even his brother had not asked any questions, which in itself was strange, very strange. Steve Smith…Shaftsbury contemplated getting in touch with the remaining Smith, but could not decide whether it would open another can of worms. Still, he had his niece involved, which in itself was paying dividends handsomely.

'WPC Sylvie can I have a word please?' Jack then left the main office and walked casually to the dark office based along the tired looking corridor where Taylor was waiting. The room had significance as it was a favorite of WPC Sylvie for making telephone calls.

Sylvie entered the room with the bright sunny smile, but upon seeing Chief Superintendent Taylor and Jack together she immediately became nervous. Butterflies began to form, gently caressing her insides, and her mouth became dry like a desert. Something was wrong. Uncle Robin had always said trust your instincts, 'Sir, before we start, do you mind if I visit the ladies?'

Jack eyed WPC Sylvie suspiciously and nodded. He had a feeling she may bolt so he had arranged for plain clothed officers to be standing outside the front and rear exits, and for some to stand at the tube station.

The suspect bolted down the stairs taking them three at a time. She fled across the road not caring for the traffic that screeched, swerved and honked around her. Her direction took her right, Jack had a hunch she would head for the tube station and hide in the security of London. She had spent her youth in the city, likely the concrete jungle afforded her a feeling of safety.

Sylvie had removed the black and white cravat and tight-fitting black tunic, dumping both in an old wooden bin. Suddenly, she felt a sense of freedom, freedom that lasted six seconds before she was clamped in handcuffs and read her rights. Those on the platform looked on in horror. A woman being arrested on their platform. It would be something to gossip about with their friends and colleagues. A proper scandal in front of their eyes, how exciting. Who was she? What had she done?

'Take a seat WPC Sylvie, or should I now address you as Sylvie Shaftsbury?' As soon as he had mentioned Shaftsbury her eyes had darted at him like a pit-bull about to attack his victim. Yet he sensed worry in them.

Sylvie was trying to calculate her odds of freedom. It appeared minor. Her palms were taking on a glossy shine and the droplets were making her uncomfortable. She could also feel sweat forming on her chest, gently and slowly. She hoped these would not be noted, as it showed certain guilt and dishonesty.

'Ok. WPC Sylvie. I won't start with the formalities as you know them very well.' Jack allowed the *very well* to sink in and hit home. He understood for the first time in her life everything was going against Sylvie. He also knew this would be his trump card.

Taylor studied his WPC, she was beginning to go a little red, almost crimson, and wet patches were forming around her hair line. He decided to go with a softer approach, dropping her official title, 'Sylvie, you know why you are here, and we want you to help us. You are an officer of the law, so help us.'

She understood the good cop bad cop routine and began to smile, her perfectly formed white straight teeth like little beacons. She knew she was in a serious predicament, yet felt nothing, if anything – she felt icy calm. This was dangerous, yet she thought it was like a pantomime, and began to laugh raucously.

Taylor studied the lady sitting opposite him and realized she was close to psychotic. Too embed yourself within a department of security so effortlessly took a special talent, a dangerous talent. To be able to manipulate those around you, required extraordinary cunning, and to falsify identification, in particular a police application and interview, meant she had a talent in deception. If she had been normal, she would have been perfect for the security services. He looked at her again. She was a beauty, there was no getting away from it. She had intelligence as well. A heady brew, yet she had chosen to take a path into criminality. What a waste. She would serve a substantial period of her life in prison now. A crying shame. Unless….

'You are well and truly fucked big time. The word loser springs to mind. Everyone outside will carry on their lives whilst you serve time. You are one silly fucking bitch.'

Sylvie could not believe what she had just heard. He had just called her a bitch, a silly fucking bitch. He never spoke like that. Why was he speaking like that to her? It was not a game. He meant it. Could he be on Uncle Robin's payroll? Her mind was scrambled. Fuck Fuck. This was not right.

Taylor suddenly stood and roared, 'I've had enough. Jack, make sure she goes down for the rest of her pitiful dog-shit life. She is a fucking waster, and I fucking hate her slag guts. She's a no-good cunt.' He then stormed out and shut the door with such ferocity it made the frame shake.

Sylvie sat open mouthed. The language used by her chief superintendent had shocked her to the core. What had frightened her was his sudden change in character. Since she had known him, he had always appeared pleasant, almost vulnerable, yet this turn of events had seriously reared a monster within. One that appeared dangerously vindictive. She was in serious trouble. She had forgotten about her DCI.

Jack studied her thoughtful gaze, and understood this cunning and slippery fox was calculating her odds, which were zero. Knowing her, she would be trying to work out an angle to maximize her probability of freedom.

He was still shocked by Taylor's outburst. It had taken him by surprise, as it had his prisoner. He had never known his boss to show such emotion. He needed to calm this situation before it spiraled out of control, 'Sylvie, you're in serious trouble, as serious as it gets. I'm disappointed, as well as impressed by you. I would never have guessed.' He smiled and laughed quietly, enough for Sylvie hear, 'Sylvie, your uncle's proper fucked you. He'll carry on, as you go down for ten to fifteen years. That's a long time Sylvie, and it seems a little unfair, don't you think?'

Sylvie sat silently. One thing her DCI had said was correct, she was in the shit seriously. Ten years was a long time, but fifteen was immense, 'What about a deal?'

Chapter 12

Seriously

The news reached Shaftsbury quickly. He stood still like a block of ice. She had been nicked, and they were going to charge her with aiding and abetting. They must have something on her, and if they had that, they had him. Fuck. What had happened? One thing he did know; Sylvie would not say a word. He needed to speak to his lawyer quickly to help her. Having met her DCI, he knew he was dogged and would not relent until he broke his niece. This in turn would cause shit to hit the fan in spectacular fashion.

Some discreet enquiries had been made, and nothing had been heard of Steve Smith. Dave and Steve, what was going on? The most feared men in England were missing. Shaftsbury knew about Dave, although he had no idea, nor did he wish to know where his body had gone, but the twin brother missing as well. It could cause serious repercussions for many influential people.

In a neighbouring room he could hear the telephone ringing. He strode casually into the immaculately decorated room and answered the red newly installed push button telephone, 'To whom am I speaking?' Shaftsbury said in an uninterested manner.

'Listen, and listen good. She's talking.'

The telephone was immediately disconnected. He stood still holding the telephone. The fluids in his mouth had dried, yet his palms were now wet. In the pit of his stomach he had a strange fluttering sensation. Shaftsbury's heart started to pound at an increasingly rapid pace. He checked his reflection in the mirror. The haunted eyes and dark circles underneath them made the long, drawn-in face almost unrecognisable. Long nights of booze, sex and cocaine had begun to take its toll. Yet this was something on another hemisphere.

Sylvie was talking, he did not believe it, she was from a bloodline going back hundreds of years. This sort of thing did not happen to his lineage. His imaginary crown was beginning to feel heavy, and his dynasty, built on ill-gotten means was beginning to implode.

He had to unravel this situation, and quickly. He wrote down names of everyone he had made contact with, trying to link them until the interloper made themselves known. Whilst studying the list one name appeared to stand out and worried him…Gary Jones. No-one knew him, in fact, no-one knew anything about the man. He was the joker in the pack, his nemesis. For some reason, he knew he was the man bringing down his empire. Since he had entered the affray, everything had gone tits up. Gary Jones, your card is marked.

Through a network of friends, he had heard of a man excellent at finding people quickly, by any means. He had been given the number of a hotel in the leafy suburbs of Essex. Evidently, a quaint place, called Warley, near Brentwood.

Shaftsbury had made enquiries, Michael Dawson had a fearsome reputation. The man had spent a sizeable period of time in prison, much of which he had been the 'governor' inside. This showed how cunning, careful and dangerous he was. He appeared to have the requisite required to end Gary Jones's existence on this planet.

Michael casually walked into the New World Inn hotel and was met with a gentle female voice calling, 'Mr Dawson. A message has been left for you.'

Immediately Michael's internal antennae became alert. Only a few chosen people were aware of his living arrangements. This message must have come from someone who was important. He looked at the message, written in pencil, 'Call Mr Shaftsbury' along with a contact number. Michael considered his options. He assumed the person had no idea what he looked like, therefore, a telephone conversation could prove profitable, and if it did not, he had lost nothing.

He made his way up-to his bespoke room. It had been immaculately turned out, as he expected. The large double bed had perfectly finished hospital corners on the sheets. They looked crisp, almost sharp. The room had a floral fresh smell, it reminded him of the flowers his grandmother had once housed. The fragrance pleased him, now to business.

He dialled the olive-green rotary dial and was immediately answered with an abrupt 'Yes.' Michael considered the person's tone, and immediately felt they could be difficult. 'Before I find out who you are, or what you require, you will need to improve your manners, otherwise, you and I will fall out, and wherever and whoever you are, I will locate you.' He was met with heavy breathing, which he understood to mean nerves and surprise.

Shaftsbury considered the caller's demands and was insulted, 'My manners? You are calling me!'

Dawson now felt an inner demon rising inside ready to explode. 'You called me earlier, do not call again you ignorant cunt. Fucking poofter', and slammed the phone down.

Shaftsbury felt excitement run through his body and began to gain an erection. This was bad, and he had spoken to a real-life bad boy. His mind began to consider the things he would do to the caller. He had to speak to him and immediately redialled, 'I feel we may have gotten off on the wrong footing.'

Dawson stood there listening to the caller begging, he was weak, 'I didn't, you did.'

Shaftsbury was near arousal. The man was very abrupt, aggressive in his manner, 'I am sorry. I am under a bit of pressure at the moment.'

Pressure, meant major problems, and possible aggravation, yet it could pay well. 'Pressure you say, how much?'

'I am having problems with a man who is causing me major problems.'

Dawson considered the information and decided to dive head first to find out about his perspective employer, 'A man? Lover, money or both?' The phone went quiet for a number of seconds. This informed Dawson the problem was probably money, and the man he was speaking to was queer.

'I am having problems with a gentleman called Gary Jones.'

Michael Dawson froze. He had hoped to find the man, but to have him drop in his lap was a miracle. He had to compose himself, yet felt fidgety, adrenaline was racing through his body. 'There is a fee.' He had to sound calm and not interested in the person's client.

'I fully understand, I will give you £1,000 for expenses, and a further £9,0000 should you complete the task. Do you consider the amount acceptable?'

£10,000 in total, therefore. I want 25 percent up front, and this non-negotiable.'

'You drive a hard bargain, Mr Dawson. I like someone who does things in a hard way. It often leads to more pleasurable results.' Shaftsbury hoped the sexual innuendo had been understood.

Dawson replayed in his mind the double entendre the man had just said. Was he fucking mad? What a dirty old man, 'Listen, and listen good. I'm going to find the man you want, and do what you want me to do to him, but that does not involve any queer shit.'

Shaftsbury immediately ejaculated. This was a total bad boy, who was rough and really dangerous. How he would like to turn him, 'I understand; we need to meet so I can give you expenses.'

Dawson considered the information, and began to smile. He knew he had to get a train using the Liverpool Street line, and a pub immediately sprung to mind, 'Meet me in Dirty Dicks at 1pm tomorrow. I'll be sitting alone with a Guinness and a sausage sarnie'. He replaced the receiver.

Shaftsbury let out a deep bellowed laugh, 'Bravo young man, Dirty Dicks, magnificent.' This one had a sense of humour. He knew the pub; it was situated opposite the station where members employed within the financial sector often congregated for working class luncheon.

The cell where Sylvie was being held was bleak, drab and cold. She had been placed in the 'Hilton' cell. It had gained its name as it was the only cell with a toilet seat. The mattress was approximately three inches thick, and covered in royal blue thick vinyl so it could be washed down quickly. The grey blanket they had given her smelt of washing power, and the material was course, making the skin it touched, itchy. The constable who had shown her to the cell had given her a new pillow. She had been on a couple of dates with him, and he was friendly. The walls of the cell appeared to close in. She could not escape the endless, darkened wait to freedom. Sitting in the corner of the chilled room, Sylvie noted the sharp corners. The walls, painted pale blue many years ago, shaped the lifeless room. The dull paint on each of the four walls carried a burden of memories where 'innocent people' drawing closer and closer to their sentence had been logging their injustice on the walls. Sylvie read the anecdotes, finally realising her predicament. Some of those she had been involved in arresting, now she was the one arrested. The irony of the situation made her smile nervously.

Sylvie could hear a conversation taking place outside, yet could not fully understand the hushed tones.

Suddenly, the clanking sound from the key being turned and the screech from the weighted 200 pound door opening afforded Sylvie the offering of DCI Jack, and a man she knew to be a lawyer.

'Miss Shaftsbury, I believe you wish to speak to someone who can make or agree deals. Is that correct?'

Sylvie considered the man facing her. He was approximately 6 feet, had greying hair, dressed beautifully in a tailored navy-blue suit and was perfectly spoken. 'I believe I should be addressed as WPC.'

'No. Miss Shaftsbury is correct. You have lost your rank, therefore your title. Do you wish to proceed? If not, I can be elsewhere.'

The information struck Sylvie like a knife through the heart. She had lost her vocation, dignity and now her rank. Suddenly, she had a feeling of loneliness and rejection. Robin had totally dumped her in the mire, she was in the biggest well of excrement ever known to anyone. Sylvie knew the moment she started to cry, she was alone. She cried slowly, tears dripping down her cheeks like little rivers, and the sobbing of her own voice echoing throughout the cell. She knew she existed, yet she meant nothing to anyone. She was alone, sinking deeper and deeper into her own pitiful well of desolation. Suddenly anger built up in the pit of her stomach and she roared defiantly. Both gentlemen were shocked by the sudden, and unexpected outburst. Sylvie turned to both, 'You want my uncle; you can fucking have him. Cunt.'

Jack Philips noted her clenched jaw and fists scrunched into a ball. She was clasping her fists so tight they were beginning to go red. She was incredibly uptight, like a coiled spring ready to explode into action. Jack glanced slyly at her lawyer. The man showed no emotion whatsoever, he looked lifeless, like a mannequin. He assumed he had seen this thing before many times, probably daily.

'I am Tom Watson, and have come to eliminate your problem. You will need to be honest with me, something you have not been – or so I have been led to believe. The moment I feel you are trying to misdirect me you will require someone else to represent you. Do I make myself clear?' The lawyer had gone from dull and dreary to an exponent of honesty, purposefulness and attack.

Jack had a good feeling about this man. He appeared to have morals and a maverick way about him. This made him a perfect adversary for Sylvie. The way his muscles had not moved meant he was purposely studying her, and whether she was a risk. There was more to this man.

'Do you understand?' It was said with little emotion, although with a touch of intensity.

Sylvie knew this man would help her; she also knew he would sense any bullshit. How the hell had she ruined her life? To be reliant on a man who could save her and ruin her equally was a nightmare situation. She was trying to calculate the man facing her. He had altered from an immeasurably meek mouse to a roaring lion. She turned her head and looked into his icy blue eyes, 'I understand.'

Jack could sense the tension in the room, it was palpable. Some situations were long drawn and monotonous, this situation was not. It was stimulating and enthralling.

'You wish to offer evidence that may allow a deal to be made, Is this correct?'

Sylvie knew once she stepped on this bomb there was no going back. 'Yes.'

'Do you understand the procedure? I will take down your statement, as your lawyer, and then consult with a judge. What exactly do you wish in return?'

Sylvie already knew her reply as she had thought about nothing else, 'I want all charges made against me dropped.' She then paused. 'And I want my job back.'

DCI Jack's mouth dropped open in shock and amazement. It had been noted by the wily lawyer, who appeared to be aware of everything, missing nothing.

'Sylvie. I can tell you now, you have absolutely no chance of returning to your chosen vocation. Absolutely no-chance. No judge in the land will support you. In fact, they will consider your request nefarious. They will then switch off, and refuse to listen any further to your request. As your lawyer, I can only advise you. If you wish to take that incredibly small and meagre opportunity, then you can instruct me to action it.'

Sylvie was stunned by the abruptness in his manner. She honestly believed he would support her, yet here he was almost mocking her, 'I'm not sure I like your attitude.'

The lawyer stood up, closed his case, 'It is not I who will serve a minimum of 15 years incarcerated. I wish you all the best with your next representative of the legal system. So, you are aware, I am the most expensive and best. I have never lost a case. Goodbye.'

This was not what Sylvie had expected. No-one spoke to her in such a derisive manner, yet here was her only chance walking out the door, 'You are not what I had expected.'

The door was closed with a resounding clang.

DCI Jack looked at her pitiful face, 'Sylvie, you proper fucked that up, that man is as good as it gets, he is considered the BEST. He sorts everything and everyone out. You are either really stupid or fucking naive. I don't know which, but what you are is proper fucked, and in the deepest pool of shit I've ever seen anyone.' He had a final look at her and walked out, leaving her contemplating her foolishness.

In an adjacent room Jack sat with the lawyer. Their part in the charade had been played. DCI Jack Philip and the lawyer sat together with a mug of tea and a plate of French Fancies discussing the developing events.

Shaftsbury entered Dirty Dicks and noted the stale smell of cigarettes, beer and working-class lunches. Those frequenting the establishment all looked like they visited the same down-market shop, or Petticoat Lane market; cheap white polyester shirts, navy blue suits, that looked a little threadbare in places, and blue ties were the choice of attire. As he looked around, he noted a man eating a sausage sandwich, or sarnie as he had so eloquently addressed it, with an accompanying pint of stout, 'Dawson?'

'Sit.'

Shaftsbury considered the manner of the command. It was something he was not used to. Dawson was ploughing into the sausage in French Bread like a farmer ploughs a field. He was a machine. Shaftsbury had not seen Dawson breath during the process. He began to sense arousal again, what was it with this oaf of a man? He then slurped half a pint of stout in one mouthful. Shaftsbury thought he was sitting with a Neanderthal.

'Gary Jones. Talk to me.'

'Do you require background information?'

'Background, foreground or even a fucking fairground. I don't really care. Just tell me about him and what you want done?'

Shaftsbury was stunned by the abruptness and ferocity. He knew Dawson was bad, but he now had a feeling he was dangerous, very dangerous.

During the next five minutes he informed Dawson of the life of Gary Jones and the problems he may have caused directly or indirectly. He also emphasized he wanted him permanently on the missing list.

Dawson studied the man closely, and decided he could not be trusted, yet here was a man who had given him Gary Jones, after many years of searching, and ten grand. It was an amazing piece of fortune.

Shaftsbury swiftly left the rendezvous with a distinct feeling of unease. The man he had just met frightened him with his intensity and lack of feeling. He appeared soul-less and full of rage. He could not put his finger on it, but felt there was a deeper meaning to the anger.

●

Dawson approached White's. Before he could knock the door magically opened in a silky movement, 'May I help you sir?'

Dawson looked squarely at the man in front of him and thought everyone in Shaftsbury's world was bent, 'Yes. You need this.'

The man appraised the card, whilst assessing the subject in front of him. He stood tall, upright, smart – well dressed in a Saville Row suit, yet there was something intimidating about him. He knew the kind; he'd had to look out for it during his time in the SAS. He slowly raised his head, 'Welcome to White's sir. Is this your first visit?'

'It is. This is not the sort of venue I usually pop into.'

The doorman quickly noted the *pop into*. He knew this man was a man who frequented public houses, and probably whore houses, not White's. He had also noted Shaftsbury had given him a membership to the esteemed establishment. He could not stand Shaftsbury. The way he floated about like a

Mr. Big Time, wanker. 'Can I show you around our premises sir so you will have an idea of the lay out?'

'No. Where's the bar?'

The doorman noted the lack of conversation, along with a deficiency in syllables. He also realized this man would cause trouble, lots of it. The hairs on the back of his neck began to stand. He had not felt like this since his secretive tours with the services. He felt alive.

Dawson sat alone at the old established bar with his Jameson. He perused the whisky glass. It was crystal. That alone told him the people who attended the club. At the prices charged they should do as well. He looked at the doorman and assumed he had been privately educated. He was very upright in his persona and quietly spoken. Probably a poof like Shaftsbury. He spoke to the barman and asked if he knew Gary Jones.

'I am sorry sir; we do not comment on other members.'

Dawson weighed up the man and decided he could be brought, 'Are you sure?' He then handed the man £5. 'Anything you can remember will be appreciated.'

'He is sporadic with his visits to the club and he is very quiet. He is also a fine chess player. I heard a rumour he lives in Dagenham, although I would be surprised as he would never gain entrance to the club coming from a working-class area like that.' Before he had finished Dawson was briskly marching towards the exit.

Dawson contacted his old home, Boyles Court, and enquired whether Mr. Stone was still employed. He was immediately informed that staff employment records were not offered.

Dawson realized this would be 'red flagged', and a warning given to Freddie Stone that someone had tried to make contact, possibly an old inmate.

Michael Dawson decided to try his luck and wait at the Thatcher's Arms. He had become a regular and had gained trust from the landlord. The public house opened at 5.30pm, and Dawson had a beer waiting on the counter, such was his early evening regularity in the establishment.

He was half-way through his second pint of Guinness, when the old black front door opened, and in strode Freddie Stone. Dawson nearly choked on his beer, making him cough immediately. This made the landlord and the new customer turn and look.

Freddie Stone looked more carefully in the bars reflective mirror that showed. The mirrors had been an ingenious idea. It allowed bar staff to see who was approaching the bar without having to turn. It also allowed those drinking the same idea.

Stone looked a looked a little closer and recognized the round red mark. What was Dawson doing here?

'Do I know you?'

Stone understood that Dawson was trying to instigate a conversation. He immediately decided to call the man's bluff.

'Michael Dawson. How are you? What are you doing round these parts?'

Dawson was caught unaware by the man's confidence. He had expected him to be defensive, yet here he was confident, unafraid and still drinking his beer. 'I thought it would be nice to see my old rendezvous.'

'Rendezvous, an interesting turn of phrase.' Stone carried

on drinking his beer, whilst studying the man in front of him. He knew this man would have an ulterior motive for *bumping* into him, and knew it had to do with the past, in particular…Gary Jones.

'Do you remember when I was a resident of the home? There was a problem with one of the other boys. A lad called Gary. Do you remember him?'

'Yes. I remember him. He was the only lad who beat me at chess.'

'Have you see him, or heard anything of him?'

'The last time I saw him, or heard from him was when he left the court. To be honest with you, I don't tend to keep check on previous attendees. It's busy enough looking after those here.' He smiled at Dawson.

Dawson looked at Stone and considered the information he had been fed, and decided it was true. Stone had always been a man considered honest and reliable. He was a man who never bent the rules and used to say, 'Rules are rules, don't break them and you'll be fine.' He also wondered why Stone had not joined the police, he would have been perfect.

'It's been lovely meeting you Mr. Stone. Look after yourself.'

'And you Michael. Be lucky and be happy.'

This made Dawson smile. The expression was something Stone had said when he was an inmate. Stone was obviously a man of routine and who rarely changed his ways. Dawson liked this. It meant Stone was happy with his life and had no problems. He had noticed he was not married, no wedding ring, he thought this the only thing strange.

Freddie Stone gave it fifteen minutes before he made call.

'Jack Philips, it's Freddie Stone. Don't know if this would interest you, but an old inmate of mine, Michael Dawson, just bumped into me and wanted to meet Gary Jones.'

Immediately Jack Philips became interested. Gary Jones was a name popping up often, yet was a man no-one knew. 'Thank you for calling Freddie. What else did he ask?'

'He wanted to know if I had seen him, which I have not. The interesting thing was Jones had seriously injured Michael Dawson when they were based at Boyles Court, therefore, there is absolutely no chance this was a social question. It can only mean trouble, yet Gary Jones was, and probably still is too wily for Dawson. He was the toughest inmate we've had, but do not underestimate Dawson, as he has a very dangerous side to him.'

'Mr. Stone, one question. Do you feel this could start a war between the two men?' The phone went quiet for a couple of seconds, before a reply was given.

'Yes. A one-sided war. If I hear anything, I will contact you. Goodbye.'

Upon returning to his present home Dawson asked the receptionist if she had a telephone book for Dagenham. After much rummaging one was produced from the previous year's addition. Dawson removed himself from the area and bound up the stairs to his room with the speed of a cheetah. His hands were shaking with trepidation. Could it be this easy? There were many Jones's in the book, yet only six with the initial G. Dawson called each number, finally dialing the last one on the list. It was immediately answered. Dawson suddenly forgot his readied speech. 'Jones, it's Dawson. You know which one. Meet me at Warley Hospital tomorrow

9pm.' The phone was disconnected.

Jones stood leaning against the wall by his telephone. How had Michael Dawson got his number? He obviously knew where he lived. As he turned he looked down at his telephone seat and book holder. The book! Dawson had got all information from the book. It was the only place where information could be gained so easily, and legally. Time had not allowed Dawson to forget his beating. It had probably eaten him up inside. Gary realized time had come to finish this once and for all. Otherwise Dawson would always be a thorn in his side.

Chapter 13

Goodbye Dawson

The meeting had been set. The two warring parties agreed to meet in the side entrance of Warley Mental Hospital. Both knew the area, although Dawson felt he had tactical advantage as he had been staying locally, yet unknowing to him Jones had already surveyed the area and selected a vantage point where he would be able view all arrivals, although only one interested him.

Gary arrived at the hospital early evening. The red brick gatehouse had been empty, devoid of life. When Gary had studied it, he thought it a magnificent structure. He quickly strode into the grounds and squatted behind the extremely pink shaggy rhododendron bush. It had been a tight squeeze, but he made it. No one had seen him. The view was perfect. The wait was exhausting, although the numbness was worse. He knew he could not move, yet occasionally he had to change position to allow circulation and to avoid cramp. Finally, his prey had arrived.

Dawson knew the hospital having used the Horse and Groom public house a few times. When the meeting had been agreed he had swiftly made a reconnaissance of the area. The meeting was planned for 9pm, therefore he decided to arrive ninety minutes earlier. He visited the pub for a couple of pints and a whisky to sharpen his nerves. On approaching the hospital, he knew the Gate House would be empty, so he decided to wait inside. Having picked the old lock in a matter of seconds, he strode in, slunk down against a corner wall contemplating what he would do to Gary Jones. The meeting place was perfect; no-one would hear a thing being inside this old building.

When Dawson had broken into Gate House it had been witnessed by Jones. A smug smile grew upon his face. Dawson, the idiot, had ensnared himself. Dawson obviously thought he was secure, yet now he had entombed himself.

The time had arrived for battle to take place, yet Jones had not arrived. Dawson did not consider Jones a man who would shy away from conflict, but there was always a first time. He sat inside until 10.30pm, before deciding to leave.

Gary slowly, carefully and gingerly slunk up-to the gate house, waiting six feet from the entrance. He knew if he made Dawson wait, he would complete his mission. One thing Dawson did not have, was patience, and this would be his downfall as he would make one slight mistake.

Dawson had waited long enough and was fuming. Fucking Jones had wasted his time. He decided to leave the inner sanctum of the Gate House. Dawson, who was totally unaware of the fate awaiting him, turned and gently closed the door.

Suddenly, he felt a stinging pain in his right thigh, like a wasp had attacked him. As he turned, his drooping eyes saw Gary Jones smiling. He tried to speak, but was unable to move his features, he was paralysed. His mind was shouting, 'Jones you absolute fucking cunt.'

'Hello Michael. How are you? Oh, by the way…2-0 to me.'

Dawson was picked up, unceremoniously, and thrown into the back of the Ford British Gas transit. Gary had acquired the van during the afternoon. It had cost him £100 to hire for the evening. An employee of the government owned body had a gambling problem. When Gary had approached him with the offer, the client had almost snapped his hand off. The only requirement was the van had to be placed back at the depot in Crow Lane.

The Propofol had been the hardest thing to acquire. He'd had to bribe the chemist who had been able to obtain the potion. Without it, Dawson would still be a nuisance…to all. Fortunately, Gary had received some information that the married chemist was a frequent visitor to an illegal gay cinema in Farringdon, a stone's throw from Smithfield meat market. After this, the man had crumbled and begged Gary to not tell anyone. Gary had informed the man this was a one off, and he would never be contacted again, and to forget Gary's face.

Slowly he rocked, back and forth. Occasionally, the wind would tug at the loose clothing moving it softly, as if it were caressing the garment. The contorted face showed no emotion, its last look a grimace that wanted to scream silently. The final sound would have been from the neck snapping. It had sounded like a piece of wood breaking.

In the moonlight, the body looked like a scarecrow. The final resting place of Michael Dawson allowed him a sensational ending. Hanging from Gidea Park Station like a ceremonial artefact.

Crowds were beginning to flock during the early morning rush hour, word had gone around of the swinging chrysalis. No one understood what was embalmed within the plastic covering. Someone in the crowd mentioned it looked like a large pendulum, which was met with a muted laugh.

The sirens in the distance had been replaced with an illumination of flashing blue lights, and black suited officers shouting at the crowds to move back. The surrounding roads were closed with blue signs stating 'Police, No Entry'.

The Scene of Crime Officer arrived and surveyed the surrounding area. It was his thinking time. The circus hadn't arrived, so he got suited up and strode towards the hanging body with his notepad. He thought, 'This is what the conductor in an orchestra must feel before a performance.' Looking up he instantly realized it was obviously a body; he had been involved in a similar case before. On his notepad were five questions; What am I seeing? What am I hearing? Which lights are on? Which are off? Who can view?

The swinging thing was slowly lowered to the floor. As it reached its destination it was grabbed and placed gently on the white plastic forensic sheet. The crime scene experts then caressed the plastic sheeting with their razor-sharp scissors, slicing through without leaving a mark. Finally, the sheet was opened, and was met with astonishment.

A hole had been drilled into the top of the skull and something poured in. Something so corrosive it had eaten away the eyes and all soft tissue inside the cavity. One of the crime scene operatives turned and removed the contents from his early morning meal.

He could not remove his eyes. During his tenure within his

department he thought he had witnessed everything, but this was something evil, depraved, frightening. Whoever did this showed no mercy, had no feeling for human life, and was incredibly, incredibly dangerous.

DCI Jack Philips had been called to the scene. He had no idea what to expect, or what was happening. His day's growth gave him an unappealing, exhausted look. Yet inside he felt alive. tinged with increasing excitement. Whatever this case was, it would be intriguing at least.

Upon arrival, he noted the crowds clambering onto buses taking them to neighboring stations, situated on the Liverpool Street line. This alone informed him it was something dramatic.

'I'm DCI Philips. You the lead SOCO?'

Philips was studied by the Scene of Crime Officer, who noted the tired and un-kempt look of the man facing him; too much tea and a poor diet, probably consisting of fried food from the station canteen, and a lack of sleep. Yet there was a sparkle – an edge to this man. He also realized the gentleman had given his life to the force, meaning policing was his everything. 'Good morning, officer. I think we have a body that is as amazing as it is terrifying.' He took a sip from his tea that he had poured from his thermos flask. The steam showed it was fresh, it was floating towards the skies. He then leant forward and took a bite from his crusty ham roll. Remnants of mustard caressed the outer rims of his lips. Salaciously, his tongue flicked out and it was removed, 'Do you want to view the body?'

Philips stood there; this was the first-time body had been mentioned. Now he understood why he had been summoned to the situation. 'I'd much rather a bacon sarnie, but a body runs it a close second.'

Both men smiled at the gallows humour.

'Touché Philips, let us peruse the once swinging delight.'

Both men strode to the waiting body. Immediately the sheeting was removed from the facing side, allowing both to study the corpse.

'Bloody hell, what's happened to its head?'

'The soft tissue is emulsified into a thick paste. The bones, namely the skull, would take 2 or 3 days to breakdown due to their density. To be frank with you DCI, I've never seen anything like this. It's a first.'

'Any ideas of time of death?'

'I would say around midnight. Whether the acid was poured whilst the receiver was still alive, we will never know.'

'Fucking hell. This is barbaric. Even I'm shocked.'

'As we all were. My assistant had to remove the contents of his early morning meal. It appears he had cereal, possibly Shredded Wheat.'

Philips looked at the man. These people are unique in their knowledge, and they had an ability to maintain personality in the face of death, 'Sounds delightful. Anything more on the body?'

'Not much until I get it back to the lab. We did remove a cheque book. Midland Bank. Michael Dawson was the name on the account, so we can be reasonably sure that is who the body belongs to.' At the name of Michael Dawson, he noted Philips's head almost spin like the Exorcist.

Michael Dawson. Another link to Gary Jones. Freddie Stone had warned him about a connection between the two,

149

'You did say Michael Dawson?'

'I most certainly did. Obviously, a dodgey fellow to end in this manner.'

Jack stood on the platform considering the facts. Everything lead back to Gary Jones, but the man was a phantom. He glanced down at the body that was now being hoisted into the body bag. What a way to end.

Gary sat in Westland's Cafe devouring his egg, bacon and bubble. He loved the breakfasts in this establishment. The place was full of builders all trying to outdo each other with their tales of craftsmanship and how much money they had earned. It also allowed him to pick up occasional pieces of gossip.

The table talking behind him were speaking about a body being found at Gidea Park Station. One of those on the table mentioned it had been hanging like a bat. This had made Gary smile. Dawson's life finished with him being compared to a hanging nocturnal animal, which seemed about right.

Gary needed to visit Bob, the Gravedigger. He had not seen him for a while and felt he should show his face. He paid the bill and left the cafe, having not spoken to a soul, apart from the girls taking the orders.

The weather was overcast, yet mild, therefore he decided to walk to the cemetery. Briskly, he strode out and reached the destination in thirty minutes. It had also given him thinking time.

'Morning Bob. Busy?'

The beast of a man looked squarely at Gary, 'Dead still need burying Gal.'

Gary wanted to smile but knew it would prove to be rude. He understood the inner workings of Bob and how he considered his vocation to be incredibly important, 'Indeed, they do Bob, indeed they do. How many have you to dig today?'

'Two done already. One to do.'

'You've done two already! It's only 9.45am. Bloody hell.'

Bob carried on digging, his shovel slicing through the earth as if it were trying to explore the ever-deepening ground below it, 'Body found at Gidea Park Station this morning.'

Gary knew that Bob was indirectly stating he knew he was involved, 'Someone from a previous life Bob, a dreadful person who needed removing.'

'Previous life, you mean Boyles Court then.'

'Yes. Michael Dawson was his name. He was a man who made money on the misery of others, in a deplorable manor Bob. He had been employed by someone I know, to remove me from life. It had to be done. This was one of those situations I actually wanted to do. In my life, I've actually only hated one man, and this was that man. He was a pariah, who was neither liked nor respected. He was a cunt.'

The grave was ever deepening, and was now waist high, 'Harsh words my friend, harsh words. This man, Dawson, did he rightly deserve his ending?'

'Yes.'

'Then I'll be digging one of these for him then.'

'Bob, you are an honourable and decent man, although for Dawson you will not suffer the misfortune of having to create his final resting place.'

Bob considered what Gary had just said. It troubled him that Gary felt the need to relieve himself of this information. He had never done this before. There was more to this story, yet he would not pry. If he felt the need to inform him, he would. He placed his shovel in the earth with such force it split a large stone, 'Gary, you are my only friend. Be careful.' He turned and carried on digging.

Gary knew this was his time to leave. It was Bob's way of saying *I need to work, go away.*

Jack Philips read a file supplied on Michael Dawson. He was amazed he had not heard the name before. He was a narcissist, he had all of the traits, yet also had a psychopathic edge, and it was the dangerous edge. He stood in the office and hollered, 'Gather round everyone, quickly.'

Immediately, there was a smack of feet walking toward his desk, and the sound of pencils bouncing on desks.

'Right everyone, you've heard about last night, and it was barbaric, even for a scum-bag like Dawson. We need to find information on the life of Michael Dawson and a certain Gary Jones. We have to know about their lives. Something, or somebody ignited this conflict, so we have to know who this person or thing is as well. Another thing bothering me is this party attended by the rich and wealthy. I may be wrong, but I feel this links in. So, find out about it. Chop chop! Time waits for no man.'

The clattering of feet going back to their desks indicated to Jack he had a solid unit. Immediately, phone calls were being made, favours pulled in and quiet conversations with colleagues taking place. This room, already busy, had become a clamour of frenzied activity.

Jack noted Drake pacing towards him.

'Guv. I've been told Dawson visited White's Club once.'

'How do you know that?'

'Old army pal of mine works their door. Told me hairs on

his neck rose when he met Dawson. Lucky Dawson didn't upset my pal. He's proper solid, no-one messed with him.'

Jack studied Drake and knew when he meant solid, he actually meant controlled in a psychopathic manner. Drake had the same ferocity about him, having been employed by the SAS. 'Excellent work Drakey. I feel you and I need a trip to London. Fancy it?'

'Ready when you are sir.'

Jack sat down whilst Drake busied himself getting ready. Over in his mind he turned over the facts. Whites was a key component; of that he was sure. Everything seemed to go back to this members' establishment. It was also not far from Dolphin Square. It all fitted together perfectly. Possibly too perfectly, but White's was key, he was certain. He also had an uneasy feeling the old boys' network would build a wall, one that may take some knocking down.

'You ready, sir?'

'I was born ready Drakey. Let's go hunting.'

As both men approached White's, the door opened majestically and Drake was met with an instant handshake, 'Pleasure to see you again. Come in. Go to the bar and I will join you.'

Philips, for the first time since working with Drake ,appeared surprised. 'What was all that about Drakey?'

Drake casually turned to his DCI, 'Nothing sir. We just served together.'

They were approached by Drake's old colleague who sat down. Jack Philips could resist no further and jumped in with a question, 'Don't think I'm being rude, but how do you know Drakey?'

'May I tell him?'

Sergeant Drake looked embarrassed by the question, and nodded.

'Captain Drake was head of my troop of 16 men. We were based in Special Operations. I can't tell you where we were, but this man saved seven men and took out a machine gun nest alone. Bravery very few people witness. He was one of the toughest in our squadron.'

Jack Philips felt his mouth drop open and wanted to say something, but he was too surprised, 'You Drakey, did that?'

Sergeant Drake turned towards his DCI with an embarrassed smiled.

'You are top lad Drakey. Always have been, and now I know why.'

'Saved my life DCI Philips. Anyway, how can I help you?'

Drake turned to his old colleague, 'Can you tell us about the man you spoke with, who you didn't strike a rapport with?'

'Dawson. Smart man, no life skills, limited conversation, working class, out of place here.'

Both officers listened to the man. He reported it in list form, as if he were back in his army uniform.

'He also spoke to the barman. I am sure money was passed to him. Speak to him.'

'Barney, where can we find the barman?'

'If you give me a couple of minutes, I will locate him and bring him to you.'

'Barney, stop the sir, we're no longer based at Hereford.'

'As long as you are sure?' He then departed seeking the barman.

'Drakey, you sly dog. I had no idea. I knew you were in the forces, but the SAS is a different ball game altogether.'

'That's a past life. One I don't think about, nor care about. The only thing it aided was me joining the Met, and it helps me analyse a person quickly, whilst knowing very few can better me, if you get my drift sir.'

A man approached wearing a white jacket. 'Gentlemen you wish to speak to me about the man who asked for information?'

'Yes, please take a pew.' Philips pointed to a spare seat. 'Can you tell me everything he wanted to know?'

'Of course, gentlemen. He wanted to know about one of the customers who occasionally frequents our establishment. The client he wanted to know about was a man by the name of Gary Jones.'

Philips could not believe it, this man was everywhere, yet no-one knew anything about him. He was a phantom, 'What did you tell him?'

'This will not go any further will it?' The barman asked.

Philips looked at the man and could not believe what he had just said, eventually he replied, 'No, nothing will find its way back to your employers.'

'Thank you' replied the barman. This was swiftly followed with, 'Dagenham. I told him I believed the Jones man came from Dagenham, although it probably was not true, as he would never gain entry to the club. What followed was odd.'

'What was odd?' Philips swiftly responded.

'He left the bar without finishing his large Jameson's and collecting his change. He left the bar as soon as I said the words Dagenham.'

Philips and Drake considered the information they had been given. Philips thanked the barman and informed him he could return to his duties. Barney returned and asked if there was anything else they required, which was met with a resounding; no', although Drake stood and placed his arms around Barney and whispered quietly, 'Who Dare's Wins.'

Barney looked at Drake and replied, 'For queen and country, sir.'

The special bond shown by the world's elite fighting machine was evident between these two men. Philips watched and admired their sense of camaraderie. It was something special to see.

Chapter 14

Holiday time

The six men sat around the old oak boardroom table in The Dorchester Hotel. The faceless men all had one agenda, Robin Shaftsbury.

All had met individually, and given their personal thoughts on the ever-expanding situation of negativity.

'Gentleman, thank you for attending this career defining meeting. There are numbers placed on the table in front of you, use these when speaking to a fellow colleague, do not, and I must emphasize, do not use their name, for obvious reasons. We are here to discuss the options regarding Mr Shaftsbury, and the ever deepening well he appears to be swimming in. Has anyone news on Shaftsbury? Yes, number 3.'

'I have heard, from reliable sources that he has attracted attention from the Metropolitan Police. More worrying, an officer by the name of DCI Philips has taken a strong interest, and is supposedly dogged, and more problematic, honest.'

'Anyone else have something to add?'

'Number 6.'

'I have learned his niece has decided to inform on her uncle's activities.'

Each of them pondered the revelation.

'Yes Number 5.'

'Number 1. Does the niece know everything? I always assumed Shaftsbury was a man of discretion.'

'Gentleman. We need to be more worried about the parties. Do you not think? You have something to add Number 2.'

'I do agree with everyone's consideration, although that will not be a problem if Shaftsbury went on a holiday, from which he never returned.'

The five men all looked at Number 2 in surprise, shock, amazement.

'Do you mean a holiday of a lifetime, whereas someone does not wish to return as they are having an agreeable time.'

'Yes Number 1. I was thinking along those lines. Shaftsbury appears to be a chap who may enjoy a long stay in an area frequented by few.'

'Number 4.'

'It could be arranged easily. I know of a travel agency, run by those with a specific skill set. They aid people with overdue and extended vacations. Very professional. The sort of organisation that understands the pre-requisites of the party who wishes the other to go on a never-ending vacation – from which they do not return.'

The men sat around the table in their own collective thoughts, considering the possibilities, and how their lives could be enhanced, bettered and prospered. None of them contemplated how they could be ruining their own lives should it go wrong. The silence was broken by Number 1.

'Gentlemen, I think we need to remove this problem, permanently. I suggest we find out everything we can and meet again next week. Is everyone in agreement?

The five men facing Number 1 all nodded in unison.

'Excellent. Shaftsbury is going on a one way vacation, never to return… Until our next meeting gentleman.'

They immediately stood behind their chairs before departing, as silently as they had arrived thirty minutes previously.

Number 1 sat in the soft leather chair and pondered the situation. Shaftsbury had to be removed, that was certain. He had grown too big, and a cacophony of ever-expanding problems had followed him. His relationship with the footballer had been his downfall. The player was too fanciful and a celebrity of sorts. If Shaftsbury had chosen wisely and become comfortable with a less prominent male, then he would be living a very recognisable life. Sadly, his ego had led to his demise. Shaftsbury had organised some spectacular parties, expensive, but highly sexed and depraved. They were beautifully bad. Power players had been met, loved and used along the way. Hence, he was Number 1. He held the cards, the secrets, he had also gathered information on everyman who attended the party.

Shaftsbury stood in the opulent reception waiting for his lawyer when he saw five men leave the Dorchester he knew well. Each had nothing to do with the other regards to business, this worried him. He became even more concerned when he the sixth man departed. This man was a power player in the world. He was a man who could make or break someone. He could ignite a political career or send a man to the gallows, with a telephone call, or a word in someone's ear.

The chief whip, from the Conservative Party, was considered a fair and honourable man by the public, but behind closed doors he was anything but. Politically, he ruled with a fearsome rod of steel, yet he was a demon with young men at the parties, and he was supposedly happily married, with a devoted wife and three grown up daughters. He loved being known as number 1. The power was immense.

What were the six of them doing in The Dorchester? They only had one thing in common, and Shaftsbury realised swiftly, it was him. They were planning his demise.

Shaftsbury considered what he had just witnessed and decided they only option was speaking to DCI Philips. He knew Philips would speak to him due to the demise of Mason. Quietly, he thought of Mason, and it brought a single tear to his eye. Since their sudden separation, he had realised how much he had loved the man. Suddenly, he knew how to avenge Mason, he would bring the house down. Fuck them all.

'Mr Shaftsbury, sorry to interrupt your solace. I believe we have a meeting.'

'I am sorry. I was in another world.' Shaftsbury suddenly gained control of his senses and grew in strength. 'Yes, in fact. This meeting may be a little longer as I have a fair amount I want you to note down.'

Ninety minutes later the meeting was complete. The lawyer sat back in his chair nervously considering the world bending information he had just taken down. This would bring down political parties, royalty, musicians, sportsmen, gangsters...everyone. The information he had been told was like a story you would read on holiday, not a true-life account of parties taking place in Dolphin Square. He looked up and anxiously faced the teller of this amazing narrative, 'Mr Shaftsbury, are you sure you want this account saved?'

Shaftsbury considered the lawyer's information and decided to give a frank and honest answer 'To be honest with you. I may not be around to see this piece of work acknowledged. There are dark forces at work that may try to end my life cycle, therefore, you must promise to see this is done, and guarantee DCI Philips receives a copy of it. Please ensure you keep three copies in three different locations. What you have been told is true, explosive and career ending.' He noted the lawyer gulp, and assumed his mouth would be dry and his palms wet. 'Please don't let me down.'

The lawyer stood and shook Shaftsbury's hand before removing himself from the room swiftly.

Shaftsbury immediately reached for the telephone and dialled the number that would connect him to Philips.

'Yes.'

'DCI Philips, you need to improve your answerable skills when liaising with someone over the speaking and listening devise.'

Philips smiled, only one person he had met would speak in this opulent and exaggerated manner, 'Mr Shaftsbury.'

'Jolly well-done Philips. If a game show needs a contestant, then you are shoe in to acquire the role.'

Shaftsbury was speaking as if it were the old boy's network, 'Shall I address you as the Riddler, or is there a purpose to you call as I am well busy.'

'Sorry Philips, I forget you are a crime fighter. Anyway, I have some news that will throw your crime fighting empire into another stratosphere, so if I were you, locate your crime fighting assistant and meet me at 5pm in The George, Borough High Street.'

The phone was disconnected. Philips sat there considering the change in Shaftsbury's perspective. Something had touched him mentally to make this sudden manoeuvre. Shaftsbury was a careful man who did not take chances, and was a man who knew people in the right and wrong places to sort problems...why now? He surveyed the busy office and knew Drake was his Robin.

Drake stood at the coffee machine stirring his beverage. The expectant welcome scent of coffee floating through the air had not reached him. He looked at it contemplating why he had not chosen the hot chocolate. He felt a presence gravitate beside him.

'Drake, throw your drink away and meet me out the front. Don't say a word to anyone.' As mysteriously as he had arrived, he left.

Drake stood there looking at his aroma less coffee. The light brown plastic cup did not enhance the heat, nor its aesthetic look, whereas the possibility of an adventure with his DCI had significant appeal. The drink was deposited in the bin and he strode towards the door.

'Guv. What's all the secrecy? I've known you many years, and you've never done anything like this?'

'Drakey, Shaftsbury called me, and he wants to meet at 5pm. There was something about his tone. He appeared more decisive, yet frightened at the same time. I can't put my finger on it, but I have a feeling this meeting could prove pivotal, crucial.'

Both men trudged along the pavement at a sedate pace, their footsteps both tapping along the empty street.

Philips noted the way Drake walked. He appeared to lurch

slightly, as if he were leaning too far forward.

Drake studied the way his DCI moved, it was with purpose and his posture was very erect, as if a coat hanger had been placed in his jacket.

Both had one thing in common, they were lost in their own thoughts. This case was becoming ever more complex. Outsiders would say compelling, but those involved would say otherwise. Both men arrived at the station.

The rasping, metallic shriek heralded the arrival of the white carriage. The doors reluctantly and slowly opened with the speed of something tired and gripped by age. Both officers gravitated towards the well-used and basic seating. The tube plunged forward at an excruciating pace. It rocked back and forth, the relentless whining and groaning as if it were hungry for oil, making both officers grit their teeth.

Sixty minutes later, Philips and Drake arrived at London Bridge and hurriedly made their way to The George. Drake, a man of knowledge informed Philips that the pub had stood on the grounds since 1542, although an inn had probably been at the location even earlier. Philips thanked Drake for the information, and privately considered the drinkers who had passed through the establishment.

The pub was a beautiful building. The white sash windows were surrounded by breath taking black boards. Both officers sensed its history. Upon entering the under sized door there was a feeling of claustrophobia. The lights were minimal, giving a sense of foreboding joy, yet it had a sense of class. Turning left, the old dark wooden table and chairs appeared occupied, yet in the far deep-seated reaches of the corner sat a man in sipping a large whisky. He was alone, he was Shaftsbury.

'Mr. Shaftsbury, may I replenish your choice of poison?'

'Philips, you are a fine chap. That would be most agreeable. Large Jameson's, no ice. Have one yourself.' A large beaming smile cut across his face.

The drink was placed in front of him. The two officers sat down with their pints of bitter. Both wrapped their hands around their glasses, taking hearty gulps. Drake wiped foam from his lips with the back of his hand. This was noted by Shaftsbury who mentally noted the caveman actions.

'Shaftsbury, I have to say. I was a little confused by your rushed phone call. I felt you wanted to tell me something, although I may be wrong. Was I right or wrong?'

Drake sat watching both men sparring and had finally had enough of this long-distance jousting. 'Gentlemen, why do you not just speak to each other. You obviously have something to say, and he wants to listen to your ramblings. So instead of both exchanging pleasantries, get on with it.'

Both men turned and stared into Drake's deepest soul.

'Well, Philips, you appear to have found your crime fighting assistant.'

Both men laughed politely.

'Seriously, Mr. Crime Fighter, you are correct. I have a story to tell that will blow your investigation to pieces. A story so amazing, it is so obviously true. I shall name names, of which some, will cause your mind to cease to believe. Are you ready?'

Both men nodded like puppets with springs attached to their necks.

Fifty-minutes later the story had been told. Not a single drop of bitter had been touched. The audience of two could barely breath with the information they had been told. It was like when teachers impart a great deal of knowledge to their pupils. This was the sort of story great tales were made of.

'There you have it gentlemen.'

Drake was the first to speak, 'Fuck me. Fucking hell.' His mind was still computing everything. 'My mind is fucking scrambled. Fuck me.'

'Drake, I realise you may have not had certain privileges in life, but surely your vocabulary extends beyond the exclamation fuck?'

Philips was still trying to piece everything together. His mind, that memorized and photographed everything, had become jammed. 'Shaftsbury, if that is all true, and for some reason I think it is. It'll bring down the house of cards to all walks of life.'

'Philips, everything, and I mean everything, is true. I ask one thing, you limit my involvement, and you put a seriously good word in for me with the judge. This information is career defining, on an immeasurable scale.'

'I can't guarantee anything, although I will try. Drake could you get us another drink?' He turned to his colleague and winked, 'Shaftsbury, what I will do as a way of thanks is keeping you in the loop. This way, you'll be able to plan an extended vacation somewhere. Do you understand what I am saying? Freedom. But you must never, and I mean never mention my name, or that I helped you in any way.'

Drake placed the drinks on the table. All three looked at each other. I think we shall name this operation – George.

•

The chief whip sat behind his desk in 9 Downing Street pondering the Shaftsbury problem. The previous days meeting had concluded the results he had hoped, regarding the irritant, and his removal from life.

As chief whip, he knew he wielded great power over his party's MPs, including cabinet ministers, being seen to speak at all times with the voice of the Prime Minister. This allowed him certain privileges, which he made full use of. He was considered a dour, dull yet disciplined man, who never allowed paperwork to pile high. His place of work was always lavishly tidy and organized. He believed everything had to be considered, calculated, corrected and completed immediately to progress everything. He loved his vocation and the power it presented.

Having attended the party held by Shaftsbury, he knew of two MPs who had found the evening most agreeable, and had made full use of everything available. The gentlemen would be used as pawns in his plan to remove Shaftsbury. Bribery would be the tool used, although this would only work if they had not known he was in attendance as well. It would be a calculated risk, but one he may have to take.

He asked one of the junior whips to locate the two gentlemen and to tell them to report to his office at 4pm. He sat smugly with his hands resting across his chest, believing he was the power behind the throne.

4pm, and neither politician had arrived. His rage held all the power of an erupting volcano, flames were almost roaring from his eyes, ready to ignite anything that came into contact with him. His brain went into overdrive as it picked every scenario of their tardiness. Everything was right – everything

– and still these two degenerates had not turned up. This was not usual. Something was not right. When the chief whip ordered MP's to attend a meeting, they did without question. The memories weighed down on him. He had to sort this out, and quickly.

•

'Gentlemen, sit please, and thank you for attending this unofficial meeting. So, you are aware, nothing will be recorded or noted during this gathering.'

This was not usual. They had been informed they had to attend a meeting at 3.30pm, which superseded any other meeting planned. They were also informed to not let the person know they would be unavailable, otherwise secrets would be drip fed to those in the media. This alone concerned both. The room was airless, cold and bland, it had housed many individuals, not the kind they usually frequented with.

'Gentlemen, I'm going to tell a story, and you're going to listen. If I get a couple of things slightly wrong, I apologize. No. I don't apologize. So is everyone strapped in for a story so magnificent, it has to be true.' The two men facing him nodded like obedient dogs. 'Excellent, so I shall proceed.'

Twenty minutes passed and the story came to an end. Both gentlemen sat ashen faced. Neither had moved, their breathing was minimal. One had adjusted his tie, believing his airwaves were being constricted. The other sat still like a statue, remembering everything about the party and praying it would never reach his family. The disgrace he would face. He would lose everything, all for a night of wild enjoyment.

DCI Philips and Sergeant Drake studied both men. It was obvious they were beaten. They could see pain in their eyes. It must have lain dormant there for a lifetime, trapped in the confusion they carried. Realizing, the love both had given, had created an immeasurable problem.

Both sat still, the emotional pain was not felt the way a cut or bruise was, it was much different, only the person with it could tell it was present. Sometimes the pain at the back of your mind was like a pulse, constantly throbbing. Other times it pushed itself forward demanding attention. Cutting your heart and mind in half. In layman's terms, both knew they were fucked royally.

Philips had already decided how he was going to use the two MP's to end this criminality, 'Gentlemen, you obviously now understand why you are here, so I shall proceed with what is expected of you. We know about Shaftsbury and the parties, the chief whip etc. What I want to know is about any-thing unusual that happened at the Dolphin Square party? If you saw anything odd taking place…if you remember any-thing that is?' He raised an eyebrow and eyed both men. 'Remember, this meeting is not being recorded or logged, so no bull-shit.'

Both men looked at each other worryingly, 'You confirm this is not being recorded officer? Once we tell you, we are left alone?'

Philips felt a sense of sympathy for the two men, 'You have my word gentlemen, for the first one, for the second I do not know.'

'DCI Philips. We'll tell you.' He looked at his colleague

who nodded. 'We have had enough of the secrets and lies. I personally want to live a life without constantly looking over my shoulder, like a frightful criminal. Shaftsbury and the chief whip hold so much power because of the parties. Regarding unusual activity. I vaguely recall a group of men entering the flat and leaving thirty minutes later. Another new gentleman arrived for approximately twenty minutes; I think he went into bedroom 2 where the gangster often frequents with very young men. I recall him departing rather swiftly. That is all I can add to your section of the tale.'

As soon as Philips heard the men talking about a man departing alone, he zoomed on it, 'The man who left alone. What did he look like?'

'Smart and handsome, but to be honest detective, I was a bit busy, so I did not take much notice.'

Philips knew this meeting was coming to an end. The men were obviously *off their heads* during the party, but they had given him some ammunition, and they had confirmed the story told by Shaftsbury, 'Gents, you can go. Thank you for attending.'

Upon returning to his office a large shout was heard, 'Guv, guv, quick I need to speak to you.' One of DCI Philips officers approached at a brisk pace, 'Guv, we've had a result. Gary Jones has been pulled in recently by West End Central C.I.D.'

'When?' The excitement could be heard in Philips voice.

'Three weeks back. He was pulled in because a young male, whose father is a commander in the Met, had to attend hospital due to anal injuries. It appears a number of men at a *certain* club abused him. One of those being Mason. When the man was in hospital, he kept on repeating Mason's and Gary Jones's name. I may be wrong, but I reckon Mason had a soft spot for Jones and tried to impress the commander's son with it. But the best is still to come…we have his address.'

'Jackpot. At last the gods are with us. Where does he live?'

'This gets better guv. He's behind us. Approximately 200-300 yards from Cross Keys Pub. Crown Street. I think it's near Sturges the Butchers '

'No fucking way. Right we're round there, now.'

Gary Jones sat on his sofa reading the *Daily Mirror*. From his viewpoint he could see two men remove themselves from a car and instantly knew they were police. He anticipated a knock on his door within the next fifteen seconds. It took nine seconds for the rap to be heard. Gary calmly stood and answered the door, without asking who they were he instantly mouthed 'Afternoon gentlemen, please come in.'

This formal and welcoming opening was not what either officer anticipated. Philips looked at the man facing him. He was well built, strong looking, with a handsome yet rugged look about him that made him look like James Stewart. 'Mr. Jones. I am DCI Philips and my colleague is Sergeant Drake. We are from the local nick and have a few questions for you.'

Jones studied both men, and decided both were professional police officers, so he had to be careful. 'Officers would you like a brew, the kettles just boiled?'

'No thank you Mr. Jones. What we need to speak to you about is very serious. Can you confirm that you are a member of Whites Club?'

Gary had been expecting a knock at his door sooner or later and had his answers planned. He also knew they had to be honest…to a point. 'Yes I am. I last went a couple of weeks back. The chef cooks the most fantastic devilled kidneys, which I love, and had.'

Drake replied, 'Sounds very nice. My mother used to make them when I was a kid. Offal was cheap, which is why we probably had them, but I really liked the taste and texture, although we had to make do with Daddies Brown Sauce for flavour.' He smiled, obviously reminiscing.

'Nothing wrong with brown sauce officer. In fact, I brought some kidneys today from the butchers, so I may give that a bash tonight.'

Philips considered the conversation taking place and decided to intervene with a curve ball question, 'Do you know Michael Dawson?'

Gary now realised why they were here, 'Michael Dawson. Bloody hell, that's a name from the past, and I mean the past. We were at Boyles Court together. Horrible bloke. A bully. We had an altercation, which he lost. I couldn't stand him. Mind you, I don't think anyone liked him. Even the guards hated him.'

'So, when was the last time you saw him Mr. Jones?

'Boyles Court, so that's ten or twelve years back. If you don't mind me asking, but why do you want to know?'

'He's dead. Found hanging from Gidea Park Station.'

'He committed suicide by hanging himself. Bloody hell.'

Both officers noted the surprise from Jones, although Drake thought it was contrived. His previous vocation had allowed him to analyse people not being truthful, and Jones stroked the left-hand side of his neck when not being honest.

Philips stood from his seat and walked towards the door

slowly before turning, 'Mr. Jones, thank you for speaking to us. Your information could prove valuable.'

Both officers left the home and pulled away both in deep thought. The silence was broken by Drake, 'Guv, he's a liar. Every time he was not being honest, he rubbed the left-hand side of his neck. It's obviously his emotional weak point.'

'Blimey Drakey, how did you notice that. I thought he was being up-front with us.'

'Guv. He's our man. Guaranteed. One thing I will say. He's a cool customer. Nothing ruffles his feathers. That's going to be our problem. It's like he's been prepped, something we were taught in the security services. I bet a high percentage of his story checks out and is true.'

'Drakey, you are becoming James Bond by the hour.' Both men laughed. 'But seriously. I think you are right. He could be our man. We need to keep Shaftsbury on side, he is central to all this.'

Chapter 15

Party people

Philips looked at the list of names who had attended the party held by Shaftsbury. It was extraordinary. He was awestruck by one or two them; the man who read the evening news from the BBC, an Olympic Ice Skating gold medallist, a minor royal, smattering of pop-stars, an Oscar winning actor, gangsters, politicians, radio presenters. The list was amazing, it was also dangerous, incredibly dangerous. People would pay handsomely for it. Obviously, Shaftsbury, Mason, the two politicians and chief whip were present, so many influential people in power, and they would not want their dirty secret spilled to the world.

There was a gentle knock at Philips door and Drake walked in, 'Guv, I've been looking through that list and I've noticed something, plus I've checked and expanded it, and something odder has happened.'

'Go ahead Drakey, what have you noticed?' This was said with genuine interest.

'Dave Smith attended the party, and he's gone missing, but more interesting, his brother Steve has gone awol as well. I'm not one for coincidences guv, but both?'

'When you mean missing. What exactly do you mean?'

'Missing, as in gone. I've spoken to some of their employees, their mum – who is near hysterical and local businesses who are currently profiting with the brothers not bothering them for money endlessly.'

'The Smith brothers are missing? Whoever would do that has got to be incredibly strong, organised and insane. Jones fits the bill.'

'Exactly my thinking guv. Jones is so calm and calculating, yet there is something wrong with him. I dug into Jones's deep past, and we are talking deep past. He was placed at Boyles Court as he killed his father – with one punch, aged fourteen. I also spoke to one of his arresting officers and they remembered him really well. They said he was cold and didn't care about the death. They also mentioned he wouldn't leave until he'd finished his dinner and made one move on his chess board. The officer thought he was cunning, and thought he treated each move in life like a chess game.'

'Bloody hell. This Jones is now our number one suspect for all that's going on, but one good thing may come of it…no more Smiths. They were slags, and a fucking menace to society.'

'It'll certainly make life quieter for all, but someone else will take their place. You know it guv.'

'Someone certainly will Drakey, but they won't have the destructive and mental edge those horrible brothers had. I've been looking at this list Drakey, and there's some big names on it. I'm not too sure how to approach it. In all my career I've never seen a list with such prominent people all involved. How would you do it Drakey?' The crumpled piece of lined paper was passed to Drake. It had a tired look due to the times it had been folded and unfolded in the previous twenty-four hours. The names were written in blue pen, and the writing had a broken look, almost child-like.

Drake studied the list, analysing the strong and weak links. He agreed with Philips, the list was key. 'Guv, I would either begin with the weak link, or go for it from the tightest link. This means the chief whip or the weakest link, which is possibly the pop-stars. The musicians will have lots to lose and could crumble as they are surrounded by sycophantic hangers on, whereas, the chief whip and like-minded people will be educated and know how to play the game, therefore, will clam up and have a legal team representing them sharpish.'

'OK. Pop Stars it is. Drakey, let's keep it between me and you. Who shall we target first?'

'Guv. The biggest. Harry Huge. He is massive, and he'll not want a scandal. Plus, there's been one or two rumours about him anyway with youngsters.'

'Huge it is. Find out everything about him.'

•

The chief whip was back at the office, having spent a weekend at the family home in rural Kent. Everyone had been present, and it had been a riot of laughter and games, yet he could not dedicate his mind fully due to problems he could be facing.

He had contacted the two politicians and demanded they meet him, one had indigently replied 'No, he was too busy'. Busy! He'll be busy searching for another job soon, whilst the other had not even had the courtesy to reply.

This worried him as he was concerned someone had got to them, but how? The only person who knew everything was

Shaftsbury, yet he had too much to lose, so who could it be. A name suddenly sprung to his mind, Shaftsbury's niece, the ex-WPC must. The whore must be talking!

The following hour involved making discreet enquiries. He found out she had decided to offer Queen's evidence to save her useless and worthless life. The bitch. The only hope he had was she did not know much. Shaftsbury's niece was a grass.

A smile grew across his face. He remembered the time she had polished him and five other men when she was ten. It had been an outstanding exhibition of cock sucking from someone so young. To think she agreed to do it for a signed picture of the pop star present, and two front row tickets to his sold-out tour. What made it even more ironic was her friend had done the same to the pop star after the concert in his dressing room. Absolutely first class.

Sylvie was the weak link. He was sure of it. She had to be shut up. He knew he had to make contact with Shaftsbury to see how he was shaping up. He dialled his number and expected no answer from Shaftsbury, as he was always out and about.

Shaftsbury picked up the telephone and answered in his soft voice, 'Hello.'

'Shaftsbury, it's the chief whip. I believe we have a problem.'

Shaftsbury had been expecting this call, and for the first time he had the edge on this devious, deceitful man,. 'How good to hear from you Whippey. What problem do we have?'

'Your fucking niece is talking to the police.'

'I cannot believe that Whippey. She is not a grass, and her

name is a proud name going back through the ages, therefore she has strong roots of discipline and courage.'

The chief whip was listening to the absolute bollocks being spouted by the man on the end of the phone. He honestly believed his niece was some sort of crusader, 'Listen Shaftsbury, she is talking to the police, someone called Philips and his sidekick, and it needs stopping.'

Shaftsbury listened intently. So, Whippey was well informed, and had obviously decided Sylvie was the weak link. The link that would bring the house down. This played into Shaftsbury hands, 'Whippey, are you sure she is talking? It does not sound like her.'

'I am sure, absolutely positive. A police officer by the name of Taylor told me. He often attends your parties. He arrives as a guest of mine, so he is never on your list, although he missed the last one. You always need someone on the inside. Something you will learn in life Shaftsbury.'

Shaftsbury knew the name Taylor very well. He kept on thinking about it until he realised, 'Ok Whippey, you have me there. I will make some enquiries about what's been going on.' He disconnected the telephone and immediately contacted DCI Philips.

'DCI Philips, how may I assist you?'

'If you are on loudspeaker turn it off Philips, you know who it is.'

'Mr. Shaftsbury you are not on loudspeaker. What is the problem?'

'Philips, you have a major, and I mean a major problem at your end.'

Philips understood the concern in Shaftsbury's high-pitched voice, 'Problem, what problem exactly are you talking about?'

'Your Chief Super, Taylor, is in the chief whip's gang. He attends the parties I lay on, although never pays. He arrives as a special guest of the chief whip. I would not know him, and this is first time I have learnt someone has attended without paying!' His voice was rising by the second.

Philips sat frozen, stunned by the information provided. His chief super, friend, was battling against him. It could not be true. He felt the air leave his lungs and stop him from inhaling and exhaling. His face dropped quicker than a corpse in cement boots. Taylor, no. 'Shaftsbury are you totally sure about this?'

'The chief whip had no reason to lie to me. He was too busy telling me about my niece Sylvie and how we had to lose her as she is a grass and could bring everything to its knees. I think he mentioned Taylor out of mistake.'

'Shaftsbury. This puts a different perspective on everything, and I mean everything. We need to tread very carefully now. Now you only speak to me or Drakey. You can trust him implicitly.'

'Philips. I know you want to arrest me, but our gentlemen's agreement does it still stand?'

'Yes.'

Shaftsbury stood by his telephone and considered the abrupt reply. It had been said without breathing or consideration. This meant Philips was a man of his word.

'Excellent. Well I shall bid you farewell for now, and until our next encounter, au revoir.'

Philips stood from behind his desk and called out to his

trusted companion, 'Drakey, lunch?'

Sergeant Drake was sifting through his mountain of paper-work, created by himself. Ever meticulous, he read and studied everything. He was reading an article about the chief whip and his busy political life, and how he juggled it with his very important and loving family, he heard vocal chords emanating from his DCI and the words 'lunch', which gener-ally meant a pie and a pint, it also meant information had been received. It was a code word both had agreed previously. Most of the staff assumed they were best mates, and did not pry.

Both officers made their way to the Railway public house. Philips ordered a pint of Double Diamond, whilst his col-league ordered a Ben Truman. This was accompanied with two very crusty ham and tomato rolls. Both men took huge slurps from their glass tankards, which left white foam mous-taches on the top of their lips. Drake's tongue emerged from his mouth and wiped away the residue component, which was followed by a mountainous bite of his roll.

Philips placed his beer on the mat and looked straight at Drake, 'I received a call from Shaftsbury, and he said Taylor attends the parties.'

Drake was mid-bite and stopped. His mind was still calcu-lating what his DCI had just said. Did he say Taylor, the Chief Super, attended the parties? He placed his roll on the plate, suddenly losing his appetite. 'Did I just hear you right?'

'Yep, you are as amazed as me, and I know it's true because Shaftsbury was concerned about an exit plan. I agreed with him.'

Drake zoned in on exit plan, but decided not to question

his superior. If he wished to tell he would, plus if anything went to court and it was mentioned he knew nothing of it, therefore – silence was golden. He picked up his beer and splashed it around the glass, studying it, 'Guv, is he on the level, he's not playing you, is he?'

'Drakey. I think he's frightened, although he's bottling it up. The chief whip is the one who's going to be our problem. I have a sense for it, and he's made his way to a significant position in government without anyone noticing his nocturnal activities. We will bring him down. The whole fucking lot of them, even Taylor.'

Drake looked at his DCI and took a bite from his roll. He studied him for a reaction, there was none. He now understood everything he needed to know. His DCI really wanted everyone, and he meant business. He had seen this before many times in his previous life. He felt reassured his boss was on his side.

•

The home of Harry Huge had been easy to locate. He lived where many rich and famous celebrities chose to locate when living in the capital, Highgate. His Georgian terraced house sat behind black, gothic wrought iron gates, offering sanctity and security. The sort of security a man who had secrets required.

DCI Philips and Sergeant Drake pressed the button and a man arrived at the gate approximately ninety seconds later. He was dressed in an outrageous array of colours that made him look a little flamboyant.

'No autographs gentlemen, sorry.' He then began to turn as if he had dismissed a child from a class.

Drake appraised the man and immediately became aware of a smell he had experienced before, a strong musky odor with herbal undertones, cannabis. He removed his badge from his inside pocket and showed it to the man standing behind the gate, 'We would like to speak to Mr. Huge, and before you say no, or he's not in – is that cannabis I can smell emanating from you?'

The gentleman shifted from side to side nervously, 'How long do you need to spend with him?'

DCI Philips was watching the butting of heads and realized Drake had comfortably won the battle and decided to interject, 'Sir, we need to speak to him. it'd be easier for your master if we liaise inside, instead of down the station, where he will possibly be recognized…don't you think?'

'He is not my master, and you can come in.'

Philips wished to laugh. The master effect had ruffled his feathers. The man understood he was Huge's lackey, but would hate it recognized by those who did not know him.

The gate opened, and both gentlemen were led into the fabulous building. They were shown into an opulent room that was lavishly furnished with outrageous colours that made it resemble a red admiral on acid. Whoever had furnished the home obviously loved vibrant colours. They were kept waiting for ten minutes before a man walked in, so over the top and loud it was embarrassing. It shocked both officers.

'Good morning officers. I am Harry Huge.' He stood in the doorway with both arms in the air, as if he were on stage, dressed in a purple silk dressing gown, which had lime green edging. 'Today I feel so fabulous it's amazing.' He then turned in an extravagant manner and poured himself a large red wine, which he swallowed in one swoop. 'How can I help you most fantastic hunky men?'

Both officers were still getting over the entrance. They felt Huge was putting on a show for them, 'Sir, please take a seat and stop prancing about. You're making me giddy.'

Huge burst out laughing showing perfect white teeth. The contrast against his holidayed brown skin made him resemble a mint humbug.

'Then I shall sit officer.' He was still laughing heartily.

Philips suddenly had enough of the hilarity taking place and decided to become serious, 'Mr. Huge, we have come to speak to you about a very grave matter.'

Huge looked at them, 'Grave, as in a place where you put bodies.' He then burst out laughing again. His eyes appeared a little glazed and resembled two shiny saucers.

Drake felt his inner temperature gauge rising and could contain it no longer, 'You were at a party in Dolphin Square, so I suggest you get serious, and fucking quickly.'

Both Huge and Philips were surprised by the ferocity of the outburst, but it worked. Huge calmed down and understood the seriousness of the situation.

Philips then gained control of the situation, 'Mr. Huge, this requires your upmost attention, as it is serious investigation you are involved in, and when I mean serious, as serious as it gets. Understand, this could result in a major prison time for anyone involved, and anyone lying or hindering the investigation will get significantly longer.'

Philips and Drake looked at Huge, suddenly, he did not appear as confident, in fact – he looked terrified.

'Did you say prison? I can't go to prison – I'm Harry Huge. Harry Huge does not go to prison.'

He had a bullish attitude about him, although the flash arrogant manner had disappeared.

'Mr. Huge, please be serious. We want to know about the party you attended, and do not tell me you were not there, otherwise I will become furiously annoyed.' Drake stared in a hard manner at Huge. The effect appeared to be working as Huge was looking subdued.

Philips took charge of the interview in a decisive manner, 'Mr. Huge, I am going to be forthright. Were you at the party?'

Huge sat uncomfortably, his hands moving incessantly, and he constantly crossed his legs. His mind was trying to calculate the permutations of getting away with his predicament. The nerve endings in his body were jangling. Huge felt his stomach shift uneasily and noticed his hands were hugging themselves, almost pinching into the skin. He released his hands but couldn't figure out what to do with them, so instead they decided to clasp and unclasp each other as if in constant need of touch for reassurance.

'Party?' Huge decided to play a defensive.

Drake was near volcanic. 'Do not, I warn you, do not take the two of us for fucking idiots. If you do, I will rip your insides out and shit down your neck. Answer my colleagues' question…now! You fucking low life prima donna low life cunt.'

Philips now understood why Drake had been so effective

183

in his unit. He was beginning to terrify him, 'I believe Mr. Huge, you need to answer my question. So, you are aware this is not good cop bad cop. This is helpful cop with seriously mad about to erupt cop. So, back to the question. Did you attend the party?'

Huge knew all his lifelines had been used, and he was beginning to become concerned about the volatile police officer who looked dangerously psychotic, 'I think I need a lawyer.'

'A lawyer? What you'll need is ten tons of lubricant where you're going.'

Huge had done it once before, and had found it something he would never try again. The thought of a closed environment full of beastly men terrified him. They would surely all want to rape him. He was Harry Huge, and he would be number one target. Having considered his options, he decided to play the police officers' dreadful game of interrogation.

'Yes, is the answer. I attended the parties.'

Both officers immediately realized the plural 'parties' had been used. DCI Philips encouraged Huge to carry on by gesticulating with his index finger.

'The parties were spectacular. They were attended by the who's who of the elite, rich and famous. All money went to Shaftsbury. Everything was on offer, if you know what I mean, and I mean everything.' This was said in a salacious manner.

Philips considered what the man had said. Huge made it appear an amazing night of decadence, yet Philips knew it was depraved.

'Mr. Huge did you note anything strange taking place?'

Huge laughed disgustingly, 'Everywhere, something strange and beautiful was happening everywhere.' He suddenly, and gently licked his lips before laughing.

The lip movement was noted by both officers, who thought it unusual as it was disgusting. Huge appeared to be remembering a previous escapade and a sly smug smile grew upon the lower end of his face. Huge suddenly felt a stirring in his loins.

Philips was beginning to tire of Huge's continuous and flamboyant attitude to law and order. He obviously felt that being a popstar offered him benefit of flouting the justice, 'Mr. Huge you need to get serious. Was there anyone acting suspiciously, or anyone present who doesn't usually attend? Think man. Think!' Philips agitated voice was making him speak loud and fast.

Huge sat seriously still. He was trying to unscramble the events of the evening. The people, the music, the drugs, the drink, the sex…the man. The man. Huge became excitable and animated. 'I remember something. I remember. Yes, I do. The man who came in late. The smart fit looking man who went into the room with the horrible gangster Smith.'

'Do you mean Dave Smith? Are you sure?'

'Am I sure. Am I fucking sure? That horrible fucking man abused me. I had to have an operation to repair tissue around my anus. He is fucking mad, a maniac. When I saw the man entering the suite, I wanted to warn him, but he re-emerged twenty minutes later. He must have showered and left the party. He was fucking calm as well.'

Philips and Drake took in the information supplied by

Huge. He had offered a lot more than they had bargained for, the personal part was not relevant, but still interesting in a weird way. Huge obviously feared Dave Smith, and was worried for the man entering his room. Yet felt admiration for him leaving shortly after, intact and unharmed.

'Mr. Huge, have you seen Mr. Smith since, or did you see him that night?'

Huge sat scratching his chin in a thoughtful manner. He was now sat cross legged on his avocado tufted velvet couch. 'No. I did not see him, but a group of men went into the suite many hours later. They looked like caretakers from a school.'

Drake cut in swiftly. 'Did you say caretakers? Did they wear overalls?'

Huge became exhilarated again. 'Yes. Yes. just like the grumpy old caretakers at school.' He began to laugh at his joke.

'How many were there Mr. Huge?'

'How many. I can't remember that, four, maybe five.'

Drake was like bear grabbing hold of a salmon. 'Were these men about 6 feet tall, athletic looking with a look of strength about them?'

'Yes. That's exactly how I would describe them.'

Drake suddenly stood up, which surprised his superior, and extended his hand to Harry Huge, 'Thank you for your time Mr. Huge. It has been most appreciated. I'm sorry for the aggression, but I don't like time wasting. Are you ready, sir?' Drake turned towards Philips and raised one eyebrow.

'I would like to replicate what my colleague has said. Thank you for your time, and we will try to not return.' This was said with a hint of sarcasm.

Before they had left the room, Huge was gone, although they could hear him belting out one of his hits, whether it was for their benefit or his own they did not know. Having not met the man they assumed it would be for his own ego.

Upon leaving, they slowly walked to the neighboring pub, The Flask. Neither speaking, lost in their own thoughts.

The deafening silence was broken by Philips. 'Drakey, I've got to ask you, but why did we leave? It was a tad strange the way you suddenly removed us from that oddball's house. Remember, I'm the DCI. '

'Guv. I'm sorry if I offended you, but I knew where it was going, plus I made a connection which we need to speak to Shaftsbury about.'

Philips grabbed Drake's arm to stop him. Both men looked at each like lovers, but this was not affection, 'What do you mean exactly?'

'Clean up team guv. The caretakers were a cleanup team.'

'What are you going on about Drakey?'

'A clean up team goes in and remove's any evidence of foul play, murder. They'll paint walls, remove blood, remove bodies, replace broken items…anything. And guv, this means Dave Smith was murdered at the party. Of that I am sure. Which means it could be Gary Jones.'

Philips was trying to contemplate everything. His brain was stuttering with the unexpected turn of events. Gradually, he was learning more and more about his friend and colleague. This man had a side to him he did not know, a secretive side.

Chapter 16

Strange happenings

Sleep comes like the falling of an axe. It comes, but Philips fought it with everything he had. The endless hours, sleep was as instantaneous as it was unwelcome. When his thoughts become intertwined with random ideas, impossible ideas, ideas on Jones, ideas on everything, he decided to get up and venture downstairs.

Sometimes we are visited by ideas that are so random and indescribable, yet upon waking, we scramble to write them down, just in case there is wisdom in their randomness. It is not that we think, but our subconscious minds can send people with problems the solutions, and a solution was sent to Philips.

One of these solutions suddenly offered some peace to DCI Philips. He finished his Horlicks and made his way back to bed, experiencing a peaceful sleep for the first time in seven days.

Philips made his way to the station and felt like a massive boulder had been removed from his shoulder. The feeling of frustration, annoyance and disenchantment had gone, to be replaced by a positive feeling of peace. He knew the man he wanted was Jones, arresting him was a major problem, yet knowing he was their man made him feel a sense of victory.

He knew Jones was perfidious, yet incredibly sagacious. This arrest would resemble one of Jones's chess games, intelligent opening moves – before capturing the king.

On the old desk sat a notebook lying open, and a stack of papers sitting under a green oval-shaped paperweight. The old swivel chair sat behind the desk. A bookshelf, bursting with files was in a corner, with yet another stack of papers under a heavy looking book on murder. A few pens were lying on the papers.

This was DCI Philips operation room. He had decided this was where he would bring down the movers and shakers who had evaded capture and enjoyed illegal pleasures.

Sitting behind his desk he sipped his hot sweet tea and began to formulate a plan. He wrote down a list of names, missing one, Taylor. The list was in no specific order. The meeting with Huge had been insightful and illuminating. Information received about Shaftsbury offered credence to everything he had told them previously. At least someone appeared to be telling the truth.

Philips pondered how he would pull it all together. Arresting everyone in one swoop was ideal, but would prove difficult, yet nicking them individually would send a message to all and sundry to take cover. Pulling Jones in for questioning was essential, yet would it prove fruitful? He appeared to be the man at the centre of it all, but nothing could be pinned on him. He had a small admiration for Mr. Gary Jones. A man who swam with the big fish, and was the biggest fish, yet acted like a small fish, so no-one recognized him. It was genius and effective. To live within five minutes of the very station that was looking for him was truly outstanding.

'Touché Jones', he raised his old stained chipped white mug to salute his nemesis.

Jones entered the club and made his way to the bar ordering a Whisky Mac. He watched the bartender professionally create the drink. Adding 45 millilitres of Scotch Whisky with 30 millilitres of Stones Original Green Ginger Wine. The ginger gave the whisky a spicy bite, yet smoothed off the edges. He sampled the drink admiring its refreshing tangy taste.

The barman was cleaning the classes until they were sparkling, casually looked at Jones. 'A strange thing happened recently sir, and I believe your name was mentioned.'

Immediately, Jones's inner antennae became alert, yet he remained calm. 'Anything interesting?'

'Not sure sir, although they spoke to the doorman, Barney. They appeared to know each other. Apart from that sir, there's nothing else.'

'I'm sure if they wish to speak to me, they will. Thank you for the information.' Jones left £1 on the bar for the barman's pocket and made his way to one of the comfortable Portobello Queen Anne armchairs to ponder the unexpected information he had received.

Sergeant Drake entered the room and strode towards his boss's office, who he noted was in deep thought. 'Morning guv. What you up-to? You had your thinking face on and was staring vacantly at the ceiling. '

'Morning Drakey. I was thinking about Jones. He is a significant part of this complex puzzle, yet he is not the enemy. If anything, he appears to be a man who removes scum bags from the street. He's a bit of a Robin Hood, and one the public will understand. We may need to get him onside, similar to Shaftsbury.'

Drake slowly moved towards the wooden chair and dragged it, the unpleasant scraping noise making a couple of people turn towards the sound, 'Is that a good play guv? Getting Jones onside seems dicey. He's bad news.'

Philips looked at his colleague, who always had his back and understood the safe move, yet this time he needed to learn occasionally a few chances had to be taken to get what you wanted, 'Drakey, if we let this play out a little longer. I believe we'll be like trawler men scooping the fish, and our net will be full of the biggest and dirtiest fish going.'

Both men sat looking at each other, both wondering what the other was thinking. The sound of silence was deafening. Drake was first to initiate conversation.

'Guv, if, and I mean if, Jones helps us. How are we going to pay him back? A man like that always wants recompense.'

'Recompense, Drakey, can always be paid, it just does not always have to be financial.'

Sergeant Drake considered the words, and understood Philips was using an army mental manoeuvre. Ego and freedom were two things all men wanted. Most wanted one, but some wanted both. Drake guessed Jones would come under the category of both.

Gary sat at the traditional circular table devouring his meal. The potted shrimps on toast were a blessing sent from the lord. White's knew how to prepare food. There was plenty of sliced wholemeal toast wrapped in cloth napkins to keep it warm. It was divine and elegantly presented. Upon finishing his final mouthful, he became aware of a looming presence.

The shadow showing on the wall was getting larger.

'Good morning Mr. Jones. I waited until you had completed your meal, which looked jolly nice. You and I need to speak about someone who may become a problem, and someone who is a problem.'

Jones studied the man and instantly knew it was Robin Shaftsbury. Why was he bothering him? Shaftsbury stood tall and proud in his Prince of Wales check suit, which had been freshly pressed. He had the air of someone with serious wealth and intelligence, 'Hello Shaftsbury, pull up a seat. How can I help you?'

Shaftsbury eyed the man. He was confident, yet quiet. Polite, but rough. Smart, but not elegant, 'Thank you, old chap. I'm not going to waste your time as I know you are busy. I'm going to tell you a story, and you can put me right if I'm wrong, but no telling fibs. Here we go.'

Five minutes passed like thirty seconds. Jones sat and did not move a muscle. He was being given a lesson in private school intelligence. Shaftsbury spoke to him in a language he understood and admired, yet knew he would never achieve. The story was totally correct apart from a couple of minor amendments. Finally, Shaftsbury completed his lecture.

'So, Jones. As you now know. You murdered the love of my life, so you are now in my debt. As I stated, a letter has been lodged with a lawyer, and if I were involved in an accident, then it will be released to relevant people in authority.'

Jones shifted uncomfortably in his chair. No-one in his life had ever spoken to him in this manner before. He had seriously underestimated Shaftsbury. He was not strong in strength, but incredibly sharp and strong in mind. Jones picked up his cup and saucer and sipped his strong tea, 'What is it you want Shaftsbury? Everyone wants something, and you are no different.'

Shaftsbury placed his Hamlet cigar in the ash tray. He was surrounded with dancing curls of smoke floating away. Sitting back in the comfort of his chair, he realized he had bested Jones, who had a confused, almost puzzled look, 'An excellent, yet basic question, and one that requires an immediate answer. You are going to remove a problem for me, or should I say us. The Chief-Whip is a man who has a remarkable memory, specifically for parties in a certain square we both know. So, I am going to furnish you with all the information you require, and you will dispose of him, in a manner you decide. How does that sound?'

For the first time in his life Jones felt backed into a corner, yet he had to admit Shaftsbury was a man who could execute a plan. If he were on Jones's side of the law, he would ensure Shaftsbury was a friend. Uunfortunately, they would never be that due to the Mason situation, 'You put it so eloquently Shaftsbury. Disposal of a human being requires a certain something, obviously something you do not have. You say the man has a remarkable memory, then this could be a serious problem, for both of us, and needs evaluating. I assume all documentation lodged with your brief will be destroyed permanently when I arrange this removal?'

'Sir, my word is my bond. Plus, you appear to be a man who avenges wrong's; therefore, it is not in my interest to ruin a new friendship.'

DCI Philips and Sergeant Drake walked confidently down the bustling London street that was filled with people being forced to walk like soldiers. The area would have been perfect for pickpockets who would have pinched purses like rabbits removing carrots from a farmer's field. Approaching the club Drake felt a hand snake around his elbow and forcefully yank him into a shop doorway. He turned towards his colleague with a shocked look, suddenly his head was directed at the club. He now understood why he had been accosted by his superior. Across the street emerging from a building were Jones and Shaftsbury. In the morning light both men looked prosperous, although Shaftsbury looked a little tired, but was dressed immaculately. Jones's dark hair touched the tailored shoulders of his blazer, which was accompanied by a crisp white shirt and plain blue tie. He stood tall and straight. His long limbs were straight but not stiff, and he held his head high. He looked like a seriously successful businessman. How misleading his appearance was.

'The plot thickens Drakey. I wonder what they're up to?'

Both men stood in amazement at the sight they were witnessing. Two men from opposing sides of the law leaving an up market establishment looking content.

'Guv, I've seen some things in my life, but this is proper strange.' Drake then scratched his head, 'There are more paths than clues in this investigation sir.' He turned slowly, not even bothering to feign surprise.

Jones strolled along the street. He and Shaftsbury had seen the officers in the shop doorway. They swiftly agreed, if asked, that they had bumped into one another unexpectedly at the club. It was inconvenient, but unexpected things happened, and everyone had to be aware of them if they arose. He was mulling over what Shaftsbury required. It irked him as he had been put into a corner, and he knew what needed to be done, yet felt like he was being played, although he would have done the same had he been in Shaftsbury's shoes.

Shaftsbury slowly meandered along to the taxi rank where he ordered the driver to take him to Henry Poole in Savile Row. He had an appointment and decided to treat himself to a new suit as his plan began to take shape beautifully. Jones had a strict discipline for time, and dining. Shaftsbury had worked out that Jones always attended the club when Devilled Kidneys or Potted Shrimp were on the menu, after that it had been easy to organize.

Having arrived back at the station, it had been decided that ex-WPC Sylvie would need to bare her teeth to help. She had been released on bail and was living at a flat in North Rainham Road. This had been agreed by the lawyer and Taylor, although he had looked at little unsure at the arrangement. The arrangement, to date, had worked fine. She was not allowed out and daily food parcels were taken to her by Philips on his way to work.

Philips and Drake swiftly left the station and made their way towards the flat that was a short walk from The Railway public house.

Drake turned to Philips and saw the shock register on his face. Philip's face washed blank with confusion, like his brain cogs could not turn fast enough to take in the information from his wide eyes. Every muscle in his body froze.

'Drakey look.' Philips nodded his head in a direction across the road.

Drake followed the brief nod and slowly turned where he saw Chief Superintendent Taylor exiting from the ground floor of a block of flats. The man looked furtive, like a well-dressed rat. 'I thought you said no one went to see Sylvie apart from you guv?'

'Exactly. He has no reason to see her, unless...'. The voice of DCI Philips trailed away mid-sentence, although it had been said with a venomous tone. His eyes were filled with utter rage, 'He's gone to put the frighteners on her, or appeal to her conscience. I believe our chief super is a fucking no good, low life, snake.'

Both watched him turn left. He appeared to be heading towards The Bull public house. It was not the sort establishment he would normally frequent. It was a comfortable place without being auspicious, and the chief superintendent always enjoyed the finer things in life.

Taylor entered The Bull and made his way to the far corner, sitting on a wooden bar stool placed around a freshly varnished beer keg, used as a table. Waiting at the table was someone he knew well from his days at boarding school, someone who had done well in business, eventually becoming the chief whip for the government.

'Gin and Tonic, with two cubes of ice and two slices of lemon just how you like it.' He studied Taylor, who had heavy eyes and appeared exhausted. He looked like a man who had the weight of the world on his shoulders, 'Any news?' He asked in a very casual and easy manner.

Taylor began to go red, as if he were about to explode. He suddenly erupted in a muted tone, 'News! News! Are you fucking for real? My best two officers are investigating a case I'm linked to. I'm having to remove paperwork, read paperwork – when no-one's about, threaten suspects, on top of the

fact there's a fucking mercenary about knocking people off.'
He glared hard at his old friend, suddenly feeling better,
'Sorry about that, but I am really up against it.'

The chief whip understood how his old friend felt. The
pressure must be immeasurable, and mounting. He looked
like a man who was struggling with everything taking place.
For the first time since they had known each other, he became
concerned that Taylor may break and spill the beans, 'George,
just keep going. It will resolve itself, and I am planning something that will help us incredibly. Don't ask me what it is. It
was something we discussed at the Dorchester regarding a
certain Mr. Shaftsbury.'

Panic seized Taylor, he realized for the first time that his old
friend would do anything to remain in his seat of power. He
sat paralyzed with the realism of the situation he was facing.
He had only attended three parties, they had been enjoyable,
but equally, they were on the brink of ending his career,
respect and more importantly…his family ties, which he
cherished. He sat there with questions jumping around, questions no one could answer barring him. His head rose and he
looked at his oldest friend, 'This has to end, once and for all.
Whatever you are doing, just get it done. Finish this ever
increasing and cesspit of wrongdoing.' Taylor swallowed his
drink in one gulp and left the pub hurriedly in a state of
shock.

Both officers slipped into the pub one minute a. They
needed to learn who Taylor was meeting.

Sitting alone was a man in a conservative looking suit that
appeared expensive. He was sipping a pint of beer and looked
in deep thought. Drake began to study the subject in the bars

mirror. It made viewing a little inconvenient, but he wanted to be sure who the man was before he told Philips. Having ordered two halves of bitter he wandered back to the table where Philips was stationed.

'Guv, I know the man Taylor met. It's the chief whip of the government. I recognized him straight away. He had an article written about him last week in *The Times*.'

DCI Philips placed his glass on the table and considered the news. Why would the chief whip wish to meet Taylor? Taylor was not a member of the club everyone appeared to belong to, so there had to be another link from the past, but what? He looked at Drakey and signaled for him to come in close, 'Drakey, we need to look into Taylor's past, something there must link to him over there.'

Chapter 17

Chief Whip

Aldington was a beautiful place to live. The chief whip considered it the eighth wonder of the world. The area was his oasis. There was no railway station, the nearest being Ham Street and Orlestone, so commuters were few and far between, and the nearest motorway, M20, was approximately ten miles away. The area was centred around the beautiful Walnut Tree public house, that had been built during Richard II's reign, although alcoholic beverages had not been sold until the seventeenth century. The place was an homage to tradition, and good old-fashioned English culture.

Every last Friday of the month the chief whip made his way to his favourite local to consume the magnificent array of bitters on sale. It also gave him the chance to catch with his cronies and allow them to put the country's wrongs right.

Having consumed a bottle of Beaujolais with his darling wife before and during dinner he was feeling upbeat and jolly. It was not a particularly pleasant evening when he left his home for the five-minute walk to the pub, yet it was something everyone had to endure, so he marched on swiftly.

Upon opening the pub door, he was attacked with the smell of cigarette smoke and the stale sweet smell of lingering beer. It was a man's smell, and one the local men found alluring.

He stayed until closing time and left the warmth of the pub for the chilled air blowing from the sea, but not before he had swiftly gulped the final splashes of his now warm bitter.

Jones was not thinking when he let out his boiling antipathy and swung his tight fist, quick and potent, into the chief whip's defined jaw; the impact like thousands of venomous blades piercing apart his clammed fist. It led him to one conclusion: that it hurt. He had thrown his body weight behind the fist and when it hit the jaw blood pooled into the man's mouth. He grasped his head and brought his kneecap up to the his nose, there was an outstanding crack. Crimson leaked from both his nostrils, and his nose was twisted right. Jones drew his fist back again and ploughed into his opponent's stomach.

The chief whip felt like he was being hit by a train head on. The battering continued until he fell to the floor. His chest gently rose and sank with each shallow breath he drew in. At the same time a sharp gasp of wind slashed his cheeks. He began to lose consciousness and drift into a dream like state.

Sweat poured from his forehead. His face was aglow, his eyes large. His mind was unusually empty of thought, his body still. What had happened? He was in the boot of a car, that was rattling along at speed, but to where, and why?

It was a seven miles drive from Aldington to Hythe. Jones's mind began to wander, deciding to unwind the window, the slap of the cold and the flash of lights shaking his mind awake. The rest of the journey was in silence; an occasional spluttering of the engine as it made its way to the destination the only noise, and the click-click of the occasional indicators. The first part of his plan had gone swimmingly well, yet he understood the perils he may still face.

He had experienced one amazing piece of fortune. The Gravedigger could pilot a small boat, something he could not. Where and when the man had learnt the discipline was anyone's guess, yet it was a piece of luck.

Suddenly, he heard a tapping noise coming from the rear of the car. It was light, like a stone tapping constantly, tap tap tap. The chief whip had awoken from his beating. Jones pulled over slowly on-to the verge, before removing himself from the vehicle. He briskly strode to the boot and lifted it.

'Please let me go. What have I done? I do not know you.' The chief whip was squinting through his heavily bruised eyes, his mouth had a cold metallic taste, yet he felt no pain. The body was an extraordinary vessel.

'You sir, have annoyed some very dangerous people, who believe you are not to be trusted. They are not like me. They are supremely educated like you, yet more dangerous than me in a way. Do you want to know who arranged this?'

The chief whip suddenly felt pain as he nodded his head wearily.

'Shaftsbury. He saw you with some people in a London hotel. So you are aware, the others are receiving the same fate as you. So don't take it personally.' Jones then produced a shiny new long blade that he plunged with such force he felt the metal of the car.

The chief whip reached for the wound, which was a mistake. A searing pain shot through his head as his fingers connected with the entrance. The bleeding continued, it looked black under the moonlight. He wished it would stop.

It had a smell, an odour, a little stale, this was how dead blood smelt. He thought of his wife and his family, and how much he had loved them. A tear tried to emerge from the corner of his eye, but there was no life left in the eyes.

Jones arrived at Hythe just after midnight. His friend was already present, having procured a boat stating it was for night fishing. He was dressed in fishing equipment; wearing a yellow pair of bib and brace trousers, black Wellington boots and a thick roll-neck wool sweater.

'Are you sure? You will be the only man on the sea dressed like a bank manager. Stick all that on. I knew you'd come like that.' He threw the clothing at Jones, 'Right, where's the deep-sea sinker?' He stifled a little laugh at his joke.

Gary had stood in the orange wet proofs given to him by his friend, 'All we need it someone dressed in green and we'd look like a traffic light.'

'Once the seaweed lands on him we've got it licked.'

Both men laughed at their gross humour, although both realised it was a serious and dangerous thing they were doing.

Jones was furiously puffing on a Capstan cigarette, which he smoked to the very end, and then threw down the stub and ground it under his heel.

This boat was their land amid the water, both men were rocked like a baby in its mother's arms. The wind was gusting with the tempo of a fiddle, dancing with long and short bows, punctuated by beautiful danger. The old boat retained the feeling of safety at sea, even with the odd creak and snap coming from its bows. Yet she was sound, seaworthy and solid enough to take to the waters.

The boat chugged and spluttered for thirty-five minutes

before it suddenly died. Gary turned in worry looking at his friend.

'Don't worry, I've turned the engine off. We're approximately seven miles out to sea.' Gary felt reassured by his friend's confidence, but neither of them had gills, so he knew he would only be reassured when they reached land again.

'Gary, time to drop your cargo overboard. Make sure you stick a few holes in it, particularly around the lungs, you need to lose as much air as you can from the corpse.'

Gary looked at his friend and wondered how he knew all the unusual and grisly facts. Gary looked at the trussed-up body that had been wrapped in blue cotton sheeting. A number of heavy weights had been added to give the body mass to ensure it sank to the bottom of the cold blue ocean.

Both men picked up the body and threw it unceremoniously over the side. The splash could barely be heard. It floated for thirty seconds before slowly making its descent to the bottom.

Bob turned to Jones. 'It may rise to the surface in three or four days, as bacteria in the stomach creates enough gas for it to float to the surface like a balloon. Don't worry, it will probably rupture within a couple of hours and sink again to the depths.' He could see the concern on his friends face 'Don't worry Gal', no-one will see or find the body, even if it is a prominent person from Parliament.'

Gary turned to his friend startled, 'How did you know who it was?'

'I read the papers, listen and watch political shows as well. I'd know the face anywhere. He was a main face in his party, although not now. The man knew his stuff. He had the sort of job that knew everyone's secrets. Obviously, he held a secret so big you were roped in to end it. One piece of advice Gal'. This bloke was big time. He wasn't a local nonce or debtor. He was main player. Those at the top will be looking for him. Whoever asked you to do this is not to be trusted, as you've done their donkey's work. They've put you in the shitter, big style.'

Gary stood frozen at his friend's choice of language. He never used industrial language. This showed how concerned his friend was. It also indicated how much shit Shaftsbury could be in, and how much shit Shaftsbury had left him in. This required a lot of thinking, and a lot of luck to right the wrong, and a lot of planning.

•

Drake hastily picked up the phone in Philips office and swiftly, yet carefully dialled his DCI's home number. He was answered with a mumbled and sleepy, 'What?'

'Guv, it's me, Drakey. Something interesting has come over the wire. The chief whip has gone missing since he left his local.'

The words were like ice cold water being thrown over him. Gathering his thoughts, he considered what he had been told 'The chief whip missing. How does someone remove the Chief Fucking Whip?' Fucking hell. Shit would hit the fan for this.

'Guv, are you still there?'

'Yes Drakey. Sorry, I was taking in what you just said. When did you get the information? Is it confirmed that he's missing?'

'Sir, it's official. I believe officers local to the Whip's home are looking for him, and we can assume the Security Services are aware, as well as the Prime Minister. This could be big sir. I think we need some help now guv, and I mean big help from big people.'

Philips was holding onto his phone as if it were going to leave him. The plastic was making his palms sweat and his mind was swirling with information, 'Drakey, come round mine, we need to talk. Have you eaten? Have you been home yet?'

'Ok. No and no'.

Fifteen minutes later DCI Philips heard a light tapping on his door. He immediately opened it knowing who it was, 'Welcome to my home Drakey.'

Drakey was welcomed with the smell of bacon wafting through the air. It made his taste bids hungry and filled his mouth with saliva. The house was welcoming from the open door to the claustrophobic hallway. Upon the walls were photographs of family members, past and present, obviously loved. Drake's surveillance of the premises was interrupted.

'Made you a couple of bacon sarnies with tomato sauce. You said you had not eaten. There's a cuppa tea on the table as well. You need to keep your wit's about you son.' Philips sat on the chair, that had seen better days and required stuffing, yet offered a view of the entire room. 'I love it here. This is where I can rest at the end of the day. From the street it is bricks and mortar topped with tile, the same as any other. Yet once I step inside it's different, a place where my heart beats a little steadier and my mind's free."

Two bites later and one half of a sandwich had been demolished. Philips allowed Drake to finish the tea and meal before deciding to speak any further. The man had not been home yet, and was proving to be a superb addition to his department. His mind wandered to Sylvie and how he had got her wrong. She could have had a major future in the force if she had been honest, yet he knew the man sitting in his living room was destined for good things. He was professional, had integrity and oozed courage. The three things all officers required. His thoughts were broken by a sudden sharp slurp of tea, which signified completion of the meal.

'Drakey, we'll have a quick chat now, and then you can bed down on the sofa tonight. No arguments. You need to rest. Anyway. I'm interested in your big help idea. What did you mean exactly?'

'Guv. We need someone from high up the tree. Possibly the very top. The commissioner. Guv, it's time we got help from someone we can trust, and to be honest, we can't trust anyone barring each other.'

Philips understood what his cohort was implying. They did need help, and it needed to be someone with impeccable values. Drake was right. The commissioner would be an excellent choice, but getting to him would not be easy. Going through the usual channels would not be simple as questions would be asked. It would require skill and cunning to take him by surprise, without causing offence and ruining their careers. Philips threw Drake two blankets. 'Time to rest now. I'll be up and about around 7.00am.'

Philips sauntered down the stairs trying to avoid the floorboards that creaked when pressure was applied. The house was so old that everything creaked, including Philips. He opened the living room to find his Sergeant dressed drinking a mug of tea.

'Hope you don't mind. I've always kept my army pattern, *down at dark – up with the lark*. It works for me. There's tea in the pot, and thanks for letting me stay last night. I was knackered, and the bacon sarnies were a treat.'

'No worries Drakey. We'll have a walk to the station and have breakfast. I'm in the mood for a Full English, and I've had an idea how to doorstep the commissioner.'

Both men entered the staff canteen. It was a cacophony of loud chatter, each table a cosseted huddle of people raising their voices to be heard above the other diners. The food was simple and basic, as was the plain decor. When the plates were delivered by the young waitresses there was a lot of food, and it all arrived piping hot.

'Drakey, our commissioner enjoys dining at Rules. He is a creature of habit and uses the same table at 6pm every Tuesday. I feel a trip to a fine dining restaurant is in order, specifically one that has a reputation for fine puddings and pies, therefore, if we go into the office until 3pm, we'll then to go home and scrub up for our venture into the West End. How does that sound?'

'Restaurant sounds nice, but do you think we'll get a table, and how do you plan to get us onto the same table?'

'I'm going to call from the office and request two extra seats be placed at the commissioners table. It's the one chance I'm going to take. It may or may not work.'

'It's chancey guv, bloody chancey, but if it comes off – we're in, big time.'

'Remember, no-one must know, like you said, we can only

trust each other at the moment.' This was met with distinct nod of approval by his colleague.

'Good evening, commissioner, your guests have arrived and are seated at your favoured table.'

'Guests?'

'Yes sir, I believe they work with you. I asked to see their credentials which they both produced. I explained to them where they should sit so your favoured seat was available.'

'Thank you, James. I had totally forgotten about the meeting with my two colleagues. Lucky I am not late.'

'Sir, I have never known you to be one second behind schedule. Your guests arrived approximately ten minutes back.'

The commissioner strode purposely, yet quietly over to the table before gliding behind it. He noted it had caught both officers off guard, who both quickly replaced their drinks on the table before attempting to stand.

'Sit gentlemen. I cannot decide whether I am intrigued, annoyed or concerned with your attempt to doorstep me in my favourite restaurant. I am also aware that I will be expected to pay for your beverage, as I assume you will not be staying long?'

'Commissioner, please forgive me for doing this, but I have a tale to tell, for which you will probably wish to buy us dinner, as it is a career defining tale for all honest officers involved.'

Immediately he zoomed in on *honest officers*. This awoke his suspicious and curious nature, 'Then may I suggest you tell your tale, and if it is a decent yarn I shall buy you both dinner. But before you start, who are you?'

'I am DCI Philips, and my colleague is Sergeant Drake. We are based at Dagenham East nick sir.'

He hated the word 'nick'. All officers used it. It was so colloquial and Neanderthal. He also realised the two gentlemen facing him were career officers, who would offer their lives to the force. This offered him some comfort, as it informed him they were trustworthy, and secondly, for them to confront him at his favoured place of dining took cunning and an inner sleuthing technique rarely found nowadays.

'I note you both have a Guinness .Would you like to replenish your drinks before you regale your tale?' Three tankards were placed in front of the officers with the dark creamy liquid. 'Gentlemen, please proceed, and remember, your evening meal will be decided on it.'

Fifteen minutes passed and his brain memorised everything. The tale was worthy of a Booker Prize. It had absolutely everything covered. The layers of scandal and depravity were unquestionably mind blowing. The commissioner looked at both men in an expectant, yet pensive manner.

The story he had listened to had many twists and turns, and had drawn him in. It had everything; corrupt officers, murder, gangsters, illicit parties, drugs, missing politicians, double agents, people removing bodies. It would make a spectacular Robert Ludlum novel, let alone an investigation under his stewardship. He felt his mind digging into the facts, evidence swirling around like a whirlpool of ferocious activity. This was what he had needed for some time, and the man seated facing him, believed in justice, and had handed him a reason to investigate like all police officers should.

'DCI Philips. I can honestly say, this is an amazing story, and one I believe. My reasons are you have named all participants in this atrocious game of deceit, plus I believe you. Therefore, I am going to support you and your colleague Drake in this personally. I will not hinder your investigation, in fact, I will give you everything you need. One piece of advice. Trust no-one. This case will have consequences for people held in the highest echelons of power, and they will not wish to be toppled from their thrones.'

Philips listened to the man, evaluating him. He was obviously privately educated and had risen up through the ranks like a phoenix from the flames. Rumours surrounded his wealth and power. He had been told the commissioner, when a police constable, had visited a well-known rapist's home and beat a confession out of him. Yet he had entered his station next day without a blemish or nervousness about him, therefore, under his cool calm exterior stood a man of menacing magnitude. 'Thank you for taking the time to listen sir. This case has become riddled with snakes, and not the pet variety. Like you said, there are people of influence stamped all over this.'

The commissioner sat impassively looking at one of few honest officers he felt he had come across. This man was going to bring him Shaftsbury. The inner fury began to envelop him. Shaftsbury, the man who had abused him during his formative schooling years. Shaftsbury had been a prefect when he had entered Eton as an inexperienced and naïve thirteen-year old boy. Yet, within six weeks, he had been initiated and broken in by Shaftsbury and a gang of friends, one ended up working within the police, Taylor. Two birds with one stone. This day had been a memorable one. Both men had obviously forgotten about him, which showed how many boys had been buggered as an initiation. Revenge was a dish best served cold, and both men would receive frozen helpings.

'DCI Philips. The Shaftsbury fellow needs careful handling to bring him down, as others will fall with him, whereas Chief Superintendent Taylor, we can probably allow to hang himself once we apply some pressure, and gentlemen this is worthy of three courses.'

The proceeding three hours involved planning, secret meeting places and codes to be left for the commissioner wherever he was. Everything must go through him or his must trusted secretary, although she would not be given the reason behind the codes. No-one must be allowed any information. It had to stay amongst the three of them until the time was right to arrest all guilty parties.

Chapter 18

Commissioner

There were invisible jail bars within his large, glazed office, which had been his prison since his meteoric rise through the ranks. He had few friends, not even close colleagues, yet he was considered a man who listened and made correct decisions in times of crisis. He was a proud and closely guarded man who listened to everyone, piecing evidence together like a million-piece jigsaw puzzle.

It was never the money that made him want to join the police. Charles Johns signed up to protect and serve. He felt a need. A calling to serve. He was possibly old fashioned, but he believed in public service.

He had witnessed the worst of humanity on a daily basis, and it had tested his beliefs. It probed his faith in the goodness of people and his everyday optimism. He was present when the fire crews cut lifeless teens from their mangled wrecks. He was there when a bleeding wife refused to press charges. He was there when prostitutes were released back to their same drug-riddled abusive lives. He also witnessed the fire-fighters rush into burning buildings, paramedics pulling miracles from thin air, emergency nurses with their speedy hands and doctors who took charge of situations most would scurry from.

He was proud to be a police officer. He was proud of his force. The day he hung his day-to-day uniform up for the final time, he realised his life would never experience the same sensations again.

He started his new life behind his desk, chairing meetings and trying to change the public's outlook. Many people behind closed doors had whispered he must be gay. The fact he was never married, or wasn't seen in the presence of females, fuelled the rumours. Yet it never bothered him. 'Small minded people spoke about small things,' he would often spout. When visiting the bar, he would drink tomato juice with a splash of Worcester sauce over two cubes of ice. He was never seen drinking a pint of beer or spirit. Again, this singled him out as different.

Having returned to New Scotland Yard, he proceeded to read DCI Philips and Sergeant Drake's files. Philips was a long and distinguished veteran of the force. He was obviously a person who believed honesty and integrity were crucial parts to a man's welfare. A man who had dedicated his life to law enforcement. Sergeant Drake's avenue into the police had taken a different route entirely. He had arrived from the armed forces, specifically the SAS. They were a force to be reckoned with as a pairing.

Having left the restaurant both officers visited the nearby Marquis of Granby for a night cap. Drake returned with two large Jameson's.

'You all right guv? You were in some sort of trance.'

Philips sat in his worn leather chair. He had the distinct feeling his commissioner had another agenda. An agenda he had been planning for some time, and whoever the recipient was would face great wrath.

'Sorry. I was miles away. Thinking in my own world.'

Drake studied the man and knew he was plotting, considering and analysing. He knew Philips was a wise, sharp officer and decided to mention the commissioner, 'Guv, I think the commissioner is a solid bloke, but something about him lit up when we mentioned Taylor, did you notice it?'

'Drakey, I'm glad you did. I thought I was going mad. Is it me, or did a sly smile go across his face when we mentioned him?'

'There's history there, and my betting is the commissioner will want to bring Taylor down, big style. He'll leave the rest for us to mop up and take the credit. Anyway, I'd like to say the *Rules* Steak and Kidney pudding was fan-fucking-tastic. Tasted even nicer when it was free!'

Both men roared with laughter and chinked their glasses before swallowing their whisky with one huge gulp.

The commissioner sat in his chair thinking of Taylor. To date, he had been considered a man of purpose, who outsiders liked and fellow officers respected, yet here he was pondering the end of Chief Superintendent Taylor, a pariah amongst the living who feasted upon the young. To think he had entered the Metropolitan Police, probably fast tracked, and been protected by those in loftier places, to carry on his devilment. Bringing him down would be a thing of beauty, and watching him suffer would be the cherry on the top. He knew the pain would be with him until the end of Taylor. Everyday a battle not to lose hope. There had been no dignity during those educational years. Etched in his mind constantly was the full horror and gravity of his past life. It took all his resistance and strength to smile for visitors attending his place of work.

Yet there was a continued ache, which could not be removed, and the ache would never leave until he found out what happened to the men who had abused him.

Now two officers had served him everything he craved, without realising. He was shocked. Taylor was an officer in the force, and a decorated one. The man was on his doorstep. He would bring him down to his knees, and pay him back ten-fold.

The commissioner spent the night on his office sofa. It was seven feet long, allowing his six feet frame to bed down comfortably. He always kept a sleeping bag in his wardrobe, specifically for occasions like this, which were happening more than he liked.

He awoke in a cold sweat. The dream had appeared real. Taylor and others were entering him in his own study-bedroom. The House Captain had been prevalent in the attack, and his name was Shaftsbury. Shaftsbury! It had to be the same man the officers had told him about. Taylor and Shaftsbury were friends from Eton. He immediately sat up, still in his bag. Invigorated. He had to set the ultimate honey trap to ensnare everyone involved, and that would involve sex and drugs. It appeared to be the thing linking everyone in this tale of depravity. He would ensure everyone involved pay for the lack of love in his life, and if it involved death, so be it.

A plan began to form. A plan so magnificent, it would bring everyone down, although it would require him dipping his toes into the other side of the law.

Gary Jones met Robin Shaftsbury in the Nags Head,

Covent Garden. Shaftsbury was sitting in the corner of the traditional looking pub sipping a Whisky Mac, accompanied by a packet of Walkers Ready Salted crisps. Jones strode in and pulled the chair aggressively away from the table making Shaftsbury momentarily jump. He sat down and stared hard at the man who was beginning to fuck him off, 'Speak.'

'Your attitude is…'

'Say one more word about my attitude and I'll decorate this boozer with your shit for nothing blood.' The menacing low growl it was stated in offered little comfort.

Shaftsbury became a little nervous, although hoped it did not show. Jones was now beginning to show the *real* Jones and it concerned, worried him. He gripped his glass, hoping it did not shatter. He now understood the menace this man could offer, had offered, would offer. The thought of it was really worrying him. He began to feel his mouth dry and words would not form.

'What's the matter with you? Cat got your tongue?'

'I, I was wondering why you had entered in such a difficult and truculent manner?'

Gary stared at the man, looking deeply into his soul. He was witnessing a beaten man. A man paddling in his own shit, created by himself. Shaftsbury was his now, totally, and the amusing thing was – Shaftsbury knew it.

'You fucked me Shaftsbury. Doing the chief whip was big fucking time, and I also think it saved your skin mightily, yet you swan about like you're the fucking king of London town. Wrong, 'cos I'm the fucking king.'

The ferocity of the sentence was not lost on Shaftsbury, who understood it was he who was now the follower. Yesterday was history, tomorrow the mystery and today? Today he was fucked, royally! The beautiful bad past had been replaced with an ever so doubtful future. The future worried him, 'It had to be done, for all our sakes.'

'See, you're talking bollocks now. You got me to off the Whip to save your sorry skin. I can't stand liars, and you are lying to me.'

The half-truths he had told Jones were beginning to haunt him. Once you're in survival mode there's a muzzle on your thinking, and Shaftsbury knew he had to start thinking fast if he was to survive.

'You fed me lie, after lie, after lie. You did it in such a way as if I were sitting in front of you holding out a fucking begging bowl waiting to be fed. I was naïve because the company I was in, and you took full advantage of my Dagenham background. I've defended you, and had hopes that our partnership could, indeed work. I shut out every word from all those mouths that spoke disrespectfully of you, and I shut them out in such a way as if I were a heavy wooden door, not even budging for the strongest mind. Yet you played me. Now you're mine. Totally.'

Shaftsbury sat rigid, unable to move. He had no reply to the tirade coming his way. He knew deep down he was going to receive something like this, but not from someone so below his social standing. The working class could certainly hold their own when backed against a wall, and his opponent was not allowing him to reply. What interested him was the vocabulary Jones occasionally used. It was not of someone who had low intellect, on the contrary, it was of someone who had good breeding, yet here was a bull of man who looked like he could demolish The Nags Head in thirty seconds, along with those currently frequenting the establishment. 'Mr. Jones please try to relax and calm down. If not for me, then do it for your heart. It'll jump out of your chest the way you are conducting operations. Now, may I say I did not lie, although removing the chief whip was a magnificent piece of business on your behalf. So, thank you. The man would have been rather troublesome for both of us.' Shaftsbury noted the rosy red look that Jones was beginning to show again and swiftly back-tracked his choice of vocabulary. 'What I meant to say was the fellow had been a thorn in MY side for a considerable period of time.' The rosy glow began to subside from Jones's face. He understood this to be a good thing, a reprieve.

'Are you gonna get me a pint, or do I have to sit here looking like you can't afford to buy me one?'

Shaftsbury jumped as if he had been plugged into a socket and readily crossed to the bar, before ordering a pint of bitter for his unfriendly guest.

Jones surveyed the pub and noted a picture that informed him a pub had stood on the site since the 1670's. He sat quietly contemplating the passing trade that had experienced the establishment's pleasures. His thought process was broken with the sudden thump of his drink being unceremoniously placed in front of him. The discourteous manner of the drinks placement informed him Shaftsbury was rattled. It amused him, although he was beginning to take umbrage to Shaftsbury's less than enduring attitude, 'You need to get a grip and calm down, and your less than hospitable attitude is beginning to wear thin.'

'If you break our deal about the letters with your lawyer. I will personally remove all family residents from the Shaftsbury dynasty one by one, until there is not one remaining.'

The commissioner sat watching the meeting taking place with his back to both men. He had ensured his table had a mirror facing him affording him the perfect view. An East End villain with an aristocratic man, a curious combination. He had trailed Shaftsbury without once being noted. Dressing down had paid dividends. He had ordered half a pint of bitter and a packet of salted peanuts, having no intention to touch the dark coloured liquid. Interestingly, the more educated man appeared subservient to the underworld figure. This was a surprising turn of events. Shaftsbury showed strength in his poker face, yet occasionally the mask would slip, whereas the other man appeared to show a malevolence and contempt towards Shaftsbury.

The meeting between both lasted twenty minutes before Shaftsbury departed. Johns stood from his chair – placing it carefully under the table, leaving his untouched beer, he casually walked to Jones. He again gently removed the chair and began to speak.

Gary looked at the man and wondered what he has doing. He then realised the man was speaking to him. 'What do you want?' The man placed opposite carried on speaking. 'Listen, whatever you want I'm not interested.'

'Excellent, I have your attention. Shaftsbury, I'm interested in Shaftsbury.'

The word Shaftsbury immediately exploded an uninterested Jones into life. 'Never heard of him.'

'That's interesting. As you were just sitting with him, and

looked like you were berating him. Please allow me to introduce myself. I am Charles Johns. I find Shaftsbury a loathsome and tiresome character who needs to be removed from society. Do you not think?' Speaking in a clipped fluid manner, he did not give Jones any chance to respond, which was what he wanted.

Gary sat staring at the man wondering who he was. For some reason he felt as if he knew his face, but could not fathom where from, 'Do I know you? I recognise you from somewhere, but I don't know where.'

'I believe you are Gary Jones from Dagenham, member of White's Club, mother sadly passed away, father's life ended,' he raised an eye at Gary when making this statement. 'Spent a period of time at Boyles Court, a Mr. Fix-it, fears no-one, has a long memory, enjoys justice, highly educated, master chess player, plays the piano to recognised standard – yet rarely plays.'

Gary was never stunned, yet this man had just summed up his life, 'How the fuck did you know about the fucking piano…and chess?'

'Mr. Jones, I am a man who does his homework, thoroughly. Allow me to introduce myself. I am Charles Johns – Commissioner of the Metropolitan Police, and you and I are about to become friends, best of friends.'

'Friends! Are you for fucking real? Friends. An amusing and amazing statement.'

'Mr. Jones. I have a strong feeling you removed the chief whip to a deeper, cooler, bluer graveyard, one in which ships sail. So, I assume I now have your attention.'

Gary sat bemused by the information being fed. This man

was serious and was not taking no for an answer. He admired the man. He was doing to him something he had done to many others. It was intriguing being on the other end of the unpleasant situation, although it did not bother nor concern him. Gary decided to sit and listen to the offerings being served.

Finally, the meeting ended. The commissioner stood and casually muttered 'Meet me tomorrow in The Savoy bar at 3pm.'

Gary moved swiftly through the revolving door. The establishment had an opulent feel, its reddish carpet had a fluffy, yet bouncy feel to it, as if it were new. Making his way to the bar he noted the Head Barman, Joe Gilmore, mixing impressive drinks behind his station, and the area was alive with people talking quietly, which was occasionally broken by the sound of polite laughter.

Gary met his 'new friend' at 3pm in the Savoy bar. As he approached the table where Charles Johns sat he noted two Whisky Mac's with two cubes of glistening ice.

From no-where a member of staff pulled his seat and welcomed him to it.

Having planted himself in the beautifully comfortable padded seat he looked hard at the man facing him. Both men eyed each other.

Charles Johns passed a very small container to Gary. He knew what his counterpart would be thinking about its size. 'It may look small, but the effects are huge. Strychnine is an absolute beast. Pour the powder into a drink or meal and let it work. Ten to twenty minutes after exposure, the body's muscles will begin to spasm. Death comes from asphyxiation. It is deadly…totally.'

Gary stared hard at the man facing him. How could the commissioner of the Metropolitan Police want Robin Shaftsbury so badly dead? He was no nearer to solving that conundrum, yet he really wanted to know what the beef between both men was.

'How do I know you'll keep your side of the bargain? You could be playing me.'

'Mr. Jones, having investigated many underworld figures, of which you are one, I have heard of a thing called a gentleman's agreement. You have mine. It is not in my interest for me to upset you. Once this is done I will leave the force within one year as my career plan would have been fulfilled fully. I will ensure you are totally protected and have the finest alibis money can buy, as you requested. I will also safeguard your freedom.'

Gary felt a sudden and unexpected softening towards the man, 'In a different life you and I could have been friends I think Charles. We're cut from the same cloth; honest, hardworking, admirable and principled.'

Charles smiled. He had thought the same. For some unknown reason he quite enjoyed the Essex villain's company. He was forthright and confident, yet quietly spoken. Like himself he had played the cards dealt from birth, whereas his had been privileged, unlike Jones's. His criminal file had made interesting as it was so minimal. Nothing stuck to the man. The Boyles Court incident had been an engrossing study. This had informed him that Gary Jones was a man who could explode if necessary when pushed too far.

'Why do you want Shaftsbury terminated? He's a slippery fucker, I'll admit, and one not to be trusted fully, but to end his life is a major thing. He must have proper upset you in a previous life.'

'Mr. Jones.'

'Call me Gary.'

'Gary, I knew Shaftsbury many moons back, and he is the proprietor of evil and cunning. To someone's face he is a charming and pleasant, but behind his eyes lays pure evil and malevolence. He is a man the world will not miss, hence the reason he must be removed, and the reason why I will protect you fully. I do not wish to speak about the acts performed by Shaftsbury, although I will say they have scarred me, emotionally.'

Gary knew not to pry further, although he had a feeling Shaftsbury had abused the man when they were younger. The emotional angle had given the game away. The commissioner appeared reflective and looked in deep thought. It must have been a time of incredible unhappiness, and if it happened when he was young, even worse. Shaftsbury was a man society would not mourn, society may even rejoice his passing. 'Charles. I will do it. Shaftsbury is a life form we do not need. He is worthless piece of skin.'

Both men picked up their glasses and chinked them heartily, like two distant friends.

Chapter 19

Digging deeper

'**G**uv, I've been thinking about Taylor and Shaftsbury. I may be barking up the wrong tree, but could Taylor and Shaftsbury have known each other when they were younger? It's the only avenue I feel they could have made contact. It's only a shot in the dark though.'

DCI Philips looked at his protégé, considering the man's idea. Everywhere they looked had turned up absolutely nothing. They had searched through records, met people, visited venues...the lot. So the idea offered was completely worthwhile and certainly an avenue worth pursuing, 'Drakey, that's an excellent idea. Younger days. Didn't we have something based about schooling. Schooling...schooling. Fuck me Drakey, that's it. They knew one another at fucking school. You fucking mastermind.'

Sergeant Drake looked at his DCI in a bemused, yet euphoric manner, 'Guv, this could be the in we need to finally end this nightmare investigation.'

'Nightmare? Beats walking the streets investigating silly crimes by idiot wannabe 16-18-year-old gangsters.'

'Didn't Taylor go to Eton? Think he comes from a pretty wealthy family.'

'Yes, yes, he did. I'll speak with their records office. See if

Shaftsbury was there at the same time. Remember, tell no-one.' Philips walked briskly to his office and closed the door behind him gently. No-one in his department turned.

Philips gingerly placed his finger in the dial, but stopped. He knew once correspondence between the school and himself had been made, then there was no going back. He knew many people in influential places had attended Eton, therefore the 'old boys network' still stood in place. He sat perfectly still, finger still in position, as if switched on, he began to dial.

Immediately, he was met with a female voice that offered a clipped, well-spoken officious manner. 'Is anyone there? Please speak.'

His mind and voice awoke as if they had been dozing, 'Sorry, the line at my end went silent.' He hoped the lie from his end would not be noticed by the school receptionist.

'We are busy. Anyway, how may I assist?'

He had to gain control of this conversation, being sarcastic or blunt would not develop this new alliance, therefore, being humble was his best move, 'Thank you for your time. My name is Jack Philips, DCI Jack Philips.' He allowed the title to embed into the lady's mind, 'I, we require information on two pupils who attended your school many years back. I am sure someone as young as yourself would not have been employed then, therefore we would be appreciative if you would search your records?'

The receptionist blushed. Compliments were few and far between nowadays at her age, yet this officer obviously understood how to play the game, and she admired his cheek. He obviously came from London, as he had the estuarine accent most from the area had, 'DCI Philips. Thank you for your compliment. It was a delight to receive. Now, how may I be of assistance?'

Philips understood he had broken the lady's resistance, and guessed she was no spring chicken, but a classy lady, 'May I ask your name?'

'It's Catherine Askew, DCI Philips,' her heart fluttered. No one had paid her any attention since her husband had died ten years previously. She imagined the man on the phone to be a career man with a wife and three children. No one paid her attention now. She had heard the words frigid and vinegar tits banded about. How wrong the perpetrators of this were.

'Catherine. A lovely name. May I call you Catherine?'

'You may Jack.'

Philips began to feel a stirring in his loins. This lady was flirting with him, and he was interested, 'Catherine, I require information on two ex-pupils. Robin Shaftsbury and George Taylor,' he heard a sudden intake of breath, 'Are you all right Catherine?'

'DCI Philips. I cannot discuss those names over the telephone. Sorry.' The phone was disconnected.

Philips was annoyed. He was unsure whether it was the lack of information or the disconnection from someone he felt a longing to meet. He sat there pondering the situation. 'Bollocks. I'm going to Eton.' He walked to his sergeant and whispered in his ear, 'Come with me, possible in.'

The journey to Windsor took ninety minutes. During the ride Philips informed Drake about everything, although he missed out the romantic part.

They arrived at Eton College and were directed to the visitors parking area. A sign directed them to the school reception.

Both officers experienced a sense of grandeur. During the journey Drake had informed Philips of the school's history; there were 25 houses – each with their own House Captain, 1300 pupils, all males ranging from 13-18, and the school had been started by King Henry VI.

Philips strode confidently to the school reception. He noted how pristine, clean and smart all pupils were. It was a far cry from the schools in Dagenham.

She was walking towards him, shoulders back, moving in an elegant motion as if this school was built on dictatorship. It was as if she felt superior and insecure at the same time.

Her cream shoes were sparking, like two diamonds. He lent forward peeking at his now tired shoes. They looked soul less.

She was not displeased at what she noted. He was as she had expected, a career officer who would be a little tattered around the edges, possibly a little un-kempt. Yet he had a sparkle about him. Some men had it, most did not. Yet he had something, 'Jack?'

'Catherine. This is my colleague, Sergeant Drake.'

Drake was confused. Catherine and Jack, were they friends, lovers, relatives? This was unexpected. They looked at one another in a lustful yet unsure manner. In the time he had known his DCI nothing like this had happened.

'Gentlemen, please follow me to one of our spectacular gardens where we can discuss your enquiry.' Catherine Askew led them to a carefully maintained wooden bench that offered a bountiful view of the gardens offerings.

'We don't get this round our way Mrs Askew. This is something else.'

'I am so glad you enjoy the view Sergeant Drake.' As she turned she saw Jack Philips looking at her. A whooshing feeling sent shockwaves through body. She hoped he could not see her heart beating, 'So, gentlemen. You want to know about Shaftsbury and Taylor? First of all, let me state they were dreadful young men. What they did to the new pupils was disgusting. To date, I am sure it still takes place. The beaks.'

'Sorry. Beaks, what are they?'

'Teachers are known as Beaks at Eton. The beaks are unaware it goes on supposedly, although I am not so sure. Taylor and Shaftsbury were in a group; of which they were the leaders. Yet, they took FULL advantage of their privilege. They abused many many new pupils. One was covered up...totally, due to the family being rather well-known. This person ended up being your boss. He was known as Charles Roberts at Eton, but changed his name to Charles Johns.'

'Our boss?' Both repeated it at the same time.

'Charles Johns... your Commissioner.' She knew she had hit the jackpot as both men's mouths dropped open.'

'Fuck me. Sorry, I don't know what else to say.'

Catherine laughed. She had not heard profanity in a long time, 'The Roberts family owned the large wireless company. They have extreme wealth. As I am sure your commissioner now does as he was the sole heir. He must be worth millions. He changed his name to remove himself from the stigma of abuse.'

'Excuse me Mrs Askew, but guv, the fucking commissioner. It's all beginning to knit together. We have something now…big. I'm going to collect my thoughts Guv so you can interview Mrs Askew further.' Drake vanished before either party could utter a single syllable.

'Catherine. This is going to sound odd, incredibly strange, but would you like to go on a date?'

She sat there transfixed. He had such an old-fashioned manner, yet he oozed charm in a tired way. He had her at *Catherine*, 'Jack, I thought you would never ask.' Her cheeks began to turn ruby red and she began to laugh nervously.

'Thank heavens for that. Being a chap who rarely, in fact, never, goes out with a lady, I didn't know how to ask, so I thought, sod it, just ask.' He began to laugh heartily. He passed Catherine his number, home and office. He got up and left, but not before whispering in her ear, 'I have a very good feeling about us,' and kissed her gently on her soft warm cheek.

Catherine sat and counted to five seconds. If he turned within that time she knew he would see her again. He turned after three.

Memories of Taylor and Shaftsbury jumped into her memory. The investigation had been inconclusive and poor at best due to the stature of the two pupils being investigated, and how prominent they were. It was concluded swiftly. The receiver of their crime had to endure a further five years of Eton. The school, amazingly, did not even change the young boy's room. Every night he must have returned to his room, with memories of being buggered many times by Taylor and Shaftsbury, initially for fun, but fun became a non-stop nightly pleasure for the two despicable and disgusting creatures.

She shook off the horrid memory and smiled, an inward glow forming through her soul. She felt younger. Before Jack, she had only loved one man, yet out of the blue she felt the same glow again. Her late husband and Jack were so very different, yet both made her feel so happy. She considered how love offers so much joy, yet can end a life. She never wanted any form of eternity until now, until Jack.

'Guv, I don't like to pry, but did you know Mrs Askew?'

'Drakey, No, but I intend to. Now let's get back to good old Dagenham and arrange a meeting with our friend, the commissioner, in the inner sanctum of New Scotland Yard.'

Both officers entered the building showing their security badges to those stationed at the solid black desk. The area was always full of hustle and bustle from the 3,500 staff employed within their Specialist Operations departments, and a smattering of invited guests. It always amazed Philips how the I.R.A hadn't attacked the impressive building. The twenty-story steely grey structure and smoked glass windows gave it a very modern twist, and the continuously spinning New Scotland Yard sign informed all passers-by what lay behind the mirrored doors.

Both officers were shown where to go once their identification had been authorised, and the commissioner's personal assistant had enquired whether he would accept the two serving officers.

'Good afternoon DCI Philips and Sergeant Drake, please take a seat. Thank you, Miss Higgins, that will be all. So, how may I help you gentlemen?' Charles detected a frostiness from both men. They appeared uncomfortable, he sensed something unfriendly from them. Both officers sat solemn faced. A genuine friendly movement from their faces had not materialised. The concern was etched all over their pale white faces. 'Come now gentlemen, has the cat got your tongue?' He looked directly at DCI Jack Philips. He did this as he was the superior officer, and secondly, his sidekick – Sergeant Drake, would offer no emotion due to background, it would have been part of his training.

Jack sat there thinking how to tackle this and decided to jump into this arena head-on. 'Sir, you knew or know Taylor and Shaftsbury. You schooled with them at Eton, and they abused you. Is that correct Commissioner Roberts?'

Charles felt a cold chill shoot through his body. An experience he had not felt since the opening night of abuse. He felt a bead of sweat form on his brow and turned to peruse the London skyline so both officers would note his nerves. Whilst standing, seconds felt like an eternity. These officers were special. They had dug up a secret buried for thirty years. He turned slowly, facing two men staring directly at him. These men had an inner strength he had not witnessed in any other serving officer. They were dogged, intelligent and honest. He decided to set a small, yet simple trap to test their honesty, 'Gentlemen, before we leave this room. You must swear that everything I tell you goes further than this room?' He eyed both, looking for any distinguishable movement or nervousness, yet none was shown.

'Sorry sir. No deal. We are serving officers, and I won't be party to any iffy behaviour or cover ups.'

'I fully agree with my DCI, Mr Commissioner. I will not,

and have never been involved in any secrets, as secrets cause even more secrets, that cause even bigger problems. So sorry.'

Charles Johns stood there smiling which confused by Philips and Drake. 'Gentlemen, thank you. I was praying neither of you would agree to my request. It was a honey trap of sorts. It was a simple test of your honesty. I am happy for the truth to come out. It has been hidden long enough. I ask one thing. Concentrate on Taylor. He is your weak link. Shaftsbury can be left to me. He is a tricky customer. And thank you. I must ask you to leave now as the Home Secretary is due. God speed.'

Both officers left the building, neither saying a word.

Drake turned towards his superior officer, and friend, 'Jack, fancy a few pints in The Feathers? I feel this investigation is beginning to come to an end and it's starting to scramble my mind. I don't think I've ever known, or ever will know, an investigation involving so many people of varying degrees of honesty, wealth and power. Power appears to be the significant player; Police officers, politicians, footballers, gangsters. They've all had power of some sort over someone. It's been as interesting as its been mind boggling.'

Jack carried on walking alongside his friend and partner calculating what he had just said, 'Do you know what Drakey, I agree. I'll be glad when it's over. Just when I feel we get a break something or someone else comes out the woodwork. The abuse thing shocked me, although massive respect must go towards the commissioner and his brutal honesty, and him wishing it not to be a secret. I think he's a good bloke.'

'Just remember Jack, he won't be telling us everything. They'll be something held back, and that something will be important. He was planning when he turned from us and faced the window. We caught him out with the abuse angle. The thirteen seconds he turned from us allowed him to formulate another option. He's sharp.'

'Did you say thirteen seconds?'

'Yep, it took him that long to work out a new plan and how to appease us, which he did by telling the truth. You have to give your captors a truth to buy time, and we were his captors, therefore, he told us the horrible truth that shocked us, and something we knew was true. He'll think it's brought him lots of time, and why did he tell us to concentrate on Taylor? He's after Shaftsbury himself. There is a lot more to this, believe me.'

'Fucking 'ell Drakey. You were evaluating the commissioner in his office. You crafty fucker. Top man. I also wondered why he offered us Taylor and not Shaftsbury. This investigation is full of snakes. Anyway, let's sink a few pints and forget about it until tomorrow.'

•

'Mr Jones, it's your friend.'

Gary understood the meaning of friend. What he really meant was *friends at arm's length*, or *friends you can drop in the shit*, 'Hello Charles, you calling me probably means bad news for us. Am I right?'

The commissioner considered Jones's reply. It was curt and to the point. He was a man of few words, a man who did not use two words when one was sufficient. 'Gary, we may have a problem. Two officers from your neck of the woods have made significant progress in the investigation, to the extent they have worked out how Shaftsbury and I are acquainted. You may have come across them. The names are...'

'DCI Philips and Sergeant Drake. They came around my pad to shake the tree to see if they could catch any information. They did not. They're the local Batman and Robin.'

Charles sat in thoughtful silence considering the ingenuity of his officers. They had certainly made a name for themselves. Those who they had met, did not speak badly of them. Just how efficient they were. 'When did you meet them?'

'A few days back. Before you ensnared me in Covent Garden.'

Ensnared, what an unusual word to use. Charles considered how intellectualism was a form of power, and how the pen was mightier than the sword. Yet in this case, he did not require a pen, he needed the sword, 'These officers are sharp, incredibly sharp, and we need to tread very carefully with these two. I have told them to concentrate on another area, yet their investigative noses will not last long before they head in another direction, therefore, you need formulate a plan on the removal of Shaftsbury.'

Jones sat pensively in his favourite armchair, which gave him a perfect view of those passing his home. He understood that thinking was best achieved when a person had reasons for solving the problem. 'I understand what you are saying. Leave it with me. Goodnight, and thank you for the tip.' He replaced the telephone on its avocado green holder and considered Shaftsbury. The man was becoming an irritant, like a non-stop buzzing gnat always nipping away. He knew this gnat had to be splattered, and quickly.

Charles Johns sat perfectly still, studying London's skyline. Here he was, Commissioner of the Metropolitan Police, hiring an underworld figure to solve his problem. What made it even more ridiculous was the underworld figure would be true to his word and solve this situation. Yet, it did need solving for his own state of mental prowess. So many years of tortuous sleeps, early morning sweats, panic attacks and dreams of abuse. He understood that during sleep we are young again. We dream of things in the past or things that will never be again. In dreams we have comfort, freedom and love. Sometimes we are visited by those we have lost, and for those perfect hours of sleep we are free again. Sadly, he had experienced nothing comforting or peaceful. He hoped he would…one day.

Chapter 20

The date

Jack Philips disembarked at Windsor and Eton railway station. The station looked like any other; dull, grey, dreary with red brick, yet when exiting the station, it was a different vision. It had a large glass overhead spectrum that leant itself into red brickwork that had obviously been completed by master craftsman. The finishing touch was the large clock immersed centrally. It was an amazing structure, obviously not recognised by the busy bee locals.

Jack had agreed to meet Catherine in the Red Lion at twelve o'clock. When approaching the old public house, he thought it reminded him of his local, The Cross Keys. It was well maintained, painted white, and appeared to have Crittall windows. The pub's entrance was painted red, obviously in recognition of its name. Jack had ensured his shave was smooth and his clothing ironed with creases resembling razors. He had splashed a little 'Hi-Karate' aftershave on his neck, something he never did it. The floral aroma was meant to attract ladies, although he only wished to attract one.

Catherine Askew entered the bar. The butterflies were beginning to work overtime, and her lack of confidence began to make her feel sick. She had only met Jack Philips once, yet she felt a kindred spirit in him. She had not sat still all morning and had barely slept the previous night. Yet here she was, walking in a public house, hoping, praying the man was here.

As she entered the Red Lion early drinkers noted her decanter shaped waistline and her silky-smooth complexion. Each recognised class.

Her nerves were broken when she heard her name called in an estuarine manner. She immediately broke into beaming smile, her snow-white teeth lit up the bar and her rose pink lips looked like fresh petals.

Catherine noted Jack's attire and let out a heartfelt chuckle. He had really tried to impress, yet looked a man who lived alone. His shoes were beautifully polished, yet still showed slight scuff marks, his trousers perfectly pressed, although one of the legs towards the top appeared to have a double crease. He had obviously cut himself shaving and had dabbed it with tissue, forgetting to remove it. The more she looked, the more endearing he became. He had a made a real effort, and coming to Windsor was no mean feat either. She had the butterfly feeling again, and this time it was nerves of excitement.

'Catherine, I'm so glad you're here. I had a horrible feeling you may not make it. Oh, these are for you.' Jack handed a bunch of flowers he had purchased from the stall outside the station. He kept on smiling.

'Thank you, Jack, these are lovely. Any chance of a drink?' She felt like a young girl on her first date. She had never felt like this before. Her heart was dancing, not beating.

'Drink, yes, good idea as we're in a boozer, sorry, bar.'

Catherine let out a deep belly laugh. The man facing her had good manners, yet was very rough around the edges, but he was trying to impress her with any way he could. Using boozer told her everything about him. It said he was honest, upright, and respectful. Not using pub made her laugh, he chose to use bar, which informed her he was linguistically intelligent as he amended his speech swiftly, 'I would love a Cinzano and lemonade with ice please.'

'Excellent choice, shall I order a Ploughman's for lunch? I'm bloody starving. Excuse my profanity. But I really am Hank Marvin.'

Again Catherine let out a schoolgirl giggle. She had never heard anyone describe their hunger by using a famous guitarist, 'A fine choice of luncheon Mr. Philips.'

Jack scampered towards the bar and placed his order, returning as quick as his legs would move, 'Hello, Catherine. I'm back, and here is your chosen poison. I would like to say you look better in the flesh than I imagined on the phone, not that I imagine people on the phone.' He laughed with his chosen phrase, yet felt heat pulsing through his entire body.

Catherine smiled. Amazingly, her date appeared to be more nervous than she was, although relieved to be in a chair, because she hoped Jack had not noted her legs shaking, 'Jack, you have made a valiant effort yourself. Are you wearing aftershave? Many gentlemen wear it nowadays. Previously, men have relied upon their musky aroma, that can be a little off putting. Your smell has a floral aroma to it.'

'Hi-Karate. It's the one in the adverts where the man has to fight women off because of the fragrance. Not sure if that's true, but I thought I'd give it a whirl.'

Catherine quickly calculated the man sat opposite never wore masculine perfumes, possibly because he was masculine.

The more she found out about Jack Philips, the more she liked him. He was happy in his own skin, although a fresh smell was appreciated by the fairer sex.

The time had reached 2.30pm and the barman called time. Those savouring their beverages swiftly consumed them, including Jack and Catherine.

Catherine took Jack around the gardens of Eton. He marvelled at the lawns and flowers. He had never seen anything so bountiful in colour. She assumed Dagenham did not have anything like this and thought it a good idea. The gardens always looked brighter after the rain. It was as if the rain was not water, but liquid magic, washing the world of its ills. Nature in her brilliance. Buttercups were glistening, grass became a deeper green – and stood like proud soldiers, roots quenched, soil replenished. It was breath-taking.

'Catherine, I've never ever seen anything so perfect. It's like something you see in the movies. It's so perfect. Everything is perfectly cut, manicured and bouncing with life. I see now why you work here. It's truly magnificent.'

The pride Catherine felt was obvious. She loved where she worked, and for someone to recognise it made it all more special, 'Shall we sit on the bench Jack?

When they were comfortable, Catherine took Jack's hand and looked at him, 'Jack, I have some news that may aid your investigation. Don't speak, please listen. There was an investigation at Eton, although it was concluded inside forty-hours. Shaftsbury and Taylor were moved to different areas, yet the abuse continued to others alongside Charles Johns. I think he was abused more than any other boy. There were rumours it was a nightly torment for the poor boy. Yet, it was not investigated again. How he rose to Commissioner of the Metropolitan Police is a testament to his courage and mind-set. He was one of the cleverest pupils to have attended Eton, whereas Shaftsbury and Taylor were bullies from the start.'

Jack sat with a dry mouth. He removed imaginary dirt from his blazer and trousers, letting the gravity of the disgusting information sink in.

Catherine studied Jack. He was white like chalk and had an expression of stunned surprise, and although she was staring straight at him he appeared not to notice her which concerned her. She prayed the information supplied had not ruined a relationship she hoped would progress.

Jack suddenly woke from his hypnotic dream and turned towards Catherine kissing her gently on her pure white cheek that had begun to turn rose pink, 'Catherine, you did not need to volunteer that disgusting and shocking information. Stay clean, remove yourself from it. A lady like you needs to empty herself from the filth of society, that's my job. Where you work and spend your life is clean, remain so. Apart from that. I love you as you are.' Jack was shocked as soon as he mentioned the final statement.

•

The wind was continuously blowing leaves around the beautifully kept graveyard like dancers being swept in the air. Bob Burns leant against his rake admiring the shapes each made. Patience was key to everything, and patience was something he had in abundance. The bushes had been trimmed and the trees offered each resident of the area protection. Bob's trained ear heard a gentle scrunch on his bowling green kept grass. Turning swiftly, he was met by Gary standing with his hand held out. 'Blimey Gary, you walk really gently, like a girl.'

'Only you could say that you fucking monster of a man.'

Both men laughed like old friends do.

'Seriously, you do walk like a fairy. Man up.'

Gary looked at his friend smiling, 'Bob, I have a job. A big fucking job. Pretty grizzly as well. Someone high up the tree, but that someone is a wrong 'un.'

Bob Burns turned swiftly. The nice Bob Burns became the nasty Gravedigger, 'Gary, the chief whip was bloody high up, but did you say wrong 'un? If so, how bad? Nonce's should all be culled. World would be better off without them. Scum bag arse wipes. Tell me then.'

Five minutes passed.

Bob was leaning on his rake in deep thought. 'Robin Shaftsbury. He has to go. Who'd have thought you'd be friends with the Commissioner of the Met' Police, and who'd have thought a man like that has been bummed many times and wanted to off that person. Mind you, shows he's got substance. You obviously want something to happen. So it's easy if I just say yes.'

Gary informed Burns of his plan to lure Robin Shaftsbury to the graveyard where his final breath would be taken and his last vision of life made. Both men agreed it appeared simple, yet effective.

Burns suggested they walk the area considering which plot should be Shaftsbury's final resting place. 'Gary, when he's popped in the hole. I wonder what his final thoughts will be?'

'Well, he'll be looking at the sky thinking. I wish I was

looking in the hole and not out of it.'

The throaty roar of laughter was made by Burns. 'Hope it's not raining.' He then began to laugh again. 'Maybe you should ask the commissioner to attend. If he does, then you'll both have something over each other, therefore you're both in the same boat.'

'Nice idea, but say he doesn't attend.'

'He'll attend. Guaranteed. He'll want to see the final moments of the man who's basically ruined his life.'

Gary stopped walking, causing his friend to abruptly cease his step. 'You're right. He'll be there in the background, watching from the shadows. Curiosity and finality will be his calling.'

'I'll be in the background watching out for you. I'll make sure it all goes well as this may be my final funeral.' The words were left hanging in the air. 'You probably want to know what's wrong, but don't ask. All I'm prepared to say is you have been my only family, and although we've done some pretty nasty things, it's always been to people who have deserved it, and this is another one of those situations. It also means I don't need paying.'

Gary was rooted to the spot as if frozen. Had he heard correctly, his best and only friend was not long of this world. For only the second time in his life Gary felt a lump in his throat. 'You are fucking with me?'

Burns looked directly, with a hint of resentment in his eye and replied defiantly 'No. Don't get emotional or soppy on me.'

Gary knew he had to act normal, yet his mind was jumping about like an early morning kangaroo.

'Gary, I have one request. The corner behind the green glossed bench in the corner is where I want my ashes placed, and I want a white climbing rose placed there as well. White means peace, and I want peace. The corner will also allow me to keep an eye on the place.'

'Burnsey, whatever you want, you can have, and I'll make sure it's as good as it gets.'

'Thank you. Now, I'll dig a hole here, and this where will put him. It'll take me an hour to dig, and ten minutes to fill. I'll go down nine feet, instead of the usual six. That allows the man who follows me to dig six feet in this space without connecting with the body. Gotta be fair to the next man who takes this job.'

Gary winced again, 'You'd like the commissioner, he's upstanding, has principles, yet has old fashioned values of right and wrong. He obviously feels an injustice has happened, and rightly so. Got to laugh though, a man like that asking me for help. It's a bit upside down.'

'Everyone needs help Gal', even the 'ole bill.'

Chapter 21

Goodbye Robin

Jack Philips walked into the station whistling. Officers turned with surprise when they saw the person making the tune. Jack Philips never whistles; these were the thoughts in everyone's mind.

One of the junior police constables acknowledged Jack in way befitting a senior officer, 'Good morning sir. Lovely day today.'

Jack stopped, turned and faced the young officer, 'Son, every day is a great day. Enjoy every one of them.' He then strode towards the stairwell with a definitive bounce in his step.

The young constable was left standing contemplating the wise words offered from someone considered a fountain of knowledge.

Opening the door to CID, Jack breezed towards his office bidding everyone good morning. In return, he received a curt nod, or an under exuberant wave. He made himself a strong black coffee and sat behind his desk lost in his own private world.

'Morning guv. How comes you're drinking from that tatty old mug. It's well chipped.' Sergeant Drake stared at his superior officer, before scratching his chin. He wondered if he was a bit pissed, 'You ok? You appear off on one.'

'Sorry Drakey. Had a triffic day yesterday at Windsor. What a place. Eton is a beautiful area. The gardens are amazing.'

'Can I stop you there guv?' This day, did it involve a certain Mrs Catherine Askew?'

'It did, and its Miss, not Mrs.'

Drake looked at his senior officer again. His tone had such a playful feel, as if he were the star of his own love story. Who'd have thought Jack Philips would be in love. If he could find someone, there was hope for all, 'I'm glad you had a fun day, but we have to sort this Gary Jones and co problem…do you not think?'

For the first time in his policing career Jack felt tired of crime fighting. Having witnessed the possibilities of life with Catherine, he'd finally realised life was passing him by with no-one to share it with, and he knew so little outside of policing. Becoming alert he responded to his colleague, 'Drakey, I think we need to concentrate on Shaftsbury. He is the pariah in this entire sordid affair. Wherever we seem to go his name pops up, and it's never mentioned in blessed terms. The murkier this investigation becomes, the seedier the involvement of Shaftsbury becomes; parties, sexual abuse, drugs, money. He is involved in it all, and he is at the forefront of it all. I know you are going to mention what the commissioner stated, but even he has a secret agenda. Everything about this case reeks of depravity.'

Drake turned and slowly closed the office door, ensuring no noise was made, 'Guv, I was going to say our chief super is the weak link. He's the one we need. He's weak. I could break him in ten minutes.'

Jack studied the eyes of Drake. He had an edge to him. His mind had entered the SAS world he had existed and thrived in. Whatever he had done in that troop he would never know, and he did not wish to know. Ten minutes! Fuck. What would he do to Taylor? 'Why do you feel this is the area we need to pursue? It could be tricky at best.'

'To be honest Jack.'

Jack...Drakey never called him by his Christian name. The man was in full flow. He had forgotten the chain of command. He was in another world. He was planning the demise of all involved.

'Taylor is the weak link. He's beginning to look a little dishevelled. It's as if he has the weight of the world on his shoulders. There are two routes. The first, we tackle him head on somewhere quietly, or, we lead the horse to water and drown him in the shit he's immersed himself in. If you want a result, I can do the first one alone? I'll get the info' from him swiftly. I was known for my swift conclusions during inter-rogations back in the day.'

Jack's mouth opened, but no words formed or fell. His mind was still calculating the world interrogation, 'Did you say interrogation? As in, interrogate Chief Superintendent Taylor?' He still could not believe Drake had spoken to him about an illegal operation involving harming a serving officer, all be it, an officer who had done wrong, 'Drakey, piece of advice. Don't mention that again. This is not the army. We're both annoyed by the situation, but always stay clean. Never, ever, enter the realms of punishment. As soon as you enter that area you are royally fucked. You are a good bloke, one destined for big things. You don't want something like that coming back and biting you on the arse…which it will, for sure.'

Drake smiled, 'Guv, you are right of course. I wouldn't want to do it, but if you ever need a skill set of defence or attack, just ask. I can do things to a man that would reduce them in seconds. But, Taylor is the one we need. He is weak, very weak.'

Gary sat looking out the window pontificating. Officers were like busy bee lives, all connecting this intriguing puzzle. Each believing their piece was more important than those they worked alongside.

•

Gary took a huge bite from his corned beef sandwich, taste buds creating a thick river in his mouth. He grabbed hold of his mug and gulped a mouthful of stewed tea that cleansed and refreshed his mouth, before devouring the remnants of his meal.

He had formed a plan to rid the world of the nuisance Robin Shaftsbury. Whether the pieces fell into place was a matter for the gods. All he knew was he had to get Shaftsbury to the graveyard and ensure Strychnine entered his body. Simple. He had considered all areas of the plan and had decided the best was the simplest. Tell Shaftsbury to meet him as he had information. Sit on the bench and offer him a sandwich, which would be laced with the drug.

He had also decided against contacting Charles Johns. Some secrets are best kept as secrets. He would just inform him it had been sorted and their arrangement was completed. He thought Johns was a person of honour, therefore allowing both parties to ride into the sunset.

Sitting alone, Shaftsbury was enjoying the peace and tranquillity of home life. This murky affair was beginning to drain him.

He was considering how man was born to thrive as one species, and how man can inherit the sins of their fathers, yet it was the prerogative of the next generation to help and develop others. The process of chaos linking to freedom and freedom linking to chaos had him in deep thought. He prayed that chaos would lead to freedom, but he had his doubts. He could not decide if the man Gary Jones was a saint or a sinner, but he already knew, but could not admit it.

His thought process was broken by the loud shrill from the telephone. He felt his heart rate begin to increase. Warily he picked up the receiver and in a non-confident manner answered. 'Shaftsbury here.' There was a slight flutter in his voice.

'Shaftsbury. Gary Jones. We need to meet. I have some information you may be interested in hearing. Meet me at the graveyard in Upminster at 3pm. Don't be late.' The call was disconnected.

Shaftsbury sat considering the vulgarity of the man. Jones's sentence structure was abrupt and contained few syllables. Each sentence was a statement. Yet the phone conversation was an order.

His day of relaxation was over. He had hoped to break in the new teenager staying with him, yet that could wait until his return. He felt a stirring in his loins. He was a beautiful boy of seventeen with a pert arse that needed filling urgently.

Shaftsbury had readied himself and made his journey to Upminster using the District Line. Upon entering the graveyard, he noted how pristine and manicured everything was. Walking carefully not to step on anyone's final resting place he admired the area. He saw a deep hole had been dug for a family grave. Gingerly he gazed into the grave. He was shocked how deep it was. He calculated a depth of eight to ten feet. His concentration was broken by a deep bellowing 'Over 'ere.' He turned to see Jones seated on a wooden bench that had been painted in green gloss, therefore blending in with the surroundings. He examined the surroundings again and thought how he should employ this gardener.

'Good afternoon, Mr. Jones.'

'Take a pew Shaftsbury. Hope you are well?' Gary passed a packet of sandwiches to Shaftsbury, 'Hope you like a ham and tomato sarnie?' He then poured a cup of tea into the plastic mug attached to the thermos flask.

Shaftsbury was a little confused. Sandwiches within the confines of a paper, how working class. Tea served in a plastic mug. This was how people from Dagenham must live. It was almost feral, 'How good of you Jones. You shouldn't have gone to all this trouble.'

'It's ham off the bone. The best. As good as it gets.'

Shaftsbury became confused for Jones's sanity. Ham off the bone. Where did he think it came from...the sky? 'How delightful. Did you say it contained tomato as well?'

'That's right. The nice juicy one's. Love a ham and tom' sarnie.'

Shaftsbury sat transfixed by Jones's description of a rather bland sandwich. Juicy? All tomatoes are juicy. Why do working class people always abbreviate words, or add an o on the end of everything when speaking to someone or about something? If they know someone named Jack, they named them Jacko. Why? 'You are too kind.'

Shaftsbury unwrapped the packet and nibbled at the sandwich. It had an unusual taste, yet it was not unpalatable. He took larger bites and understood how the tomato and ham off the bone may be a delightful experience in one's mouth. It had taste and substance.

Shaftsbury felt his cheek go into tiny spasms. The muscles throughout his face had a severe, painful feeling. His leg then began to go into a slight convulsion.

Jones noted a change in Shaftsbury's demeanour. He had wondered how long the strychnine placed within the sandwich would take to react. Quickly was the answer. 'Shaftsbury, you ok? You look a bit confused.'

Shaftsbury was concerned. Was he having a stroke? He felt jumbled. He wanted to ensure Jones did not become concerned with his state of mind. It was like he was in a bad dream and his world was spinning. The pain in his face was growing, He began to speak but the words would not form.

'What? I didn't understand what you said. You need to lay down.' Jones was intrigued by the state of Shaftsbury and how quickly the drug had reacted with him. Strychnine was powerful, fucking powerful.

Jones decided to inform his victim what was happening. 'Shaftsbury, you have ingested Strychnine. It was supplied by Charles John's, the Commissioner of the Metropolitan Police. A person you buggered senseless at Eton. Now do you understand? For the record, it was me that got rid of the Smith brothers and Michael Dawson. The hole you were admiring is yours. Good 'eh? And you are a bum boy fucking piss taking nonce.'

Shaftsbury's body was convulsing quite badly, yet his mind was alert. He wanted to use a profanity so bad it shocked him. He shouted by nothing came out. His mind was shouting 'You fucking cunt. You won't get away with this. I'm Robin Shaftsbury. I'm a known person in the top circles.'

Jones was amazed at the fight in Shaftsbury. He was genuinely surprised. His body was thrashing like clothes in a washing machine, yet he was trying to speak. Jones laughed at the things he assumed Shaftsbury would be saying to him in his mind.

Shaftsbury felt himself floating like a bubble. He had been picked up by someone who was not Jones. This someone had incredible strength. They had picked him up like he was a miniature bale of hay. The floating feeling had changed to a plummeting emotion. A violent snap was heard by all. Shaftsbury heard someone say, 'His spine's broken.' He had been dropped in a hole and was facing the pale blue and cotton white sky. He was unable to move and realised he was going to die alone. A huddled heap of ripped clothing and broken bones, he lay alone utterly terrified in his final resting place. His Malcolm wasn't there to soothe his fears. It was just him, alone in a strange place with strange people. He had never considered how he enjoyed the company of others, now he did. He then thought of Malcolm, and how they would be reunited.

Red-hot silent tears ran down his face, each one carving

furrows on the now soil covered tender flesh, it was like salted raindrops flowing towards the drain.

He felt the damp earth, and could feel it seeping through his clothing, he didn't care, yet the first mouthful of soil did worry him. Being buried alive terrified him.

The soil was landing on him at a rapid rate. He wanted to plead but knew it was pointless. The soil was creeping up and the earthy fresh smell surrounded him. He noted two earthworms trying to burrow into his clothing.

The throwing of soil stopped. His eyes opened to see Gary Jones looking down into his grave, 'Robin, you are not a bad man. A depraved greedy one, but not bad. I know that. If you pray for forgiveness I am sure you will meet Malcolm Mason again. You have now realised I am going to bury you. I am going to ask you something I have never done before. Would you like me to recite the Lord's Prayer? If you do, blink.'

Bob Burns was shocked by his friend. He had never done this for anyone before. Why now? It was so out of character.

Robin Shaftsbury blinked three times.

Gary recited the Lord's Prayer, and did the sign of the cross. He looked at Shaftsbury and decided to say 'God speed.' He knew these were the last words the man would ever hear.

Shaftsbury was at peace. He did not wish to die, but understood why it was happening. The thought of meeting Malcolm again made him smile, albeit a small growl like smile. His final thoughts were of 'His Malcolm.'

The final shovel of earth was thrown into the hole. It was three feet above the body, which had stopped wriggling like a worm. Something which would be wiggling inside it shortly.

Bob Burns examined Gary, unable to contain his curiosity

any longer, 'Gal, why did you do the religious thing. It was so out of character.'

'That man was a sex case at school, and ran depraved parties for profit as an adult. That's about it.'

'Aren't you forgetting the chief whip? We'd go down forever if anyone found out about that. Luckily they won't.'

'I don't know. He was just different. I also think the footballer love thing was strange. Seeing a person in love was different.'

Burns looked in disgust at his friend, 'It bothered you so much you offed him.'

'Maybe you are correct. Anyway. How are you? That's more important.'

'Gary. I told you, don't ask. But as I said before. That's it now. No more private burials.'

Charles Johns sat quietly at his desk. He had just finished his daily update on the previous day's events, and possible events that may happen over the forthcoming days. He sipped his Ribena with hot water, in deep thought. His secretary had been told he would accept no calls from anyone for 30 minutes. She knew this was his quiet time, something he called *PRT,* personal reflection time.

The telephone rang. It was answered immediately, 'I am sorry. The commissioner is not accepting calls for 30 minutes.'

'Thank you for the information. If you could inform Charles, it's Gary his friend. He'll speak to me immediately.'

The personal assistant was now unsure. No-one addressed The commissioner as Charles. In fact, she was sure no-one had ever mentioned his Christian name. What made it even more suspicious was the ending *friend*. She was sure her boss had no friends. 'I am sorry sir, but in 25 minutes he will be available.'

'OK. Thank you for your time. Could you do me a favour. Buzz him and tell him it's Gary. If he does not respond that is fine.'

'I am sorry. He genuinely is unavailable.' The phone line disconnected. She left her seat and rapped on The commissioner's door.

'Come.'

'Sorry to disturb your PRT Mr Commissioner, but I just had an odd telephone conversation with someone named Gary. He said he was your friend. I informed him you were unavailable, but he was insistent. I believe he will call back in 22 minutes.' She noted a change in her boss. He appeared to be going red.

Charles sat there, fuming. Why had she not put him through? Bloody woman was so correct it was getting him down. Suddenly, an icy feeling came about him. 'That is ok. If it is important. I am sure Gary will call again.'

She stood there noting a difference in his persona. Her commissioner appeared really angry, yet totally calm. She had never witnessed any emotion within him, yet this person Gary, had certainly stirred something within him. It was interesting, yet she felt a sense of danger. Something did not feel right.

Exactly 21 minutes later the telephone rang and the caller was immediately put through to the commissioner.

'Mr. Jones, how are you?'

Gary knew he was speaking to Charles Johns the Commissioner due to his clipped well-spoken English, 'I'm good Charles. Are you alone?'

'Gary, I am endlessly alone, and no-one, I repeat no-one, can hear our conversation. What brings communication from your good self?' Gary Jones's vocals were so distinguishable. The East End accent he so dearly held showed his living area.

'Charles. Your problem has disappeared, and will no longer be bothering you, or anyone else.'

Charles Johns, the Commissioner of the Metropolitan Police sat there stunned. His Adam's Apple went south. He felt like his blood had stopped running throughout his body. The man who had almost ruined his life was no more. Tears began to roll down his face. 'Gary Jones, thank you. Thank you so much. We must meet. Dinner on me. Rules restaurant, tomorrow evening 7pm. Are you free?'

Gary was sure he heard a sob in the man's voice. He then realised Bob Burns had been correct. Shaftsbury did deserve to go. Whatever had happened between the two had obviously played a major effect on Charles Johns, 'Charles, that'd be smashing. See you then.' He disconnected the telephone allowing the man time to compose himself.

The commissioner's personal secretary walked in. She placed four documents on the desk in front of him asking for signatures. She noted red blotched marks on his face. He had been crying, 'Sir, would you be able to sign these, and should I hold all calls for 15 minutes?'

Chapter 22

Too many questions

With Jack Philips it was by the book. When the team needed to get something done it was organised with precision. He held all the cards. If they went through the procedure, he would have the arrest of Chief Superintendent Taylor pronto.

Through the light wintry mist came his form, five-feet-ten and a little round about the middle. The boss stepped into the station, a place he called home. In the confines of his pocket were the collection funds made from the local spieler's, all cosied up in the brown envelope. Everyone assumed he was a goody-goody, yet he was up to his eyeballs in corruption. Greed was good, if handled correctly.

From out of the shadows appeared four police constables, Jack Philips and his assistant Sergeant Drake.

'George Taylor, I am arresting you on suspicion of sexual abuse of a minor.' There was a sudden in-take of breath from all those present. No-one knew what the arrest was for. 'You do not have to say anything, but it may harm your defence if you do not mention when questioned something you later rely on in court. Anything you do say may be given in evidence'.

Taylor felt his legs give way, but he was still standing. The officers had him gripped tight, 'Philips, what is going on? I demand an answer.' He was panicking and it was showing in his voice. Although he roared at his officer, there was a slight tremor.

'Officers, take him to interview room 1.' It was offered with a lack of feeling, as if it were a drunk and disorderly case. The fact it was a potential sex case, and one who was a big fish locally in police world made no difference to Jack Philips. In his eyes, George Taylor was a criminal.

Taylor's pockets were emptied. The depth of the envelope startled those in attendance. The envelope was opened and the money counted. The desk sergeant reported '£490 in cash'. It was loud enough for all in the vicinity to hear. Many heads turned and they all thought the same. 'Did he say £490 cash?'

The interview room was barren, cold and unwelcoming. Facing Jack Philips and his apprentice made George Taylor laugh. As if they would have anything big enough to keep him. The chief whip had told him to calm down as everything was in place, yet what was in place? The man had gone missing, 'Come now gentlemen, you've had your fun time. Now release me.' The final statement carried an edge.

Both officers stared hard into his eyes. He had bullshitted them since day one. Now, it was his turn. 'Mr. Taylor. You have been arrested for sexual abuse. A complaint has been made by Mr. Charles Roberts from abuse he suffered at Eton.'

Taylor stiffened. Charles Roberts, that was certainly a blast from the past, 'Sorry, I have no idea who you are speaking about.'

'Really? Records show that yourself and Mr. Robin Shaftsbury were keen on welcoming pupils to Eton, unfortunately this boy suffered abuse many, many, many times.'

Robin Shaftsbury. His two investigators had certainly done their homework, 'I am still unsure where this is going officers.'

Jack eyed Taylor knowing he was beginning to become nervous. A small pool of sweat had formed at the base of his hairline, and he kept crossing his legs. Jack decided to play the trump card early. He thumped a picture on the table. The noise made an echo within the room, 'Who is that?'

'That is Commissioner Charles Johns of the Metropolitan Police.'

'Well done Mr. Taylor. You are correct. Score one point.'

Taylor became angry, 'Do not be obtuse with me Philips. Remember who I am?'

A second picture was laid delicately on the table before Jack responded quietly, 'Who you were, not am. Anyway. Who is in this picture?'

Immediately, George Taylor recognised the picture. It was of Charles Roberts in his Eton uniform, 'I think that may be the Roberts boy, although it was many moons ago. Much has happened since.'

'Excellent. You collect a second point. That is Charles Roberts. Now, tell me. How do the two pictures link? Any idea?'

Taylor attempted to not look at either picture, but his inner curiosity got the better of him. He leant over and looked at both. There was something about them, but he could not place it, 'I genuinely have no idea. Should I?'

Drake leant forward. His aftershave could be smelt by

Taylor. His breathing remained calm, 'Take a good look, and when I mean a good look. I mean a fucking good look.'

Taylor became a little nervous. Drake had hardly blinked and his persona was calm, yet there was a dangerous feeling emanating from him.

A loud bang shot around the room. Making the other two occupants jump.

'Look at the fucking picture man. Not at the blue walls. Are you attempting to wind me up? If you don't look at that picture, I'll pull your eyes out and fucking eat them. Look!' Drake had become violent in his interview technique. His hand was red from slapping the table in fury. He had regressed to SAS form.

Taylor placed his head down and studied the picture. There was something but he could not understand the significance.

'George. Do you trust the commissioner? Do you like him?'

The response was immediate, 'Of course. He's a decent human being.'

Jack leant back in his chair, realising the confusion going through Taylor's mind. 'Then why did you abuse him?'

'What are you talking about? Abusing who, the commiss...' It could not be. He studied the pictures again. He was finished. They were the same person. It was the eyes. 'They're the same.'

Philips and Drake left George Taylor in the confines of the interview room to stew. Both men sat down with a strong cup of tea in Jack's office, exhausted. The investigation trundled through their brain like a speeding train, with no intention of stopping.

Jacks' focus was scattered, filled with nervous expectation. Concerned, yet jubilant. He could not hold a conversation or sit still while his thoughts danced in a plethora of directions. Taylor. Who'd have thought Taylor was a sex case? It was amazing, as it was shocking and deplorable. The deafening silence was broken by Drake.

Through red tired eyes he looked at Philips, 'Guv. This investigation is beginning to run its course, thank heavens. We just need to speak to Shaftsbury and Jones.'

Both men examined the other. Looking at the dark rings around the eyes and wearied look. The investigation was taking its toll, along with their poor diet and late nights.

'We need to find Shaftsbury and speak to him sharpish. But before we do we need to charge Taylor. We have enough. The commissioner's words alone will send him down. We'll let him go. He won't go far.'

Both officers entered the interview room to find their ex-chief superintendent with his head in his hands. He had the look of a beaten man. His hair looked a little shiny and it showed a balding area in the middle.

Taylor lifted his head as if it weighed heavily on his shoulders, 'Come to gloat?'

Jack felt a moment of sorrow for the man. He had dedicated his life to policing, yet here he was broken, finished, 'We are not here to gloat. We are here to do our job. Unfortunately, the next job is to read your charge sheet for the crimes you have committed. Due to your service and longevity to the force we are going to allow you bail. Obviously, you will have to adhere to all conditions we set. Handing us your passport etc.'

Taylor's head suddenly bolted upright, 'You patronising prick Philips. Do not tell me what I already know.'

Jack carried on, his tone unchanged by the outburst, 'You will have to report to a police station at agreed times twice a week, live at your home address only and not contact certain people.'

He stood, as did Sergeant Drake. He took two steps, stopped and turned towards his ex-superior officer, 'Patronising prick! It's not me who's going to do time for being a fucking nonce, and police officer as well.' It was like a release valve exploding. Opening the door, he calmly walked out.

Drake turned on his heels and faced Philips, 'Where did that outburst come from? I've never heard you give someone a verbal doing. Mind you, it was long overdue, and I agree with everything you said. The nonce bit was harsh, but funny as well. The look of shock on his face was worth the admission alone.'

He sat there a tenth of the man he had been four hours previously. Having ensured Sylvie would not open her mouth had been the correct thing to do. The silencer had killed the noise, and only people from ten feet away would have heard the sound. The look of shock on her face as the bullet entered and exited her forehead had made him grimace. She had been a fit looking lady, who should have settled down instead of playing with the big boys. Now she was a faceless woman. He knew Philips and Drake would learn of her murder shortly, yet they could not pin anything on him, although they would know it was him. He was in the shit big time, at least he would not go down for murder. He knew he would only serve three years at the most. A smug smile grew across his odious wet face. He would have his justice when released from prison. Removing Charles Johns – aka Roberts, from all walks of life would be a magnificent thing of retribution. He suddenly felt a slight hardening within the confines of his underwear. He may even fuck him as well.

The shrill from the telephone broken his concentration. He eyed it warily, studying it for a number of seconds. A sense of nervousness overcome him. His throat became dry and he felt a longing to not answer. 'Hello, Charles Johns speaking.'

'Mr Commissioner, it's Jack Philips.'

Charles had grown accustomed to Jacks tone. He would recognise it anywhere. 'How may I assist you?' He kept a very formal tone. The secretive side of him always assumed someone may be listening.

'We've charged George Taylor sir.' There was a slight hesitancy, a pause, 'You still their sir?'

'Sorry. Philips, I was in a state of trance. To think, after all these years it finally comes to an end.'

Jack heard an extraordinary gasp of air. It was as if the person he was speaking to was able to breath clean air for the first time in many years. 'Thought you'd like to hear the news. Of course, there will be a court case, and your evidence will be key, although a member of staff at Eton has also agreed to speak up on your behalf.'

The commissioner immediately became alert. Did he say a member of staff? How intriguing.

He leant back in his chair and considered all pieces of the human chess board he had played, and each had mastered their moves beautifully.

Taylor was going to prison; he would ensure that. Philips

and Drake had done their job, that would require a commendation or a promotion. Shaftsbury had gone missing, and only Jones knew that resting place. Jones appeared to be a man who would keep his word. He was old school; therefore, an oath would not be broken. There was no-one else to manoeuvre.

A smug grin grew across his face. He felt like a dead weight had been lifted from his shoulders. Hopefully, it would allow his life to prosper. Having dedicated his life to his career, he thought it time to dedicate some time to himself.

The cell was cold. He felt like his blood had frozen. His hands occasionally began to shake. Taylor sat looking at the confines of his new home. He would never last in prison. Someone of his stature would suffer immeasurably. Inmates would find joy at bringing him down. He felt his body begin to tremble uncontrollably. There was no other option, tears began to cascade down his face.

Removing his trousers, he knotted them around his neck, tied the other end to the bars of his window and stood on a chair. His body shook violently. Suddenly, he found clarity thinking, realising it was a coward's way out, yet the shaking of his body was too ferocious, the chair fell forward. The body thrashed like it was having its first swimming lesson. Finally, the movement stopped.

The cell door opened, welcoming Philips and Drake. Both stood transfixed. Taylor was hanging against the wall, obviously dead. The ligature had constricted his neck. The tongue was protruding, causing it to dry. Death by suspension hanging had tightened the ligature around his neck causing Taylor to lose consciousness within thirteen seconds.

The emergency button was pressed, yet both officers knew it was too late.

Drake turned to his superior officer and bluntly muttered, 'Fucking coward.' He then turned and walked back to the office showing no emotion.

Chapter 23

End game

Gary was sitting quietly in the Cross Keys reading his dog-eared *Daily Mirror*. There were small circles surrounding today's horse racing selections. Jonjo O'Neill and Peter Easterby had horses running that day, both favourites of Gary. He suddenly became aware of a presence. The shadows were looming over his table and crawling towards him. He glanced up to note DCI Jack Philips standing like a Roman centurion, 'Afternoon, don't just stand there, take a pew. Where's Tonto?'

'If you mean Sergeant Drake, he's at the bar buying us a well-earned pint. You included.'

'Has he won the pools?' A sly smile grew across Gary's face.

Jack acknowledged the sarcasm and smiled, showing his teeth, 'Nope, thought you may like to know that George Taylor hung himself in his cell.'

Gary considered the news. Hung himself. Fucking hell. He regained his poise 'Blimey, that takes some courage. Person must be at the bottom to do that, or have no way out. Why'd he do that, if you don't mind me asking?'

Philips was expecting the question and had pondered his response. Having considered all options, he considered to go with the truth, 'He got webbed up with an old sexual assault,

265

and a nasty man you know, Robin Shaftsbury.' He studied Jones for a reaction, but received nothing. He was a man of ice.

Jones realised he was being profiled, although it made no difference. He showed no emotion, physically or emotionally. He closed his newspaper and folded it, before carefully placing it on the dark beer stained table. He chose his words cautiously, 'Robin Shaftsbury. I know him. He's a member of White's. He's not a trustworthy man. In fact, he's one to be avoided.'

Three pints of bitter were placed on the table. Splashes of the dark liquid flew onto the surrounding surface. These were accompanied with Golden Wonder Ready Salted crisps. 'Get stuck in. You can't beat crisps with a pint.' Drake took a massive slurp from his jug handled pint glass before replacing it carefully, 'Jones, you are well dodgy. I know it, so stop piss balling us about.'

Gary looked at Sergeant Drake and let out a huge laugh that made two men standing at the bar turn around, 'No-one speaks like that to me. You crack me up.' He was still laughing and beer was flopping over the sides of the glass like water leaving a ship.

Suddenly, all three were laughing for no reason. It was like a release valve had been removed, and all the tension they had been experiencing was being removed from their inner being. Philips had tears running from his eyes, he tried to sip his beverage but instead it dribbled down his face like a speeding river.

Regaining his composure, Gary grabbed his drink and took a huge gulp, 'Fella's, I know you want me for some reason, although I have done nothing wrong. I am a man who collects debts for people, therefore I am an industry. I don't have a big house or flash car, although I am a member of White's, that is my extravagance, and that is about it. whatever you think or believe. You've even been in my house, so you know what I'm like.'

Drake studied Jones, and for the first time in his life he could not read the man. Usually, if someone is lying they'll have a little motion. It could be; watery eyes, rubbing a part of their body, nervous laugh or become fidgety, yet this man had no signs, he was unreadable. He was like a man who had served. This thought had crossed Drakes mind, yet there was something amiss. He was too cold and had a lack of feeling, in fact – he had no feeling. His thought process was broken by the unexpected clinking of glasses.

'Gents, whatever happens, I hope our fucking paths never cross again.'

Both officers placed their jugs on the table, their conversations frozen in the dirty cloud of smoke, and stagnant stench of cigarettes hidden within the collaboration of secretive odours. A sharp smell of drink wafted towards them, like black plumes fighting their way from the windows of a burning building. The merest hint of beer soaked into long stained carpet danced amongst publican and drinkers. It was as if time had frozen. The moment was broken by Jack Philips.

'Jones, Drake is right, you are dodgy. It's obvious. But in life you get bad dodgy and good dodgy. Luckily, you are the latter...I think.'

The final statement was left hanging in the air with a tangible feeling of doubt. The three men looked at each other. All trying to ascertain what the other was thinking. Trust, doubt, suspicion was all present.

Gary stood up from the table and held his hand out, not sure whether the officers would accept, 'It is time for me to leave. I honestly don't know what kind of parting this is. Perhaps we will walk on diverging paths forever, onwards to new adventures.'

Both looked at him. Weighing up whether to shake the man's hand, and if it was appropriate, 'Do you really think we should shake hands? I am not sure our paths won't continuously cross. I feel as if we are linked, and now we know you, we'll obviously want to stay in touch, for old times' sake.'

Gary laughed gently, 'Jack Philips. I shall enjoy our continuation of play, and Sergeant Drake, the same goes for you. Dagenham's very own Lone Ranger and Tonto. All the best gents.' Gary then removed himself from the bar.

Gary left the bar and made his way to his home. He became aware of steps behind him increasing in pace. He suddenly felt a sharp pain. He knew a knife had met his flesh. The tip of the blade sank deep enough to make him yelp.

'You silly ole cunt. Fink you're top dog? Well you ain't, you've 'ad your time. Time to die cunt.'

He crouched on the floor not believing what was happening. Did they not know who he was?

The blows and kicks kept coming, they were beginning to hurt now. He could taste the blood running into his mouth. Blood had that stale, almost sickly taste that was unpleasant, although he must not let them see it hurt. He tried to stand but a sharp kick caught him on the jaw. The crack could be heard, it was broken, that was certain. It made the sound of a thick branch being snapped. He tried to stand again and heard one of the lads nervously say, 'Turn it in now or you'll kill the ole fucker, then you'll get a ten stretch.'

That was a mistake their first and last mistake. They had underestimated his resourcefulness, mixed with his inner craziness. Gary's inner demon willed him up. He began to stand and charged at the young wannabe killer. During the charge he had picked up an old white discarded plastic spoon and snapped it. He then lunged at the young wannabe top dog and plunged the handle of the spoon in the lads left eye and screwed it round three times making sure it pierced his useless brain. He then fell to the floor. Realising that time maybe ebbing away he thought, 'No one ever bettered me, I am just too fucking hard. I am Gary Jones, London's number one.'

His eyesight was going foggy, the last thing he remembered was a pair of white trainers running from the scene, with all the strength he could muster he turned and faced his victim. The stained plastic spoon stood prominently from the lad's eyeball. It resembled a swan's neck.

He woke to find himself in Oldchurch Hospital. A policeman was sitting in the room next to him looking incredibly bored. His throat was dry, he tried to lift his left hand to reach for a glass of water but found it could go no further than eight inches. The officer immediately became alert. 'Do you require a drink sir?'

Gary nodded. He could not understand why his arms would not move.

'Sir, I have a straw. Take a sip. It will refresh your mouth.'

'Thanks. Why can't I move my hands?'

'Sir, your arm is broken as is your jaw. You are currently in a private room. No one can see you.'

Words bumbled from his mouth, 'Why?'

'To be honest sir, I have no idea.'

Gary studied the young police constable and believed him. The man sat down and carried on reading his paperback book, taking no interest in him. This informed Gary the man had no idea who he was guarding. How the fuck would he extricate himself from this predicament? For once in his life Gary had no idea, he was totally baffled.

Suddenly the door opened sharply in a swinging motion, a deep tone, 'Would you like a cup of tea officer?'

Gary head spun round in flash. He knew the deep-rooted vocals of that person at one hundred paces. Standing in overalls was his best friend. He had forgotten what a huge presence he was. He noted the police officer staring at his huge feet, before slowly working his way up-to his head.

'Cheers. Don't take offence, but you are the biggest nurse I have ever seen.'

Bob Burns, the Gravedigger fixed the man a stare, 'Been big since birth.'

'Anyway, thanks. I'll take a ten-minute break.'

Both nurse and patient watched the officer happily leave for an unexpected and welcome break.

'Jones tried to offer a thank you smile, whispering, 'Am I glad to see you.'

Immediately, he was hoisted from the bed, and clothes were thrown at him unceremoniously, 'Stick that on and get in the chair, look dopey.'

'Dopey, are you for real?' Speaking sent shockwaves dancing through his jaw.

'Just have that usual look you have, that'll be enough.'

Gary looked at his friend. No-one spoke to him in that manner, only this man, who remained emotionless, yet always had his back. Before he could consider the implications of their actions he was whisked down the corridor at such speed nurses had to skip from their path.

Upon leaving the hospital a waiting ambulance was in place. The rear doors were opened with precision and pace. Gary was hoisted into the back like a piece of meat, before the ambulance departed as if a Royal Mail van had an important package in the back.

In the distance, both occupants of the van could hear sirens blaring. Occasionally, they heard an ambulance, although a majority of the sounds were the enforcement kind, their sirens did not resonate as much.

Gary realised how lucky he had been. He was still sore from the trouble. It felt like someone had their hand inside of him and was gently squeezing his organs. He was breathing slowly and deeply until it passed. Yet he was alive. To live another day.